KISSING MIDNIGHT

"A dark velvet caress for the senses, *Kissing Midnight* is a powerfully seductive, decadent paranormal romance. Emma Holly's name on the cover guarantees a smoking-hot read!"
—Lara Adrian

"An epic that in true Emma Holly fashion will wrap you in the sensuality and mystery from the first page ... Full of sensual moments between several couples that only heighten the suspense and romance and will leave every fan breathlessly awaiting the next installment of this magnificent saga! ... Pick up *Kissing Midnight* for a powerfully emotional read that is action packed and steamingly hot!" —*Joyfully Reviewed*

BREAKING MIDNIGHT

"An enthralling read that will keep readers hooked from beginning to end." —*ParaNormal Romance*

"This book has everything! Passion, lust, humor, love, hate, anguish, greed, power, hope, plus a great cast of characters that brings each word and emotion to startling, vivid life on the pages ... An outstanding read!" —*RBL Romantica*

SAVING MIDNIGHT

"[An] exciting and erotic trilogy ... Holly outdoes herself by deftly taking her readers into the age of werewolves and vampires that is totally unexpected ... [A] fantastic voyage ... Decadently delicious ... A fabulous tale filled with touching and expressive emotion."
—*Night Owl Reviews* (5 hearts, Reviewer Top Pick)

continued ...

continued . . .

BEYOND SEDUCTION

DEVIL AT MIDNIGHT

EMMA HOLLY

BERKLEY SENSATION, NEW YORK

THE BERKLEY PUBLISHING GROUP
Published by the Penguin Group
Penguin Group (USA) Inc.
375 Hudson Street, New York, New York 10014, USA
Penguin Group (Canada), 90 Eglinton Avenue East, Suite 700, Toronto, Ontario M4P 2Y3, Canada
(a division of Pearson Penguin Canada Inc.)
Penguin Books Ltd., 80 Strand, London WC2R 0RL, England
Penguin Group Ireland, 25 St. Stephen's Green, Dublin 2, Ireland (a division of Penguin Books Ltd.)
Penguin Group (Australia), 250 Camberwell Road, Camberwell, Victoria 3124, Australia
(a division of Pearson Australia Group Pty. Ltd.)
Penguin Books India Pvt. Ltd., 11 Community Centre, Panchsheel Park, New Delhi—110 017, India
Penguin Group (NZ), 67 Apollo Drive, Rosedale, North Shore 0632, New Zealand
(a division of Pearson New Zealand Ltd.)
Penguin Books (South Africa) (Pty.) Ltd., 24 Sturdee Avenue, Rosebank, Johannesburg 2196,
South Africa

Penguin Books Ltd., Registered Offices: 80 Strand, London WC2R 0RL, England

This is a work of fiction. Names, characters, places, and incidents either are the product of the author's imagination or are used fictitiously, and any resemblance to actual persons, living or dead, business establishments, events, or locales is entirely coincidental. The publisher does not have any control over and does not assume any responsibility for author or third-party websites or their content.

DEVIL AT MIDNIGHT

A Berkley Sensation Book / published by arrangement with the author

PRINTING HISTORY
Berkley Sensation mass-market edition / November 2010

Copyright © 2010 by Emma Holly.
Cover art by Danny O'Leary.
Cover design by Leslie Worrell.
Interior text design by Laura K. Corless.

ISBN: 978-0-425-23781-6

BERKLEY® SENSATION
Berkley Sensation Books are published by The Berkley Publishing Group,
a division of Penguin Group (USA) Inc.,
375 Hudson Street, New York, New York 10014.
BERKLEY® SENSATION and the "B" design are trademarks of Penguin Group (USA) Inc.

PRINTED IN THE UNITED STATES OF AMERICA

10 9 8 7 6 5 4 3 2 1

THE VIEWING LIST

Sunset Boulevard

One

⌁⌁⌁⌁⌁⌁

1950

It was a perfect cinematic night in the suburbs of Ohio: fat white moon, wispy silhouetted clouds, stars like pin holes drilled through a huge backdrop. The house Grace Gladwell lived in was a stone's throw from where she sat, its yard so newly sodded the turf lines hadn't filled in yet. The proximity of the rancher should have darkened her mood, but—ensconced as she was in the front seat of handsome Johnny Dorsey's Buick convertible—she actually felt happy.

Johnny must have felt hopeful he'd finally have a conquest to tell his friends about. He shut off the ignition and let the straight-eight engine go quiet. He and Grace had been dating for the last three months, almost since the day she'd transferred to Lakeview High. The spring night was warm, and he'd thrown his letter jacket into the back of the Roadmaster. His gaze followed hers upward, then returned to her face.

Grace knew he wasn't used to seeing her relaxed. With a smile of his own, he twisted toward her on the leather seat.

"This sky looks like the one from the movie. You know, when William Holden and the woman who wasn't Gloria Swanson strolled through the studio lot."

Grace laughed, because she couldn't remember the second actress's name, either. Johnny might play football, might come from a clean-scrubbed family and hold doors for girls, but he and Grace shared a trait or two. When they went to a drive-in, they watched the screen.

Tonight's picture had been *Sunset Boulevard*.

Feeling uncustomarily close to him—though feeling close to anyone tended to make her nervous—she scooted around like he had, her knee bumping his beneath her petticoat-poufed skirt. Johnny's slightly sweaty hand dropped immediately to her knee. Grace enjoyed the warm squeeze he gave her, though she knew she shouldn't encourage it. She tossed her head to distract him.

"'I *am* big,'" she said, imitating Norma Desmond's melodramatic delivery. "'It's the pictures that got small.'"

"You could be a movie star." Johnny's thumb swept her bare kneecap. "Everyone at school thinks you're pretty."

Everyone thought she looked like Rita Hayworth, with her wavy red hair and her grown-up breasts. Grace appreciated the compliment, but being an actress wasn't what she dreamed about. She laid her hand over Johnny's to keep it from climbing higher. "Can I tell you a secret?"

Johnny leaned closer. "You can tell me anything, Grace."

"I want to be a director. I want to be in charge and tell the actresses what to do. I want to make people forget their troubles for an hour or two."

"Well," Johnny said, obviously startled by her passion.

"But why shouldn't you be a director? We'll call you Grace Hitchcock."

"Oh, please don't tell the kids at school. I'd die if they knew. It's just a silly dream."

He stroked her nose with one finger. "It isn't silly if you really want it."

She could have loved him then, this nice, normal boy who would have been horrified to know the minefield she was forced to walk every day. He'd have been horrified just by how many towns she'd lived in and how hard it was to think of anyone as a friend. He must have seen what she was tempted to feel for him. His eyes grew more liquid, more heated as she held his gaze. The moon shadows made his lashes look ten feet long.

"Grace . . ."

"I should go."

"Not yet," he said plaintively. "Your curfew isn't up for ten minutes."

"You know how strict my dad is."

"The light isn't even on. He's probably asleep."

Against her better judgment, Grace let him kiss her, let him pull her carefully over him as he slid down on the seat. Just this once, she wanted to feel cared for. Johnny was strong from playing sports all year, tall and muscled and— at seventeen—almost a man. Though he wasn't rough with her, he was hard all over, including under his jeans. As she sprawled atop him, the ridge behind his zipper grew. She knew what the bulge was; she wasn't totally naive, but the sensation of that part of him getting bigger shocked and excited her—more than she expected. When she squirmed her hips a little, her body overcoming her good sense, he groaned like she was torturing him.

"Grace," he panted hotly beside her ear. "Grace, I'm so gone on you."

She knew he was. Knew he wanted them to go steady and be a couple like other kids. She didn't love him, but more than anything, Grace wished she could say *yes*.

Instead, she wriggled from his arms and pushed away. The car door opened with a creak as he reached for her. She didn't dare turn around. The soft rub he gave her back was tempting enough. "I have to go."

"Grace."

"I have to," she said, ignoring his coaxing tug on her ponytail. "I'm sorry."

She ran around the lemon yellow car in her saddle shoes, then leaned over his door for a last, quick kiss. She was gripping her pink purse so tightly her knuckles ached. "Go home, Johnny. Please."

"I'll wait for you to get inside."

She kissed him harder, opening her lips to let her tongue push into the warm cavern of his mouth. She didn't do that often; her being the aggressor got Johnny too worked up. Tonight was no exception. His breath broke and came faster, one hand rising boldly to cup the fullness of her breast. "Grace . . ."

His voice was hoarse with longing.

"Go," she repeated, tearing away from him.

She hurried up the front walk on trembling legs, waiting on the stoop until he shook his head and drove off. Only then did she slide her key into the lock.

She knew the house being dark didn't mean she was safe. The dangers she faced liked to lie in wait.

She got as far as the kitchen entrance before her father struck.

"Whore," he said. The back of his hand caught her across the cheekbone, hard enough to knock her off her feet.

The blow hurt, but her first thought was that if he'd

bruised her, she'd have to stay home from school. She didn't want to; school was her escape, but no one could be allowed to suspect the hell she lived in. The one time she'd tried to ask for help had only earned her another move.

"Johnny and I didn't do anything," she said, scrambling back from where she'd stumbled, farther into the living room. "It was just a kiss, was all."

Her father grabbed her upper arms through her sweater set and hauled her up. He was a big man—fat really, though no one dared say that to him. Grace could smell that he'd been drinking. Maybe he'd lost his job again. "I saw that boy touch you. I saw you lying on top of him in his car."

"He was only hugging me. I promise it was nothing."

"George?" her mother said, querulous. She stood at their bedroom door, hair in curlers as she pulled her quilted robe close to her. The gibbous moonlight outlined her like a ghost. Grace knew she'd be no help. Helen Gladwell was little more than an audience for her husband's rage.

"Your daughter's a whore," he said, so furious he was spitting. "A whore and a damned liar."

He threw Grace back when he said *liar*. The liquor had stolen his usual caution but not his strength. Five foot five and slender, Grace hurtled toward the painted brick of the fireplace. Her skull struck the plain wood mantel, then cracked a second time as she dropped to the field-stone hearth. She wanted to cry out, but all that came was a moan.

"George!" her mother shrieked.

Time went funny, and suddenly her mother knelt by her side, clutching Grace's hand to her breast. Grace's head didn't feel right, and something warm and wet pooled beneath her hair. Her mother was sobbing hysterically.

"It wasn't enough?" she demanded of Grace's father. "It

wasn't enough that I gave up everything for you? You have to steal Grace from me as well?"

"*Mom*?" Grace tried to croak.

"She's playacting," growled her father.

She wasn't, though. Grace felt a pulling sensation deep in her gut. A moment later, her life's last scene faded to black.

SIX MINUTES

Two

Grace stood at the bottom of an outdoor amphitheater, looking up the bowl and across a broad fan of empty seats. The sky above her was cloudless, the sun a concentrated circle of blinding white. Beneath its glare, the grass that carpeted the theater's steps glowed like emeralds. The seats themselves were ornate and old-fashioned, upholstered in deep red velvet and painted with pretty pictures of chubby cupids where the rows met the two side aisles. Gold-leaf scrolling framed the little paintings, twinkling a bit in the bright daylight.

Lacking anything better to do, Grace climbed the shallow steps. Her favorite seat was ten rows back and in the center. Today she didn't have to squeeze past a single pair of knees to get to it.

She sat with a sigh of pleasure. She was wearing what she thought of as her play clothes: rolled-up dungarees and a soft button-down white shirt. Her saddle shoes were scuffed to perfection and her red hair was down. Prepared to enjoy a show, she looked in the direction of where a screen should have been. She saw the faintest glitter hanging in the air, but nothing solid seemed to be there. Instead, a dreamy landscape dotted with palm trees rolled into a blue distance. The recently rescued "Hollywood" sign perched partway up one of the low hills.

Well, she thought, *if this is Hollywood, the movie should start soon.*

"Popcorn?" suggested a deep male voice.

Grace should have been frightened; no one else had been here a second ago, and—in her experience—surprises weren't good things. Illogically, she turned with an unfamiliar sense of excitement. The fair-haired man who sat beside her was broad shouldered. He wore a beautiful tuxedo with a white bow tie, very like the one Norma Desmond bought William Holden when he became her kept man. Despite the clothes, his face wasn't William Holden's—or any other face she knew. His features were worn but nice, as if he'd been living well and enjoying it. Grace thought he looked good-tempered, with a glint of humor in his kind blue eyes.

"I'm your guide," he said. "You can call me Michael."

Grace accepted a handful of popcorn from the bag he was holding out. It was delicious, buttery and hot with just the right amount of salt. Feeling a need to be polite, she swallowed before she spoke. "If you're my guide, what is this place?"

When Michael smiled, deep lines crinkled around his eyes. "This is an in-between place. A place where things . . . get decided."

A flash came back to Grace of her father throwing her at

the fireplace. The violence seemed like something that had happened to someone else. "You mean this is purgatory? *Am* I going to hell for kissing a boy?"

Michael crossed his right leg casually over his left, the shift turning him more toward her. "Do you think you should?"

"No! At least, I wouldn't send someone to hell for that."

"What would you send them to hell for?"

"For killing someone, I guess. You know, if it was murder. Or a kid. I don't think it's right to hurt them."

Michael nodded, his gaze focused on the depths of the popcorn bag. He was shaking it a little. Grace had the sense that her answer disappointed him.

"Why would *you* send someone to hell?" she asked.

When his eyes came up, Grace's heart contracted inside her chest. His expression was the most intense she had ever seen, like a ray gun shooting hot blue fire. He wasn't disappointed like she'd assumed, but she couldn't have said what his emotion was. It was avid, compelling, as if what he felt was too powerful to squeeze under one label.

"I wouldn't send anyone to hell," he answered. "I'm made of mercy and I can't judge."

"You can't?"

"It isn't part of the nature I chose for myself. Come to that, it isn't part of the nature you started with."

"That can't be true. I judge people all the time."

She'd braced her palm on the armrest between their seats, and her fingers tensely rapped the wood. Michael laid his hand over hers. The instant he did, his touch ran through her bones in delicious waves, calming her until she relaxed.

"Are you judging now?" he asked. "Would you kill your father if I gave you a gun?"

"Of course I would!"

Michael raised one gold brow.

"I would! He killed me."

Except . . . she didn't feel dead, and she didn't feel angry. Her father seemed small now, unimportant. But maybe this was some sort of trick.

"You did something to me," she accused.

Michael shook his head. "I can't do anything to you. Only *for* you. And only if you allow. This is simply the effect of the human part of you fading. You can't hold on to anger or fear now. In fact, if you stay here long enough, you'll grow more and more like me."

Grace wasn't sure she liked that idea. Michael seemed nice, and not being frightened put her on cloud nine, but she was human. She was *herself*, whatever that meant. Young as she was, she'd hardly had a chance to find out.

"You don't have to stay," Michael said. "Everything is voluntary."

"You want me to stay. You want me to be like you."

"No," he countered very firmly. "Neither choice is wrong. Neither choice is less."

Grace's eyes strayed toward the place where the movie screen should have been.

"I can show you your life again," he offered. "If you think that would help you make up your mind."

Grace's nose wrinkled with distaste. "Can you show me how my life would have turned out if I hadn't died?"

"Mm," he hummed. "*What if* is tricky. Even here, tomorrow hasn't happened yet."

"All right," Grace said. "I just wondered . . ."

"About the boy?"

"I wondered if we would have stayed together. If Johnny was my one true love."

Her odd companion burst into a laugh. "Sorry." He waved

one hand in front of his contorted face. "It's just the universe isn't that stingy. For that matter, neither is the human heart. If you wanted, you could have quite a few 'true loves.'"

"One is plenty when you've had none."

"You think you've had none?" His grin grew broader. "You think this one brief life is all you get?"

Her human side might have been fading, but Grace was annoyed enough to fold her arms. "Show me then. Show me the loves I've had."

Michael cocked his head at her, still smiling but thoughtful now. "Showing you all of them would take more time than you want to spend. Why don't I show you your oldest friend? Maybe when he was last your age. The one who's been more to you than a lover. The one you meet up with again and again."

She looked into her guide's sky blue eyes. His face with its lines and crinkles was just a mask. His eyes were the windows to the truth of him, to the kind of soul she could scarcely dream about having. Wiser. Sweeter. Forever joyful and never tired. For just a moment he seemed familiar, as if *he* were her oldest friend, as if he never left her side. But that was impossible. She wasn't important enough for that.

Still, the word called to her. A friend was better than a lover. Better than a parent or a spouse. A friend was Grace's personal holy grail.

"Yes," she said, convinced this was what she wanted. "Show me the boy I meet up with again and again."

Three

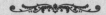

1460

Despite the cool autumn breeze that blew off nearby Lac Léman, sweat ran down Christian's muscles in steady streams, soaking his padded gambeson and causing it to itch liked Hades against his skin. He had been training his father's men since morning. He was young for the responsibility—maybe too young—but Gregori Durand preferred to leave his own flesh and blood in charge. Since Christian was his only living son, that meant the honor was his.

Though currently engaged in blocking a downward cut from a six-foot blade, Christian caught sight of trouble from the corner of his eye.

"Hold," he said to his training partner.

"Gladly," William laughed, allowing the blunted tip of his weapon to drop to the bailey dirt.

They fought in chain mail rather than plate armor, plate being more expensive to repair. Conveniently, depending on your point of view, the iron-ringed hauberks were no lighter than forged steel. Added to that, the two-handed swords they swung were twice as heavy as normal blades. The reason for this was simple. Stamina in battle spelled the difference between life and death. If they used more weight during practice, normal weapons felt easier. To gain that advantage, today they suffered. Though William was larger than Christian, his face was just as red and sweaty beneath his helm.

"Left arm!" Christian called to Charles, who was struggling ineffectually against a taller veteran.

"*Merde*," Charles cursed. The soles of his boots slipped in the dirt as he went down flat.

With a happy chortle, Hans—the veteran—pressed the axe head of his halberd into Charles's mail-clad chest. Charles's orange hair—the bane of his existence, according to him— had straggled from beneath his coif to plaster his face.

"He is stronger than me," Charles said as Christian came to stand over him. "And Christ knows how many stones heavier."

"You would not notice if you remembered you had two arms. In any case, you are faster than he is. Why did you let him close with you that way?"

"We have been at this for hours," Charles complained. "Forgive me if I grew weary."

"Battles do not halt because you are weary," Hans and Christian chimed in unison.

Laughing, Hans offered his felled opponent a hand up. The numerous scars that seamed his cheeks made his grin a fierce thing to see.

"Walk until you catch your wind," Christian said to Charles. "Then go work with the pell."

Charles groaned, because the pell was a hacking post and—while not as dangerous as combat—it was one of the more grueling exercises he could be set to.

"Left arm strikes only," Christian clarified. "I shall tell you when you may cease."

"*I shall tell you when you may cease,*" Charles repeated in mincing tones, but Christian knew he would obey. Charles only pretended to be contumacious. When the need arose, he always fought valiantly.

"You stay with me," Christian said to Hans, which wiped the grin from the warrior's face. "Charles did not give you enough of a challenge."

"Ha!" Hans barked, recovering his humor. "The day you challenge me is the day I retire." With his hands spread wide on his halberd's shaft, he brought up the weapon and began to circle. At forty and a few years of age, he was built like an old prize bull. Even through his chain mail chausses, Christian saw his thigh muscles bulge. "Do you worst, stripling."

"Christian," someone hissed through the continuing clatter of mock combat. "Your father comes to the yard."

Christian lowered his sword and turned. His father was indeed entering the bailey of their fortified hillside house. Like his son, Gregori Durand was swarthy from his mingled French and Italian blood—a common enough mixture here in Switzerland. Thanks to his departed mother, who had been a Habsburg by-blow, Christian was a mite taller than his father but far less broad. In contrast to his offspring's litheness, Christian's bearlike sire walked as if each step ought to shake the ground.

Today he dangled a writhing burlap sack from one meaty hand.

The frightened yelps that issued from it had Christian's stomach sinking like a stone.

"*Scheisse,*" Hans muttered beside him. "He found Lucy."

Knowing there could be no delaying this confrontation,

Christian closed the distance between him and his father. Gregori's expression was, as always, icy. His father never showed his temper by losing it.

"Would you care to explain this?" he asked coolly.

"She is but a hound," Christian said, striving for equal calm even as his heart thudded in his chest. At this point, any pretense of continuing to practice ceased. All the men were turned to him and his father, not drawing closer but watching. Whether by accident or design, the five who most often fought in Christian's *rotte* stood nearest. Hans was the exception among his silent supporters. Hans served in whatever group needed him.

Wanting to prove he was worthy of their espousal, Christian squared his shoulders. "I thought the vineyard owner's children might like to play with her."

"I gave you an order," his father said. "Are you saying you cannot obey me any better than this dog?"

"She is still young, Father. She did not mean to ruin your hunt."

"What she meant does not matter. She acted without discipline, and she cost me my prey. The other dogs did not fail me the way she did."

The other dogs lacked Lucy's spirit—and her love for humans. She was smart and playful and brought out the boy in men who had earned their keep killing strangers for more years than Christian had drawn breath. Lucy had slept on one or another of the mercenaries' pallets since she was a puppy, had shared their food and sent them into gales of laughter over her antics. Christian did not know a single member of their household who had not slipped her a treat or two.

Except his father, of course. His father had no love for any creature that Christian knew.

"I will take the whipping," Christian said. "This is my fault for letting the men make a pet of her."

His father stared at him, his eyes as black as wet stones. The back of Christian's neck tightened. Too late, he saw he should not have offered this.

"You will take the whipping," his father repeated, his face gone blank.

Not knowing what else to say, Christian bowed his head in submission.

"Very well," said his father. His hand gestured toward the men. "Hans, tie him to the pell."

The veteran soldier cursed too softly to make out which saint he was blaspheming. He did not, however, hesitate to lead Christian off. All of them knew better than to stand against their commander, for each other's sake as well as their own. Christian did not resist his mail tunic and shirt being stripped from him, nor did he protest when his best friend Michael was ordered to wield the single-strand raw-hide lash. This was simply another in the endless series of tests his father was forever requiring them to pass. *Whip your friend. Kill this dog. Grovel until your knees grind down.* The reward was never approval, but just living another day. Christian even understood why his father did it. This world was a hard and bloodthirsty place. Only those who commanded fealty could survive.

Hans's motions were brisk as he bound Christian's wrists together with a thick hemp cord. Christian hugged the pell, the hacked wood post a support he would be grateful for soon enough.

"Ready?" Michael asked, the single kindness he would permit himself to give.

Christian nodded and clenched his jaw.

His father ordered him to take twenty strokes, and Michael's strong right arm ensured they were hard enough to suit the elder Durand's taste. Once destined to become a monk, Christian's golden-haired friend grunted with the force it took to break Christian's skin. Luckily, Michael's aim was precise. The leather stayed on his back and shoulders and away from kidneys and spine. This whipping would neither kill him nor leave a disabling scar. Christian would live to earn other ones.

His breath whined through his teeth by the fifteenth lash, his body jerking helplessly at the pain. Christian tried to contain any other noises, not only because they would betray weakness to his father, but because the evidence of his suffering would distress his friend. Though Michael was a few years older than Christian, his heart would never be as hard. Keeping silent was a luxury Christian fought for. Salt-sweat stung his wounds like acid as Michael was obliged to cross stripes he had already made.

"Nineteen," he counted, his voice ringing out as if he, too, were being struck.

Then he brought the last blow down.

Christian's back was throbbing, the fiery heat of the lashes like snakes writhing on his skin. He flinched when the blood from one rolled into the next.

"Water," someone said quietly. A moment later, a bucket of blessed coolness was poured on him.

Hans cut his wrists free, gripping Christian's elbow just long enough to help him lock his buckling knees and stand. The scarred old warrior's face was angry, but only if you looked closely. Nostrils flaring, Hans stepped away and stood at attention as soon as Christian faced his father. Christian was shaky, but his head was high. He blinked until the sweat cleared from his vision.

To his amazement, his father laughed.

"I give you this, son," he said, almost sounding pleased, "you are no swooning lad."

Christian had one shocked heartbeat to enjoy this rare piece of praise. His father's expression sobered as he once again lifted Lucy's sack. He thrust it squirming in Christian's direction with his usual flinty look.

"Now," he said. "Kill the dog."

Afterward, Christian sat in the dirt with Lucy cradled in his lap. She was . . . She *had been* a short-haired hound, white with liver-colored splotches. Her once perpetually wagging tail hung limp, her body cooling under his petting hands.

Christian's eyes were dry. If he had cried even as a child, he could not remember it.

"We will take her," Philippe said. "Matthaus and I will bury her outside the walls under a nice tree."

"Bury her deep." Christian's instruction was distant but steady. "Else, some animal will dig her up."

"We will," Philippe promised, easing Lucy's slight weight from him. He glanced back over his shoulder to where Matthaus waited, slim and tall . . . or perhaps his gaze scanned the shadowed archway where Christian's father might again emerge.

Christian found it difficult to care. Other hands helped him up, careful to support him without touching his bleeding back. Christian's eyes met Michael's. His friend's face was tight and angry over the beating he had been forced to inflict. Christian suddenly felt exhausted, as if he could drop where he stood and never get up again.

"Be not troubled," he said to Michael. "No one else could have whipped me as well as you."

Michael snorted out a bitter laugh, then cleared the gawking servants from the bailey entrance with a sharp command.

"Find Cook," he snapped. "The young master's wounds need tending."

The staff scurried away even as the men half carried, half dragged their young master in. Gregori Durand's fortress was a thick-walled square built around a large courtyard. His men-at-arms slept on the upper floors, three or four to a chamber close to the weapons stores. They had never been attacked at home, but they all knew it might happen. No one could doubt they had rivals among the area's mercenary bands.

In these parts, war still brought in more gold than wine.

Christian was one of few with a private room, a narrow, stone-lined chamber with a single window—monklike quarters, at best. The two most massive of the men, Hans and William, laid him on his bed facedown. Despite their care, Christian hissed with pain as the muscles of his back shifted.

"St. Sebastian's balls," Hans swore darkly. "If your father weren't such a good commander . . ."

He was, though, sharp as a Venetian dagger on the battlefield and off. Gregori Durand found them contracts and got them paid, not always an easy matter when the merchant they had been escorting decided he would rather spend their fee on a new mistress.

"'s fine," Christian mumbled into his mattress. "I shall sleep in tomorrow."

Only Michael stayed while Cook came to clean his wounds and dress them in bandages. He sat on the bed after she had finished, not touching Christian but probably wanting to. Ferocious though he was in battle, Michael had a tender heart—and a tendency toward guilt left over from his former failed calling.

"I am sorry," he said now.

"You had to whip me," Christian said. "If you had not, Father would have demanded worse penance."

"No. I am sorry your sacrifice failed to save Lucy."

Christian's hands curled into themselves. "She was just a dog. I should not have let you men get attached to her."

"Stop."

Michael's order was sharp. Christian rolled onto his side to look up at him. His friend's lean, ascetic face was flushed with intensity. "Do not turn into him, Christian. Your father is no better than a beast. In truth, he has less soul than that dog you killed."

"Do you want me to weep for her?" Christian asked, hard with scorn. "Do you think that would change anything?"

"I want you to feel. Or pray. Anything human." Michael covered Christian's clenched hand. "Your mother would not want you to grow cold like this."

Against his will, Christian's gaze slid to the wooden crucifix that hung on his wall. This and a small gold ring were all that remained of the woman who had brought him into this world. He had been seven when she died in childbed, trying to birth the third of his brothers who had not lived. He still remembered his father saying *good riddance to weak stock*. A burn flashed across his eyes, but he tightened his jaw swiftly.

"Let her pray for me," he said. "Let her look down from heaven and pray for me."

Christian tugged his hand back, and Michael rose. He paused, seeming as if he would speak. But the one-time monk could not bring himself to preach. As he put it, his flesh had always been too weak to counsel others to holiness. Instead, his breath sighed out of him and he left.

Christian knew he had disappointed his friend. He also knew he could not have responded any other way. He wanted to survive, wanted to protect the men who relied on him. If that meant hardening his heart, so be it. From what he could see, God and the saints were a capricious lot anyway.

He rolled onto his face again, ordering his fists to relax. His right hand stroked the coarse wool blanket on which he lay, fingers petting it until he recognized what he did. Pain seized his rib cage worse than any scourge. He could feel Lucy's fur again beneath his fingers, could see her eyes turned trustingly up to his. She had thought herself safe up until the instant he snapped her neck. She had thought herself safe with him.

The first sob tore from him, so harsh and strange he barely knew what it was. Tears came with it and he could not stop them, though he fought hard enough. He could scarcely breathe through the fit of sorrow, the violence of it taking him aback.

Stupid, to cry for a dog. Stupid and pointless.

His sole consolation was that no one was there to see.

Grace was on her feet, standing on the grass-clad stage beneath the magical movie screen. She felt as if her cells were going to explode. Never had she felt more called to action—or more helpless. Considering her recently ended life, that was no small claim.

"I should be there," she said, so sure of it her voice vibrated. "You said he was my friend. I should be there to comfort him."

Her tuxedoed guide came toward her down the broad aisle steps, his expression smooth and unreadable. "These events happened long ago."

"You said you could do things for me if I allowed it. I'm willing to be sent to him."

"I can't send you like you think, Grace, not as a person."

"But you *can* send me."

He glanced at the screen where the young man named Christian lay racked with grief on his narrow bed. "I can send you after a fashion. If that's what you truly wish."

"I promise you, it is."

He looked at her, considering. "I didn't expect you to ask this. There are . . . limitations on this sort of thing. Time will stretch but not indefinitely."

"I accept the limits. Don't you want me to help him?"

She knew she had to convince him. She'd never had a friend that she could remember, not one she'd been allowed to keep. Dead or not, she wanted to know this one.

Michael smiled, slowly, sweetly, his face abruptly so lovely that it hurt to look at it. "I would like you to help him, yes."

His words had power. This place she'd ended up in—the emerald grass, the plush red seats, the flickering screen— melted around her like colored sugar left in the rain. For just a moment she was frightened like the old days.

Holy cow! she thought.

And then her feet found solid ground again.

Four

Recovering from her little panic, Grace looked with fascination at her surroundings. Dying might not have been fun, but thus far the aftermath had been interesting. Now she'd traveled to another time, with sweaty men in chain mail and giant swords. Despite having her doubts about reincarnation, it looked like she was going to meet a friend from a former life. As the kids at school said, that was Fat City.

She was only a teensy bit disappointed that the Middle Ages were homely.

Christian's room was a far cry from knightly splendor. Longer than it was wide, she could have touched both walls with her arms outstretched. For furnishings, it had a bed, a worn chest with leather buckles, and a three-legged stool. A set of solid wooden shutters blocked the window, but there was no glass. Surprisingly, the draft didn't chill her. It should have; her clothes had changed again, and she wore a thin white nightgown. Her feet were bare on the plastered floor, but they, too, seemed immune to the cold. Her body felt as if it had no temperature at all. It also seemed lighter than normal, as if she floated in water.

Time must have passed while her guide did whatever he did to transport her here. Christian's storm of tears had abated. He breathed heavily, wearily, his hard arms wrapped around a small pillow. His hair was shoulder-length, straight and black and caught behind his neck with a leather tie. It looked coarse but healthy, with blue black highlights shining in the strands.

Suddenly shy, Grace hesitated to call his attention. He appeared older than she was—twenty, maybe, though this was hard to judge, given the mature development of his physique. College boys didn't have this many muscles, that she knew of: big ones, small ones, layered and interlocking in a fascinating sun-browned puzzle. The bandages couldn't disguise the dramatic narrowing of his torso, nor did she fail to notice that he was barely dressed. Christian's lower half was clad in a garment as light as the shift she wore. Tied around his trim waist, it extended midway down his thighs and then stopped. His legs were long and muscular, stirring an unexpected urge to drag her mouth up their light cover-ing of black hair. The rounds of his buttocks looked tight enough to bounce quarters on. When he shifted at some dis-comfort, she just had to lick her lips. His spine ended in two dimples where its curve dove into his hindquarters' crack.

The shadows that area harbored drew her eyes irresist-ibly.

Feeling uncomfortably like a Peeping Tom, Grace real-ized she could register temperature, after all. Her face was blazing, along with certain lower parts. Apparently, she'd underestimated what desire could be. Johnny's most enthusiastic embraces hadn't affected her this strongly.

"Christian," she whispered, tearing her guilty gaze from his taut rear end. "Christian, I'm here to help."

He scrambled up so quickly from the dark gray blanket that the movement must have hurt his back.

"Who are you?" he demanded, one forearm swiping his tear-marked face. "Why come you here garbed like that?"

His right hand held a dangerous-looking knife. Grace had no idea where the thing had come from. She hadn't seen it anywhere nearby. The well-honed sheen of its blade had her heart jumping.

"Um," she said, the uncertainty that swept her unwelcome. "Don't you recognize me?"

"Are you one of Charles's whores? Is this his notion of a jest?"

"Hey," she said. "I didn't put myself in this nightgown. And it's not like *you're* wearing any more."

He looked down at himself and then up at her. For some reason, this caused her to blush harder. Clearly, he wasn't modest. His underthings were too transparent to cover his front parts any better than they had the back. Whatever his age, the sexual organs cradled by that cloth were a man's.

"I grant you are a comely wench," he conceded, "but I have no spirit for bed sport tonight."

"I'm not offering you *bed sport.*"

He laid the huge knife on the mattress. "I am tired," he sighed. "I mean no insult, but I bid you go."

Well, this was awkward. Possibly Grace should have asked her guide a few more questions before she leaped into this. Then again, how was she to know she'd need to when everything that had happened since she'd died was at least half dreamlike?

"No," she said unimaginatively back.

Christian made a growling noise that spiked her temperature again. There were barely two strides between them. He closed them, his arms coming up in preparation to steer her away. Grace dug her heels in, determined to stand her ground for once.

They both gasped as loud as gunshots when his body passed straight through hers. All she'd felt when it happened was a slight tingle.

"Blessed Mary," he breathed. They'd whipped around to face each other, and he was backed up against the door with his eyes gone wide. Swallowing hard enough to jerk his Adam's apple, he waved his trembling hand through her form again. Her body didn't stop the motion any more than it had before.

"Holy cow," Grace said, gazing down at his wrist disappearing disconcertingly into her belly. "I guess this is what he meant by not being able to send me here as a person!"

"Specter," Christian accused. "Why have you come here? Is it because of Lucy? Are you my punishment?"

"I'm not a punishment," she huffed, backing away until his hand slipped free. "And I'm not a specter!"

Christian's brows lowered. His eyes were so dark she thought they might actually be black. "You are not corporeal. And that gown could easily be grave clothes."

Much as she would have liked to, Grace couldn't argue this. "All right, maybe I am a spirit, but I'm not a ghost. I died and met this man—an angel, I think. He said you and I had been friends before."

"I assure you, we have not met."

"He—" Grace struggled not to mumble with embarrassment. "He said we'd known each other in another life."

"Another life! I see I am to be haunted by a lunatic."

"I haven't come to haunt you!"

"Why else would you travel hence? I am not a man with whom angels do business." He laughed, short and sharp. "That is, unless they seek vengeance."

"I told you, the angel said we're friends. I came to . . . offer you comfort."

Christian's muscles bunched impressively as he crossed his arms. Grace fought not to shiver at the breadth of his naked chest. It had a nice smattering of hair on it.

"I need no pity," he said. "Certainly not from a denizen of the otherworld."

The sneer in his tone drew Grace's attention up. His face had grown handsomer with his anger, his sharp, thin nose as proud as an emperor's. His slash of a mouth was cruel—or it would have been if she hadn't seen for herself the depth of attachment he was capable of. Her own anger bled away as she remembered him cradling the poor slain dog.

"Maybe you could consider me company. I mean, I know what it is to want to be alone with your troubles—"

"Do you?" He cut her off scornfully. "Do you really?"

Grace pulled herself straighter. "Doubt what you like about me. That I'm an expert in."

Their gazes locked together, both narrowed, both certain of their own rightness. Grace wasn't accustomed to staring directly at other people. She'd been trained young not to issue such challenges. Keeping her eyes on the floor was safer, but she forced herself to hold Christian's gaze. No point not to, since she no longer had a body that could be hurt. Something passed between them as their standoff lengthened, thickening the air with electricity. Grace had the fleeting and strange sensation of increasing weight in her limbs.

Whatever *he* was feeling, Christian's lean cheeks darkened. "You bear the hair of a witch," he said.

"Fine," she countered, searching her brain for some

period-appropriate insult. "You have the manners of a toad."

She wasn't sure he cared about his manners, but his nostrils flared. "I want you gone."

"I'd rather not be dead. Looks like we're both doomed to disappointment."

"You refuse to depart?"

"I'm not refusing," she gritted in exasperation. "I don't know how to leave. Someone else sent me here. And since I am here, maybe you could put something on!"

Christian spun away from her in frustration, stubbornly ignoring the wild pounding of his pulse. He was arguing with a ghost. An honest-to-goodness specter had taken up residence in his room.

Like anyone, Christian had heard tales of supernatural beings: sirens and succubi and beautiful death omens who collected soldiers' souls on the battlefield. He simply did not comprehend why *he* would meet one—or why *his* ghost had to look like this.

If she had been more ghastly, maybe he could have run. Instead, she was young and pretty and, apart from her raiment, all too innocent looking. She was, in truth, precisely the sort of female he did not let himself dream about. He was a damned soul, a mercenary who killed for coin. By his very nature, women like that were not meant for him.

His member thickened, deepening his resentment as he yanked his hose up his legs. With no doublet to tie the points to, the garment drooped, but he saw no reason to dress more formally for a shade. If she disliked the look of his body, she could go back where she had come from!

He braced himself before he turned to her again.

The girding did no good. Her beauty hit him harder the second time. Her witch's hair was as dark as rubies, its shining waves spilling down her arms. Her eyes were a clear light green, wide in their frame of lashes, big in her creamy-skinned, sculpted face. He could not fathom by what means she appeared so solid. Her lush red mouth looked perfectly kissable, light glinting off the edge of one pearly tooth as her lips parted.

His gaze slid lower, helpless not to take in the rest of her. By heaven, her breasts were lovely, full and round and sitting high on her rib cage as if begging to be cupped. In contrast, her hips were narrow, almost boyish . . . until they ran into long, shapely legs. Whether a man be saint or sinner, he would have to be dead not to want to be wrapped in those silky thighs—wrapped and squeezed and clutched in amorous congress until the very last of his breath gasped out.

Christian swallowed at the thought of that. He was young and such things happened, but even he was taken aback when his pike hammered up in the space of two hard heartbeats. Her linen shift did little to shield the dark red triangle at her queinte.

If, as she implied, an angel had dressed her, the creature must have had a devil's intentions.

"Shirt?" she suggested with the little huff she had used before.

Christian forced himself to toss his head in a lordly manner. She might have twisted him into a knot of desire, but he did not have to admit it.

"You are a ghost. What care I for your maidenly modesty?"

Her cheeks blazed pinker, her gaze dropping briefly, interestingly to his chest. Goose pimples broke out around his nipples, which he could not doubt were erect.

"Fine," she said, her voice husky. "But you should return to bed. You won't heal well unless you sleep."

Come there with me, he thought in spite of himself.

"You expect me to sleep with you in my chamber?"

Her pretty green eyes narrowed. "I have no body. I couldn't harm you even if I wished. And surely you're not suggesting a big, strong knight like you is too cowardly to try."

"I am not a knight, I am a mercenary. Men like me fight for money and not the Lord."

His interloper shrugged with affected calm. "All the more reason not to act like a frightened goose."

He glared at her, knowing she was attempting to manipulate him. Gingerly, he lowered himself onto his mattress. He *was* tired—exhausted—but who knew what a ghost would do once his guard was down? Only a fool would trust one to tell the truth. Come to that, there were not many living people he would make himself vulnerable to.

His hand bumped his knife, reminding him it was there. He pushed it warily beneath his pillow. This weapon, at least, would not work on her.

"I'll swear on whatever you want," she said. "Whatever you old-time folks believe in."

This apparition spoke very strangely, though he found he had no trouble understanding her. Oddly, her dialect seemed to untangle even as it slid into his ears.

"*Old-time*," he repeated under his breath. On impulse, he snatched down the cross that hung above his bed. He did not know if it would protect him, but it was better than nothing.

"Good," she said as he pressed it against his chest. "Now lie down and relax."

Christian's jaw tightened. She had no right to give him orders. For that matter, he should have been shouting for

Michael. His closest friend had not studied at the monastery long, but perhaps he knew a ritual that would banish her.

"Please," she said. "I came here to be with you."

To his surprise, her lower lids welled with tears—a devil's tears, for all he knew. He fought the weakness inside him, but its grip was too strong. The simple, shameful craving for kindness pulled him onto his side on the blanket and closed his eyes.

A silence followed, during which all his muscles tensed with the knowledge that the shade was still there. He told himself he could call his men any time. Or leave. Leaving might be a fine idea. His friends might or might not see her, but he would not be alone with her.

The faintest sense of weight depressing the mattress caused the hair on his arms to rise.

"You are sitting on my bed," he said, his eyes still shut.

"Hush," she answered. "Even a ghost can't stand forever."

He had only her word for that. He opened his mouth to protest, but a tingle like he had experienced when he walked through her caressed his hair.

"Specter, you touched my head!"

"Hush," she repeated as if her teeth were clenched. "This is what I came for. No one should have to bear every weight alone."

He snorted, because what people should have to bear rarely matched what they did. "I am too tired to stop you," he announced proudly. "I will deal with you later."

"I'm not afraid of you," she retorted, which was ironic—considering she herself did not sound convinced. "My name is Grace, in case you're interested."

He steeled himself against a brush of curiosity. What

sort of ghost would care if he knew her name? "I am only interested in getting rid of you."

"Maybe I'll be gone when you wake up."

"Maybe you are a hallucination in the first place." He was so sleepy the words trailed off into a jumble. His shoulders jerked, the tension that had been coiled in them unexpectedly releasing. The phantom tingle of her hand slid onto his arm. It was almost warm, almost heavy, its rhythmic strokes soothing. His erection was slowly fading, though its nerves continued to hum. Lulled, he rolled forward onto his face.

"Your wrists!" she gasped, cradling one. His skin was raw from tugging against the rope that had bound him to the whipping post. The bruise did not hurt when her tingling touch skated over it. For whatever reason, he could feel her more clearly now. She had cool, slender fingers—gentle and slightly shy. She *was* comforting him, ludicrous though that was.

"Stop that," he grumbled, the words slurring.

He would never know if she listened. Sleep swept over him in a thick black tide.

Five

Christian lay beside Grace when she woke the following afternoon. Not having much experience being a spirit, she hadn't known she could sleep. She remembered sitting by Christian, stroking his hair and hands for a good long time. She could feel them, just a little, and the sensation had been pleasant. Her nervousness about pushing herself on him, when he so obviously didn't want her there, had faded with the last day's light. She'd grown peaceful, almost happy, and then the world had blanked out.

If she'd returned to the in-between place where she'd met her angel, she didn't recall it now.

She pushed up from Christian's bed where she'd been resting. He slept on, still on his stomach, snoring softly from exhaustion. His head was turned to the side on the pillow, his features squashed. His lashes fanned so thick and dark against his cheeks that she felt jealous.

"Michael," she whispered, clambering over Christian

without disturbing him. "Michael, what am I supposed to do now?"

Dust motes swam through the beams of light that filtered past the edges of the wooden shutters. She heard distant shouts outside, the rumble of wagon wheels, the clatter of clay dishes. Despite her own incorporeality, this other world was amazingly real to her.

"Michael," she hissed more loudly. "Did you really mean to just leave me here?"

"Who are you talking to?" Christian mumbled behind her.

Grace spun to him, noting with a little lurch that the dust motes didn't stir when she did. "To my guide," she said. "The angel who sent me here."

Christian rubbed his sleep-creased face. Stubble darkened the dramatic planes of his jaw. She could hear the bristles rasping beneath his palms. He was sitting up on the side of his bed. The imprint of the wooden crucifix he'd slept on was clear and red on his flat stomach. Also clear was the startlingly large erection poking through the flap of his underthings. The pants he'd pulled on last night were constructed in separate legs and didn't cover him well at all. Half asleep as he was, Christian seemed unaware that his private parts were exposed.

Grace had heard boys joke with each other about "morning wood," but this was a baseball bat! Christian's penis was thicker than she'd imagined a man's could get. Longer than her hand and veiny, it shuddered like a living creature from the pumping of the blood in it. Grace wasn't convinced even the head of that marvel would squeeze into her.

The size of his "marvel" notwithstanding, it wasn't fear that had her flesh ticking and squirming between her legs. As she wondered if he started every day this way, she felt a rush of warm wetness there.

"Grace?" Christian said, but she couldn't tear her gaze from his organ's crest. Its skin was taut and shining, as if it had been polished . . . or maybe licked. "Grace, did you hear me?"

Had he asked her a question? She looked into his leanly handsome face. Those black eyes of his could pierce any woman's soul.

"Are you daft?" he demanded. He glanced down at himself, belatedly registering the state of his body. "Oh, Christ." To her disappointment, he grabbed the pillow and shoved it over his lap. "You should not stare like that, wench. A man might draw the wrong conclusion."

Grace blushed hot for a moment before she laughed, perhaps a bit hysterically. "I can stare all I want. No man can hurt me now."

"*Did* one hurt you?" Christian asked.

Grace quieted abruptly. "No. Not . . ." She stopped, at a loss. She understood what he meant, but didn't know how to answer.

Christian's expression grew closed and proud. "Forgive me. Your past is not my concern."

Whatever her unsureness, she didn't want to hurt his feelings. "My father used to hit me," she said. "But that's all it was. Just hitting and calling names."

Christian's gaze searched hers so deeply she had to fight not to wince. "Your father is the reason you lost your life."

"Yes," Grace admitted. Her voice was husky, and she felt inexplicably ashamed. She shrugged one shoulder higher than the other. "It doesn't matter. The angel promised that, in time, I'd forget to be afraid and angry."

"Murder should not go unpunished," Christian said sternly.

Because it seemed pointless to argue, Grace said nothing. Christian stared at her a few seconds longer, his hands tightening—perhaps unconsciously—to cram the pillow deeper into his lap.

"Your angel did not answer when you called?"

"No." Grace's cheeks heated for where her mind had drifted. "I'm sorry. It looks like I'll be staying here for a while."

Christian grunted and rose. Seeing him straighten, she realized he was as tall as he was muscular, perhaps a shade above six feet. Giving her his back, he threw the pillow onto the bed and stalked to the door. When he opened it, she saw someone had left a jug of water and a deep tin basin on the floor outside.

"If you do not wish to see me," he said, "you should turn away while I wash."

She did wish to see him, but she supposed this was his way of asking her not to stare. She faced the blank stone wall as the sound of dripping water and a dampened cloth set her fantasies rioting. When a muffled groan broke from him, suggesting what he was washing now, Grace couldn't contain her grin.

"Need help?" she teased, the boldness rising unexpectedly.

Her offer had more of an effect than she'd anticipated. His next groan became a curse. The slapping of the cloth stopped . . . and then sped up determinedly.

"I think," he said, his words coming breathily, "that it was not by an angel's grace that you came to me."

His play on her name made her laugh, but "Oh, Jesus," he added without warning and more deeply. "Oh, holy Christ and the saints."

My God, she thought. He was . . . he was masturbating in the same room as her. Medieval people certainly were more casual about their lusts. Then again, to judge by the hoarse noises he was making, not to mention the speed with which he washed his "marvel," his current fit of cleanliness felt better than he'd been prepared for. Grace should have covered her ears, but found she wasn't that considerate. Could his need really be so pressing that it couldn't wait? Did all young men do this in the morning, or was his urgency worsened by her presence? He'd admitted he thought her a comely wench, but that was before he'd discovered she was a spirit. Had his attraction truly survived the shock?

Grace was forced to conclude it had.

"*Unh*," he grunted with real volume now, his breath coming in hard pants. "*Unh. Unh.*"

He was rubbing himself so quickly, so desperately, that the cloth sounded like a whip.

"Christian," she whispered.

Her voice pushed him past the barrier of his pleasure.

"*Scheisse*," he gasped as a splash of what she assumed was seed hit the floor. More moans came from him as the splash repeated, until finally he sighed, long and torturous. The sound seemed as regretful as it was relieved.

For half a minute, while he caught his breath, neither of them said anything.

"Forgive me," Christian said at last, his tone unsteady. "I should not have done that, but when you stared at me . . . In faith, my prick grew too ardent to subside on its own, and when I touched myself with the cloth, my need was too great for me."

Incapable of facing him, Grace hugged her arms around her middle, oddly grateful that she was solid to her own embrace. "I never heard a man do that before," she confessed.

"Never?" The nearness of Christian's deep male voice made the back of her neck prickle. "You died a maid?"

She nodded, her lips pressed tightly together.

"I did not know," he said. "If I had . . ."

"Don't apologize." She forced her shoulders down from their hunch. "Maybe it wasn't nice of me, but I liked listening to that."

He laughed softly through his nose. "You see, Grace? It is as I said. No angel sent you to me."

She turned, able to confront him now that he was joking. "Thank you." When his eyes widened at her heartfelt manner, she saw she ought to clarify herself. "For calling me by my name. I know you didn't invite me, but I appreciate not being shouted at."

He blinked, more than surprise flickering behind his black coffee irises. She thought the fleeting look might be compassion. If it was, it faded before he spoke. "Whatever happens, Grace, I shall never shout at you again."

He sounded coldly angry, but not with her. Grace's throat was too tight to speak. With the sense that maybe he was her friend, after all, she nodded in gratitude.

The mystery as to whether Grace was visible to anyone but Christian was solved when Michael stuck his golden head around Christian's door.

"You *have* arisen then," he said. Perplexed, he squinted at his friend. Christian had been standing in the center of his cell-like room conversing with Grace. At Michael's words, she drew back wide-eyed against the wall—*into* the wall a bit, to be precise. If Michael had seen her, he would not have asked his next question.

"What are you doing? Charles claimed he heard you making strange noises."

Christian should have told him about Grace then, should have sought his help in banishing the shade. The words would not push themselves from his throat. If no one else could see Grace, she was his secret.

"Nothing," Christian said. "Talking to myself."

"Talking to yourself," Michael repeated dubiously. When Christian did not change his story, Michael shrugged. "Come down to supper, assuming you are done pretending to be the Maid of Orléans."

The lately martyred Joan of Arc was not what occupied the others' minds as Christian and Michael reached the hall. Christian's father laid a generous board. His men sat shoulder to shoulder around the long trestle tables, tucking into the hearty fare all soldiers relied upon. The standard under which they fought—a boar on a yellow ground between two red stripes—hung high on the painted wall above the dais.

Gregori Durand's absence was evidenced by the raucous humor of the company.

"O, merciful Saint Onan," Charles cried, leaping to his feet as soon as Christian appeared. "Forsake me not, lest my manly parts burst with lust!"

He accompanied this speech with genuflecting motions. Then, in case his meaning was mistaken, he added a lascivious hip thrust to drive it home.

"Very witty," Christian acknowledged as he took the space on the bench that Philippe and Matthaus had made for him. Someone slid him a trencher heaped up with stew. Taking it, he felt grateful Grace had remained behind. He was not certain he could have kept from blushing if she were there.

"You waste the strength of your good right arm," Hans counseled from the table's end. "Everyone knows the lasses in town would gladly spare you that labor."

"O, Christian," one of his father's men sighed in dulcet tones. "Is that a pike in your braies, or are you happy to see me?"

Christian grinned at the inanity of the chaffing, resigning himself to more of the same for the duration of the repast. He was glad the men felt comfortable enough to tease him, though he knew their awe at his luck with women was partially genuine. Bereft of any gift for love-talk, he had—nonetheless—a knack for gazing into females' eyes and luring them to him.

A sudden thought surprised him into laughing, causing him to choke on his venison. If he had not been so skilled at luring women, perhaps he would not be haunted by one now!

"We should go into town this eve," Charles suggested, his orange hair glowing in the light from the high windows. "Remind the wenches why they miss us."

"Not too late," Michael cautioned. "Tomorrow is no holy day."

"Saint Onan's day," Charles put in predictably—which set off another round of jests at Christian's expense.

He was almost restored to his normal humor by the time he rose from his seat, the only difference being a disturbing keenness to return to his room.

Not to see if Grace was there, he assured himself, but instead to hope she was not. With his stomach full and his ears ringing with male laughter, it was possible to believe he had imagined the visitation, maybe due to a fever from his whipping.

"I will bid Cook to change your bandages," Michael said.

Christian clapped him on his shoulder.

His habitual caution snapped back in place when a broad, dark shadow detached itself from a turning in the passageway to the stairs.

"Father," Christian said, startled to meet him there.

Gregori stood in his path, blocking the way. Though the light was dim, the seams and hollows of his brutal visage seemed deeper than usual. The idea that Christian's indomitable sire might be getting older was unsettling.

"They laugh with you, son," he said, "but that is not the same as following you in battle."

Sometimes it was, but Christian had the sense not to utter this. He tried not to think of Lucy, knowing his anger over the young hound's death would show in his face. "Do you need something, sir?"

His father gave him one of his silent stares. "What could I need," he mused after a moment, "that *you* would have the power to supply?"

To this, there was no answer. Christian bowed respectfully to his sire, then moved to squeeze past him. Gregori allowed it, but it was a near thing. Christian hated the fact that his scalp was prickling with fear-sweat as he edged by. Too many childhood beatings lurked in his mind, too many memories of helplessness.

"Familiarity breeds contempt," his father called after him.

Christian's stride hesitated without his willing it. His father would see the hitch and know what it signified. However much he had grown, Christian was still his dog to kick.

He fisted his hands and continued walking, smoothly, steadily, refusing to increase his pace even after Gregori Durand could not possibly witness it.

The Durand abode's main entrance, which led by way of a tunnel into the practice yard, was guarded by not one but two heavy iron gates. The walls to which these gates were bolted were thick and clad in rusticated masonry, much like the ponderous architecture quarrelsome Florentines preferred. Though a house rather than a castle, the residence's defensive nature was obvious.

Christian doubted anyone but he paid that mind this

evening. As he and his friends emerged, they were more interested in making merry. Christian was accompanied by his closest associates: Michael, William, Charles, Philippe, and Matthaus. Only Hans was missing, the older man claiming that carousing was for the young. Grace was in Christian's chamber, where Christian had most sternly ordered her to stay. Part of him regretted leaving the ghost alone, a regret intensified by the forlorn obedience his adamancy had inspired. He imagined Grace's father had cowed her, and now he was doing the same. The parallel did not sit well, but what to do with her confounded him. He did not want her trailing after him while he made up his mind.

These were not the only thoughts that had him unbalanced as they trod the well-worn road down the hill and around the lakeshore to town. His recent encounter with his father also disturbed him. Christian could not help thinking his sire had been issuing a warning.

He was gnawing his lower lip when Charles's freckled finger poked his shoulder.

"Come, now, Sir Gloomalot," he chided. "How will we draw the fairest damsels to our table if you resemble a rain cloud?"

Christian raised one eyebrow. "Are you implying you cannot draw them yourself?"

"Of course I can . . . once they see past my hair and discover my other charms."

"More like your gift for nonsense," William scoffed. His huge shoulders shifted within his marginally too-small blue tunic. William's dagger, an accessory without which none of them left the house, hung from a scabbard on his leather belt.

"You only wish you had my silver tongue," Charles retorted, smoothing his looser green tabard down the front of his chest. Beneath the pleats, his hose were particolored, one red and one white, in the eye-catching style he favored. "I was simply referring to Christian's ability to hasten the process of enticing butterflies into my net."

Christian rolled his eyes, his gloom shaking from him at Charles's foolishness. They were entering the narrow, winding street that led to their favorite tavern, the half-timbered walls of the surrounding buildings lit in passing by the lantern Matthaus carried. Their goal awaited beyond a shuttered apothecary, its entry bracketed by torches. Their short boots gritted on the cobbles as, one by one, the friends ducked through the ironbound door.

Once inside, more ducking was required. The Crowing Cock's low ceiling was made lower by wooden beams. These were prettily painted with the symbols of local guilds. The Durand boar gleamed among them in the tallow light, thanks to Christian and his friends spending so much coin here.

Fortunately, Christian's father's cronies drank elsewhere.

"Table," William said, pointing to a square one opposite the fire. Three men sat at it, tanners by the acrid smell of them. William's size shuffled them off with only a few grumbles.

"Good man," Charles praised, pausing long enough to slap William's shoulder before pushing through the crowd to find—and no doubt flirt with—the barmaid.

Christian lowered himself onto a bench at the table William had commandeered. As he did, he ran his gaze around the noisy room. He wasn't expecting trouble, but this was need as well as habit for him: to always know who was beside and behind him.

Life with his father had ingrained that.

At the table's other end, Philippe and Matthaus were

setting up a Nine Man Morris board on which to play each other. Matthaus was grinning, an expression Christian seldom saw on his roughly handsome and pockmarked face.

"Those two," Michael sighed, sitting next to Christian.

Christian knew he referred to the rumors that when *those two* shared a bedroll, more than sleeping went on. "They are discreet," he said. "And they harm no one. In any case, I have heard some say the same about us."

"About us?" Michael sounded so surprised Christian had to chuckle.

"They say you are too pretty to resist on those long campaigns."

"I?" Michael's mouth was gaping. "If that is true, why am I not fighting off wenches the way you do?"

"Your former calling keeps them at bay. Women fear you would rather take their confession than their virtue."

"Ballocks," Michael scoffed, though his face had turned thoughtful.

"Tears of Our Lord," Charles interrupted, returning with a jug of the local sweet red wine. He filled their cups with an easy hand and sat on the other side of Christian. "By the way, my friend, I believe you have a new admirer."

Charles tilted his head to indicate the murky corner just past the hearth. Herbs hung in drying bundles from the rafters there, casting broom-head shadows on the smoke-stained walls. At the farthest table, a figure sat, sprawled casually back in a slatted chair.

Christian's shoulders tightened. He had not noticed this person when he surveyed the room. He—or she—was dressed all in black, from pointed shoes to short velvet tunic to the ebony ostrich feather that curled on a small round cap. Built very slightly, the figure leaned forward. Christian saw it was a woman, despite the male attire. When the firelight hit her features, they were surpassingly delicate.

That she had been staring at Christian, she did not try to conceal.

"Traveling minstrel," Charles informed him. "Her lute is resting against the wall."

"Minstrel?" William turned his shaggy head to look. "That is a peculiar occupation for a woman."

When the woman's gaze slid over William, his hulking shoulders jerked as if he perceived a threat.

"Brr," he said. "She has funny eyes."

They were dark eyes, almond shaped and slanting like a princess who had been carried in a fancy litter down the Silk Road. Odd lights glinted in her irises, swimming up and sparking in a rhythm that did not match the dancing of the fire.

Christian was carrying his rondel dagger rather than the larger cinquedea—or five-fingered blade—that he kept under his pillow. Without thinking, his fingers curled around the grip. His thumb slipped between the ears of the pommel, which were designed to impart more force to a stabbing blow. The rondel was a favored weapon among assassins. Christian had always been fond of it.

"I will see what she wants," he said, rising.

"I daresay I can guess," Charles joked.

As Christian reached her table, the woman reclined again in her chair, her strange eyes seeming to laugh at him silently. She showed none of the fear most woman would have when caught alone, but instead an almost masculine bravado. Up close, she was uncannily beautiful, her skin smooth and perfect and ivory white. Her small bowed lips were red as blood in all that paleness.

"I was wondering when you would notice me," she said.

Her hands were as dainty as the rest of her, her fingers slim and graceful as she stroked the scored table top. Her hair hung as loose as Eve's in the Garden, straight and black as the finest silk. Until he stepped to her, the strands had disappeared into the inky velvet of her tunic.

"Do you desire a service of me?" Christian inquired.

When her lips stretched around her smile, her teeth were as white as Grace's. Unlike Grace's, her incisors looked like a cat's, a fraction more pointed than they should have been. Christian's gaze snagged on them until she spoke.

"I desire quite a lot of you, as it turns out."

In spite of his native caution, the archness of her manner stirred an answering warmth in his groin.

Sensing this perhaps, the woman licked her lips and leaned forward. "Your soul is a roaring flame on a cold, dark night. You have no idea how your hunger glows before eyes like mine."

Christian did not remember deciding to sit, but he was seated—on a hard little stool opposite her chair. His forearms were on the table, to either side of a bejeweled goblet. *Her* goblet, he assumed. The Crowing Cock had nothing like it on offer. Between his arms, the surface of her wine shivered with the hard beating of his pulse.

"You make me glad I stopped here," she said. "Geneva itself cannot offer such charms as you."

Her voice curled into his ears like a mystic's smoke, but when she touched his hand with her tiny seductive fingers, he jerked back as William had. He had felt something drawing on him at the contact, as if she had the power to suck the strength of life from him.

"A thousand pardons," he said, pushing a little shakily to his feet. "I am afraid you have mistaken me for someone else."

Her curving smile did not falter. "Never. I always recognize kindred souls."

His tongue was not quick enough to answer. He bowed and withdrew a step. "I must take my leave," he said.

"Christian," she said, stopping him before he could turn.

His scalp prickled violently, though he knew many of the tavern's patrons could have revealed his name.

"I will be here," the woman promised, "sipping at my wine, any night you tire of the succor your hand can bring. I shall be here, utterly available to you."

She was guessing, a lucky arrow shot in the dark.

His nod was a jerk of his head and neck. He backed away from her to rejoin his companions, trying not to retreat too quickly. The woman seemed to fade again into the shadows, but he sensed her still watching him. Tense, he rolled his shoulders as he sat.

"Too rich for your blood?" Michael asked sympathetically.

"Too something," Christian agreed.

Charles opened his mouth, laughing.

"No," Christian advised, laying his hand on his friend's forearm. "Do not give her a try yourself. I think she is dangerous."

Charles twitted him for that, but his eyes were already seeking out the barmaid. Charles liked simple, blowsy women, not adders in the grass. Christian tossed his wine back in one swallow, wondering how long he had to wait before they returned home.

Six

❦

Grace sat alone in Christian's chamber. Before he left, Christian had opened the shutters so she could look out at the road and the giant lake, but without him there, that soon palled. Her guide wasn't answering her calls, and a whole world stretched outside this room to explore.

There was no TV here, no movies, no Nat King Cole crooning over Mona Lisa on the radio. If Grace didn't entertain herself, no one would.

"No reason to be a mouse," she said practically, pushing up from Christian's three-legged stool.

It occurred to her that one advantage to being a spirit was that no one heard you talking to yourself.

Through trial and error, she discovered she couldn't float or fly, but she could walk through walls. Many of the rooms she passed through were as dull as Christian's—apart from the start she took at finding groups of people sleeping there. Most were soldiers—mercenaries, Christian had said—each of whom kept a frightening knife or two close at hand. Grace saw a lot of gruesome scars and heard a lot of bodily noises, making her glad her ghostly nose wasn't functional.

None of the rooms impressed her until she got to the dining hall. There the ceiling rose to a dizzying height, with thick, age-darkened beams to support the roof. Three tall men could have stood inside the hearth, could have danced a jig in it, if they wished. The fire had been extinguished for the night, leaving the great space quiet and dark. Grace could see everything anyway, including the colors of the intricate patterns painted on the walls, which said volumes about her changed circumstances.

Grace wasn't alive anymore. She might not even be human.

For all she knew, she'd never find out whether *All About Eve* really was Bette Davis's comeback.

She hugged herself, shivering for reasons other than a chill. What was she supposed to *do* here? Perform some divinely appointed task? Pester Christian for the rest of his life? Maybe she was meant to rescue him from some danger. Grace didn't mind that idea. She kind of liked it, in fact. She just wondered what would happen to what was left of her afterward.

She didn't understand why heaven wasn't any more responsive here than in Ohio. Shouldn't *that* have been an advantage to being dead?

"You are a fool, Philippe," someone chuckled low and dark behind her.

It wasn't Christian. It was one of the men who'd left with him earlier. He had a companion, yet another of the oversized, supermuscular males who seemed to populate this place. This one—Philippe, she expected—crowded the male who'd spoken into the paneled wall. Grace's mouth fell open. The pair were pressing their bodies full length together, their arms locked fist to fist and stretched above their heads.

Neither appeared unhappy with this mutual bondage.

"If I am a fool," Philippe rasped, his hips grinding the other's as if he meant to dig through, "I am only a fool for you."

His friend rumbled out a groan and kissed him, their mouths and muscles warring in a battle Grace blushed to see. They were fighting to get closer, grunting and heaving their weight into each other until they writhed. The man who was trapped against the wall tore one hand free, squeezing it between his hips and the other man's. What he was gripping wasn't hard to deduce.

"Yes, Matthaus," Philippe gasped, his head flung back in a pained sort of ecstasy. "God in heaven, it has been too long."

"It is always too long," Matthaus returned. His hips thrust forward in a hard rhythm. "I could take you twelve times a day."

In answer, Philippe clapped one hand around his rear, increasing the very enthusiastic pressure with which they strove together. Without warning, Matthaus made a choked, high sound, his face twisting strangely as his body went board-stiff.

Inexperience notwithstanding, Grace had a pretty good idea what had just happened.

Philippe did, too. He waited until Matthaus relaxed, then slid down him to his knees with a soft chuckle.

"You always go first," he said, his hands untying something at the other's waist. "It is fortunate I know how to help you rise again."

Matthaus moaned as Philippe's face disappeared into his parted clothing. "*Yes*. Lave me there with your tongue."

Grace had been frozen, but now an upsurge of embarrassment reminded her what she was doing.

Get out of here, she thought to herself. *You weren't invited to this party.*

She wasn't sure how it happened, but the hall blinked out of sight around her. In an instant, she was transported to Christian's room.

Christian felt as rattled as a bunch of knucklebones a giant hand had thrown. Between his father and Grace and this odd encounter at the Crowing Cock, he scarcely knew which end of him was up.

He should not have been walking faster as he approached his chamber, should not have felt his heart beating harder as his prick swelled ungovernably. Most definitely he should not have experienced a bloom of warmth within his breast at finding Grace inside. Her company had no business assuaging him. Her company was not even real. Strange though the woman at the tavern was, she was a far more suitable match for a man like him.

At the least, the minstrel had been alive.

Grace twisted from the window as he came in. Her cheeks were as flushed as if he had caught her in a forbidden act. The deep pink stain was like a punch to his heating groin, an all too pleasant one. A thousand thoughts of what she might have been doing blazed through his mind.

"Christian," she gasped.

He closed the door behind him. "Has something happened?" he asked carefully.

Her hands were clutched together beneath her bosom, which her gown did not shield any more effectively than before. He struggled not to stare at her rose pink nipples—or to notice that they were furled.

"I was walking," she said somewhat breathlessly. "Around the house. I popped back here, and I don't know how."

"You *popped* back here."

She nodded and blushed harder.

The laugh that rushed up in his throat surprised him. "You were spying, and you saw something personal."

"I didn't mean to spy. I was bored up here on my own."

The plaint was half apology. He stepped to her, remembering only at the last moment not to try to stroke back her deep red hair. He did not know how he could have thought her a witch. She was clean and sweet, almost radiant in the candlelight. Christian wanted to bathe in the sight of her. Her lashes dropped shyly at his nearness, her high, lush breasts rising and falling more swiftly in her sheer kirtle. Christian's prick finished hardening with a vigor that tempted him to groan. Be she maid or not, if he could have touched her, he would have fallen on her like an animal.

"Did you enjoy yourself?" she asked, speaking to a spot somewhere on his chest.

Christian's head felt muddled. "Enjoy myself?"

"Wherever you and your friends went out."

"*Enjoy* might not be the appropriate term."

Grace looked up at his acerbity. Every thought escaped him. Her eyes were the green of polished peridot, her dark red lashes heightening the color. With an effort, Christian cleared his throat.

"I feared you might be drawn with me," he said. "When I left the house."

She blinked as if she, too, had trouble following his words. Then she shook her head. "I don't seem to be tied to you that way."

"You could go anywhere you pleased when you went walking? Even outside the walls?"

"I don't know. I didn't try. But I saw no sign that I wouldn't be able to. Do you . . ." He watched her slender throat move with her swallow. "Do you want me gone that much?"

He had braced when she did, his shoulders tightening like a spring. Maybe he dreaded his answer as much as she dreaded hearing it. "You have no other acquaintances in this region? No friends you might like to . . . see?"

She snorted bitterly through her nose, the sound an eerie twin to one he might have made himself. "I don't know anyone here but you."

Sudden moisture glittered on her lower lashes. She turned away and pressed her fist to her mouth.

"Sorry," she said with that same brief laugh. "This is pretty darn pathetic." She shook herself, pushing her shoulders back. "When I was alive, I didn't get a chance to make friends. We were always moving from place to place. I didn't dare let anyone get close. I couldn't afford to let them know what my life was like. My father—" She stopped, then shook her head as if determined not to speak of that brute again.

"When the angel showed me what your father had done to you, when he said you and I were friends, I jumped at the chance to come. I didn't think about what would happen next."

A chill moved down Christian's spine. "The angel showed you what my father did?"

"When he had you whipped." She waved her hand, her voice lowering. "And the dog. I saw what he made you do to Lucy."

She faced him again, and he was the one who now felt compelled to turn away. "I would not have had an innocent girl see that."

"I know you didn't want to hurt her. I know he left you no choice."

Christian's arm tingled where she touched it. He felt almost too stiff to move. "You saw me weep for her. That is why you offered me comfort."

"Yes." Her hand fell away, leaving an odd cold spot. "I assumed you knew."

Had he known? Had he simply not wanted it put in words that she had witnessed his weakness?

"Christian." Her low, throbbing voice shocked through him like a crossbow bolt. "There's no shame in crying for someone you care about."

"What about in being too weak to protect the people who rely on you?"

"Whatever you do, there's always someone stronger."

"I do not accept that," he declared. "May the Almighty strike me down if I ever do."

He had never spoken of these things, not even to Michael. It made him shake to have done so, a fine, tight tremor that vibrated in his marrow. When Grace stepped around to his front, his hands clenched without thinking.

"I'm not sure," she said slowly, "that God would strike you for anything."

This was not what he expected her to say. His throat was thicker than he wanted it to be.

"I am damned," he said. "I have known that since I was seven, when the last of my three younger brothers died. Whatever my mother said, I knew there was a reason heaven wanted them and not me, a reason *I* would be left alone. Considering what I turned out to be, the cause is no mystery."

She stared at him, not speaking for so long that he thought she would remain silent. He wished she would . . . or that he had himself.

"I've wished some people damned," she said at last, "but you aren't one of them."

She broke him as easily as if she were a ten-foot ogre with an enchanted sword. Tears spilled down his cheeks in two long, hot streams. He wiped them, but they kept coming. He remembered holding some of those younger brothers, the two who lived long enough. So small, so fretful, like little sacks of beans in his awestruck arms. As a boy, he had let himself love them, to hope each time that one would stay with him. Always he had been wrong. He choked for air as Grace reached up to dry his cheeks, but naturally that did nothing.

The kindness in her eyes did something. Ridiculous though it was, that was his personal aphrodisiac.

"I have gone mad," he confessed with a shaky laugh. "In the midst of all of this, I would ravish you if I could."

"I would let you," she said.

He closed his eyes, tormented by a desire he truly did think would madden him. He looked at her again, at her lifted face with its cheeks blushing like sunset. Her lips were parted, her pupils huge. His breathing shifted, no tears in it anymore. He made a rash decision.

"Let down your kirtle," he growled.

She flinched, but she did not flee.

"I want to see your breasts," he explained.

"Are you going to touch yourself like you did before?"

"Yes," he said, the word a hard rasp of sound.

She wet her full, red lips with her pointed tongue. Her gaze slid down to where his prick pushed thick and aching behind his hose. "Would you let me watch this time?"

"Yes," he said as harshly as before.

She licked her lips again and took one step back. She was still close enough to touch, had that been possible. Clearly nervous, she shrugged the loose neckline of the kirtle over her shoulders.

The instant her breasts were naked, his hand dug into his braies.

"Is this all right?" she asked shyly.

He couldn't look away from her. Blindly, he found his

throbbing length and fisted it. Incited by her participation, the snug pressure of his fingers was even more welcome than before. He was used to swiving women, to being inside of them, but he had never felt this level of desire with others, or this level of pleasure. Unable to wait, he started working his pike, pulling with the tight, hard force his incredible need required. Her shape was lovely, the tightness of her puckered nipples, her collarbones, the faint golden down glinting on her curves. Her breasts looked like they would be just a bit heavy . . .

"You are beautiful, Grace." His voice was so rough, so broken by the urgent rhythm of his efforts to ease himself that he had to wonder if she understood. Wanting her to, he pulled in a fuller breath. "I am honored to be the first man to see you."

She bit her lip, hesitating. "I can't see you well enough," she confessed.

She nodded at his jerking hand and prick, which must have been obscured by his barely disarranged clothing. He had thought he was at the limit of lechery, but at her gesture heat lashed through him with renewed force. Cursing this additional flood of desire, he released himself, fumbled his points free from his doublet, and shoved his hose and braies down his hips. His prick thrust from the nest of hair at his loins, nearly on fire with its hard demands.

Grace's eyes hooked on it.

"Better?" he demanded.

"Yes," she whispered. Her tongue swept out tormentingly yet again. "Please go on as you were before."

Grace loved his laugh, shaky though it was. It was low and male, tugging recesses deep inside her and leaving them warm and wet.

"I could not halt," he said hoarsely, "not if the world were ending."

The urgent motions of his right hand emphasized his claim. He was completely bare to her now: cock, balls, the tendons straining in the hollows of his strong inner thighs. His feet were planted wide for balance, kicked free of his discarded clothes. It was impossible to find his half dress silly. He was too virile.

Grace couldn't help dropping to her knees, and never mind how fast that made her seem.

"Grace," he moaned, but she couldn't look up to see what her change in posture had done to him. What he was doing to himself had her complete attention, his white-knuckled grip pushing all the way down his thick, reddened shaft. When he reached its root, he tugged the whole of his cock up and out again. His penis was very hard, but he was still flesh, and his fingers compressed his skin. He tightened them each time he crossed the flare that marked the separation of shaft and head. Then, at the top, his fist engulfed the crest and squeezed, each time, over and over, as if he most liked the pressure there.

Grace's fingers curled into her palms watching it.

His crown was wet and shiny in the candlelight, not from sweat but from the tiny beads of fluid that were welling steadily from its slit. As that wetness grew, drawn up and down by his working hand, the sound his fist made became a slap.

"Grace," Christian groaned. "When you lick your lip like that, I go mad."

"Don't finish," she pleaded, moving nearer. "I'm not done watching you."

She was so enraptured by his intimate performance that she didn't think twice about bracing her ghostly palms on his thighs.

"*Grace!*" he choked out.

This time his voice was so agonized she had to lift her gaze. His expression was every bit as contorted—and ecstatic—as that man Philippe's in the dining hall.

"Can you feel my hands?" she asked.

"They tingle," he gasped, beginning to grunt in the helpless, guttural fashion she remembered vividly from before. The muscles of his stomach tightened until she saw every one. "Grace, put your hands on my ballocks."

She only just understood him. She cupped her spectral hands around his updrawn scrotum. When it had risen, she didn't know; his testicles had been hanging lower when she last looked. She didn't have a chance to ask him. His entire body jerked at her touch, shoving her hold slightly *inside* his flesh. Her hands buzzed, her skin pulsing wildly all over. He must have felt the interpenetrating contact as strongly as she did.

He made a sound—not quite her name, not quite a growl—thick with the sort of yearning epics were spun around. Aching for him more than she had for anyone in her life, Grace gathered her nerve to press her ephemeral lips to the tip of him.

His seed exploded from his penis in a shocking rush, shooting through her with an odd tickling sensation. Between her legs, her body clenched, but she couldn't reach the same culmination, not without more help.

Exhausted, emptied, Christian dropped to his knees on the bare hard plaster in front of her.

"Grace," he said, trying pointlessly to take her face in his hands. In stark contrast to before, when he had looked strained, his eyes were heavy and relaxed. "Fare you well?"

She nodded, though she was shaking.

He smiled, his slash of a mouth now fuller from his satisfaction. He brushed one tingling fingertip down her cheek. "You have a garden of roses blooming here. You make me wish I had the power to pleasure you."

"That's all right," she said hastily.

He drew his hand down her front, his longest finger trailing directly over her left nipple. Grace jumped at the feather light but very personal touch. She had her palms pressed anxiously to her diaphragm, one on top of the other. Christian laid his large hand over her smaller ones. When he did, it felt as if a breeze were whispering over them.

"Perhaps you could touch yourself," he said huskily.

She shrank back from him in alarm, sitting on her heels with her head wagging. Christian's eyebrows rose.

"You would deny me the delights of watching you?"

"I can't," she gasped breathlessly.

His gaze slid down and up her body, lingering on her bare, trembling breasts. Grace had never seen an expression that fiery—not even on a movie screen. Christian was a prince, darkly elegant and dangerous. She tensed when his eyes locked with hers again.

"Do you think heaven would punish you for seeking release?"

His question seemed serious.

"I can't," she repeated. "Not with you here."

He continued to search her face, the insidiously seductive heat clearing only slowly from his features.

"You are shy," he concluded.

She nodded, teeth sinking into her lower lip.

His smile was deeper this time, the shallowest of dimples appearing magically in one cheek. Her nipples tightened as he leaned closer.

"I see I shall have to devise some other method," he murmured next to her ghostly ear.

Seven

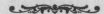

Christian wondered what sort of weak-willed mooncalf reveled in the company of a ghost. He must have been demented to do and say what he had last night. Once the cold light of morning dawned, with its promise of sanity, he should have been terrified by Grace's continued presence, should have feared for his already blackened soul. Instead, when she asked him—eyes downcast and hesitant—if she might stay with him that day, he had said she should please herself.

He had said it gruffly and with apparent bad temper. Inside, though, he had been disconcertingly gratified.

Grace wanted to be with him. Her sweet face had lit up and her smile had glowed, made happy by his grudging acceptance. He had almost glowed back, turning away and grimacing at the last instant. Her story of angels and age-old friendship could not be true. Christian might not live up to the name his mother gave him, but he knew the concept of other lives was a heresy. In any case, *nothing* lasted forever, not in the world of men. His reaction to the apparition was only lust—and a rather twisted lust at that. He had refrained from easing himself again that morning, but only just. It seemed that nothing could damp the effect of waking up with Grace next to him, especially when she looked so very real and tousled and warm.

"What are those doors?" she asked now, pointing.

Christian had been taking inventory of their stores, a duty his healing back allowed. The task had brought them to the rear of the house, which was dim and empty at present. Thankfully, Grace had been quiet while others were about. Christian was not a garrulous man, but it was strangely difficult to restrain his impulse to speak to her. Doing so now was an equally odd relief.

"Those are the garderobes," he said in answer. "They empty into a trench below."

"*Garderobes*," she repeated as if the word did not fit her mouth.

Arrested by her manner, Christian stopped walking to look at her. "Where *did* you reside when you were alive?"

"Um," she said, her hands twisting together in front of her.

Her nervousness spurred his interest. "That is not a hard question."

"I know. It's just, you didn't believe me about the angel, and I don't think you'll believe this."

Christian crossed his arms and lifted his brows at her. His challenge should have intimidated her, but the light from a nearby arrow slit revealed more ruefulness than fear on her pretty face. Neither emotion mattered. If he was fated to be haunted, he deserved answers.

"Fine," she said, crossing her arms to match his. "Have you ever heard of Christopher Columbus?"

"No. Was he the mayor of your town?"

For some reason, this made her laugh. "Sure," she said. "Christopher Columbus was our mayor, and my town was really, really far from here."

"If you do not wish to tell me, you should simply refuse. I do not like when people lie to me."

Her laughter died at his frown, and a tiny part of him regretted this—a part he squashed as ruthlessly as he could.

"I'm sorry," she said, her arms unfolding. "Please trust me when I say you'd like the truth even less."

"You should trust *me*," he countered. "I could have tried to have you exorcized."

Her face grew sad then, which caused an unpleasant tightening in his chest. *She* thought he was her friend. Even if she was deluded, even if a sane man would keep his distance from her, it was unmanly to kick at her.

"I suppose you could have." She gazed up at him, then squared her shoulders. "I keep forgetting to look at this from your perspective. Even someone from my . . . town wouldn't relish being trotted after by a ghost."

"Was your town known for specters?"

She grinned at his wide-eyed response. His question must have been as dull-witted as not recognizing the name of her region's mayor. Seeing she had pricked his pride, she reached out to pat his forearm, where his sleeves were pushed up. Christian did not have time to gird himself. The weight of her hand was no more than a feather against his skin, despite which it sent a strong rush of feeling straight to his groin. If she did not release him, he was going to harden, maybe worse than he had that morn.

"It was just a town," she said softly. "Chances are its people weren't so different from the people here."

She was coddling him as if he were a child *and* evading a straight answer. Though he did not wish to as much as he ought, he shook free of her humoring hand.

"Grace," he said, a warning growl in it.

"Christian?" The voice was male and unwelcome. William had come up the stairwell. No doubt he, like Michael before him, thought Christian was talking to himself. On the battlefield William was a lion, with a natural genius for strategy. In other arenas, he was not the sharpest of knives. The expression on his big bluff face at that moment was confused. "Your father wants to see you in his office."

Christian tensed but tried to hide it. A summons from his father was never good.

"You stay here," he hissed to Grace beneath his breath —alas, not quietly enough.

"As you like," William said, sounding surprised. "Might as well take a piss."

Grace's green eyes went big, her suddenly intrigued gaze following William's strides to the garderobe.

"No," Christian growled, easily guessing where her thoughts had traveled.

"But I've never seen one," she pleaded, laughingly.

"No?" William said, his hand already on the privy door handle. "You have some reason why I should not empty my bladder?"

"Talking to myself again," Christian huffed, narrowing his eyes at Grace. "Reminding myself how much I dislike spies."

"Assuredly," William said, not sounding sure at all. "Not too fond of them, either."

"If you took me with you," Grace suggested, her smile

truly wicked now, "I'd have no chance to spy on your large friend—or his, ahem, presumably gargantuan equipment."

Christian blew out an outraged breath. Did Grace honestly believe he would fall for this flimsy ploy? Her baiting manner and bold claims aside, she was blushing as bright as a rose.

"You would not dare," he declared.

"You'll never know," Grace teased back with a toss of her dark red hair.

He could not credit her behavior. She was enjoying crossing swords with him! Worse, some small part of him enjoyed it, too. She *did* trust him if she could show this much spirit. She was not frightened by his anger.

"What would I not dare?" William asked, perplexed.

"Nothing," Christian snapped as Grace bent double with amusement.

He reached for her wrist without thinking, meaning to tug her away from temptation. They both gasped when his fingers wrapped solid flesh. Her wrist was delicate, her skin as smooth as silk from the Orient. It was warm, as well, though not as warm as his abruptly sweating palm. He was touching her. Christian was *feeling* his apparition as real as day. Tiny but intense shivers rolled down his spine. Grace's gaze was chained to his as he slid his hold up her slender arm.

She was solid all over, it seemed.

She shivered when he fanned his thumb across the inner bend of her elbow. She was breathing shallowly, her full lips parted to draw in air. Between her small white teeth, he could see the glistening tip of her tongue. The longing that stabbed through him was unbearable. Had his prick been any harder, it would have split.

"Christian," William said, still lingering outside the privy. "What *are* you doing? You look brainsick."

Christian jerked his head to William. His heart was thumping in a panic, his fingers contracting ungently on Grace's arm. Obviously, William could not see Grace any more than before, but if she continued to be corporeal, would that change?

Christian was not certain he could stand to share the sight of her with William.

"I am leaving," he said as steadily as he was able. "My father will grow impatient if I delay."

He kept his grip on Grace as he walked rapidly to the stairwell, pulling her after him.

"Christian," she gasped.

What she was protesting, he did not know—perhaps the way he was hurrying her. Unable to stop, he hastened down to the next turning of the spiral stairs. Once he reached it, he backed her tight against the stone wall.

The moan that broke from him was low and rough. Her body was firm beneath his, giving and rounded but also slim as a girl. Her warmth caused a conflagration inside his veins, one that worsened as she grew warmer herself. The hands she placed on his waist were deliciously tentative. Set amongst all that heat, her maidenly shyness made him feel ten times the man he normally was. It was his nature to plunder, and she was a prize no marauder could have passed by.

"Christian," she whispered as his head sank toward hers.

"I *have* to kiss you," he said.

He was almost afraid to do it. Would she return to mist if he broke this spell? Would he be left with a ghost again? Her breath wafted over him, her lips trembling palpably. He cupped the back of her silky head, his fingers spreading, her gorgeous hair spilling down his arm. The scarlet locks fell to the center of her back, thick and cool and gleaming as if they recently had been combed. With the sense that he was changing his life forever, he pressed his mouth over hers.

Such a tiny sound issued from her throat that only his ears could have caught it.

"I won't hurt you," he promised, drawing back from paradise just far enough to speak.

Tears glistened in her eyes, beautiful but unshed. "I believe you, Christian."

She rose on her toes, her soft, full breasts sliding up his chest. Her hands branded him with fire as they shifted onto the back of his brown doublet. It took one galvanic heartbeat for him to sweat through his shirt. Needing to hold her more than he needed breath, he wound his arms around her, between her back and the wall. Helpless not to, he wrapped one hand around the curve of her bottom and lifted her.

This time, when their lips sealed together, he was the one who moaned.

God bless her, she gave him entry, letting him lick her, letting him stroke and suckle the small, sharp tongue that had been inciting his worst cravings. He tried to be gentle, even tender, but when her fingers curled around his shoulders from behind, her surprisingly strong arms tightening, he could no longer take the care her innocence deserved.

His hips surged against her, his friction-greedy prick rubbing and thrusting against her mons. She was a maid. His aggression must have alarmed her, but rather than object, she changed the angle of her head and pushed her own sleek tongue deep into his mouth.

Christian's knees threatened to buckle. Her kiss was eager, and not without natural skill. Unbelievably aroused by both, his hand clenched in a spasm on her hindquarters, crushing her closer to his groin. Grace cried out and kissed him harder, the movements of her hips beginning to answer his. Christian's breath came like a bellows. With a choking sound he could not repress, he yanked her smooth legs up to his waist level. Her linen kirtle was loose enough to allow this, though the folds and gathers that bunched between them maddened him sorely.

"*Merde*," he cursed, breaking free of their last kiss to begin another impatient one. Their tongues engaged in a battle he could not get enough of, though his excitement was already at fever pitch. He felt the pressure of impending climax build in his testicles.

Grace seemed disinclined to slow him. She clutched his head as they kissed, her fingers kneading the most tantalizing sensations into his scalp. Her touch felt so good chills chased each other across his skin. Grunting very much like a bull in rut, he heaved his body against hers. Her gown was damp where it met the bulge thrusting out his braies. Wanting to feel her responses better, he yanked some of the gathers in her gown away. By luck as much as intention, his rhythmic shoves had parted her nether lips. Her swollen pearl was a hotter bump on his underridge. Struggling against the inclination of his eyes to roll back with bliss, he tried to aim the strongest pressure of his erection there.

He would not enter an innocent so hastily, but he wanted her to break with pleasure, wanted her to explode and gush. She had not done so the other day, and the omission had been wearing on him since. If the needs that drove him would have permitted it, he would have dropped to his knees and ravished her with his tongue.

"Go," he groaned into her mouth, his muscles trembling with how close he was. He thrust more rapidly against her mons, desperate to bring her apace with him. "I pray you, beloved, go."

Something cupped his suffering prick. Her hand had squeezed between them where they were so determinedly rubbing their mutual itches over each other. When her fingers curled around the shaft, the sensitive crest of his organ drove straight into the mound underneath her thumb. With all their writhing, he had broken loose of his braies, and the contact was skin to skin, his bare tip against her bare palm. The most unholy ache swelled like gunpowder in his groin. He peaked before he could stop it, before he could gasp for air. Pleasure blinded him as his seed burst free in a fusillade, shooting into and over her hot, damp hand.

Even in his throes, some part of him knew she had not joined him. Trickles of perspiration rolled down his temples as his body calmed. He was spent then, but bereft of his full reward.

He knew this failure to bring her to climax could easily obsess him.

"Perdition take you, Grace," he swore once his lungs agreed to function. "Why did you do that?"

She was looking nervously up at him, standing on her own two feet with her pretty teeth digging into her lower lip. Immediately contrite, he cupped her cheeks in both hands.

"Forgive my harsh words," he said. "You did not know you would push me so quickly over the edge."

"I liked doing that," Grace insisted, a trifle rebelliously.

Christian let his hands slide to her slim, straight shoulders, his thumbs caressing her collarbones. "I am not angry. I simply wished to share that delight. You are young, and perhaps you are not aware, but women are as capable of enjoying the carnal act as men—more so, some philosophers say."

Grace squirmed slightly in his hold. "I know that," she mumbled. "I'd just rather try things on you."

He laughed, surprised by the relish he took in making the sound. He cradled her face again, bending to kiss one fiery cheekbone.

"Allow me the same privilege," he whispered into the shell of her ear. "Let me try a thing or two on you."

His hand slid over her breast, stroking it through her kirtle, brushing its pebbled nipple with a slow massage of his palm. Her eyes grew wider as his touch circled, her mouth falling open for quickened breaths. Christian's lids felt weighted as his gaze was pulled between enchantments. Innocent or not, he could not doubt she was responsive; every inch of her declared her readiness for love. The veins in her throat pulsed, the slopes of her breasts shaking. Carefully, he gathered up her gown with his other hand. Over her knees it rose, up her thighs, baring flesh as smooth as carved pink marble.

His chest grew tight as her triangle of scarlet curls was revealed. His recently sated prick was twitching, lifting in surges between his legs. She was so beautiful, so obviously aroused. Her pubic hair was spiked with moisture, her little bud of pleasure peeping out from those most delicate petals.

She gasped when he gently cupped her mons veneris, but—to save his life—he could not lift his eyes to her face. Watching his own actions with bated breath, he allowed his longest finger to burrow where she was most wet. That wetness increased even as he found it, spilling hot, sleek cream over his knuckles.

"Shh," he soothed as the muscles of her lovely thighs attempted to bar his exploration by tightening. "Grace, I promise you will like this."

He sent his thumb toward her hooded pearl, sinking just the tip of one finger into her entrance. He achieved both goals at the same instant—which proved too great a test of Grace's valor. Squeaking like a mouse, she jerked back from him.

With no small dismay, he saw she had retreated halfway into the stone wall.

"Grace," he said sternly. "Make yourself solid again now."

"I can't," she panted. "I don't know how I did it before."

Christian glowered at her from beneath lowered brows.

"I don't! I swear it was an accident."

"Methinks your *accident* was suspiciously well timed."

She muttered something he suspected contradicted him, then looked up and crossed her arms. Her glare was every bit as belligerent as his.

"At least step out from the wall!" he exclaimed.

She stepped, planting her little fists on her waist. This new pose did nothing to lessen the distraction of her round, red-tipped breasts. The sight reminded him how quickly he was recovering from his premature and rather forceful release.

"Your father will be waiting," she huffed at him.

"*I* am waiting," he said, but he could not disagree with her. His breath sighed out in resignation.

He did not bother trying to convince her to stay behind.

Christian's father's office was a long, beamed room on the second floor. Its two tall windows overlooked the court-yard, and they were relatively broad. Lit by the generous illumination, the furnishings were simple: a long desk, a few chairs—mostly wood with leather-wrapped seats and backs. At some point, the plastered walls had been painted a bilious green, a dreary color Gregori seemed uninter-ested in improving on. Two globes on stands enlivened the equally somber carpet—one celestial and one representing terra firma as it now was known. A dozen books lay scattered about, fresh from the new "movable type" presses in Nuremberg. Some of the Durands' clients, primarily those from Italia, liked to cultivate the appearance of being learned. Gregori had collected these Greek and Latin texts to impress them. As far as Christian knew, he had not opened them himself.

The only personal decoration in the office was a wall display of battered swords and knives, which were the actual fighting weapons of Gregori's father. Christian had not met his mercenary grandfather. He had been dead by the time Gregori's first and only living son was born. Occasionally, Christian wondered if the men had been much alike. Christian's father never spoke of his progenitor that he could recall.

As Christian waited for Gregori to look up from his ledgers and acknowledge him, he tried to ignore Grace's curious progress around the room. His resolve was shaken when she leaned into one of the deep windows to look out. The light from the opening shone through her sheer kirtle, limning her body as clearly as if she were naked. The halves of her bottom were as high and tight as they had felt in his gripping palm. The curving shadow where her parted thighs met caused him to swallow hard.

A click signaled that his father had set down his quill.

"You kept me waiting long enough," he observed.

Christian inclined his head. "My apologies, Father."

Gregori stared at him with his cool snake's eyes, probably waiting for an explanation. When Christian neglected to supply one, he pursed his lips, settled back in his seat, and went on.

"We have a new commission, a woman who wishes to be escorted to Florence." Christian's father pressed his fingertips together in front of his bullish chest. "She asked for you specifically."

"For me?" Christian was startled into asking.

"Yes," said his father. "And I have to wonder why that would be."

"I do not know. No one, man or woman, has spoken to me about a job."

"She mentioned meeting you at the Crowing Cock."

Muscles tightened in Christian's neck. "I met a female *minstrel* in that tavern the other night."

"Apparently, she is eccentric but no mere minstrel. She offered twice the normal fee for our services, providing you were included among the guard."

"I do not know what to say. I had no notion she intended this."

"Did you not?" His father leaned forward over his desk, his dark eyes keen and suspicious. "You are only twenty. You might not realize that is too young to strike out on your own, much less to set yourself up as my rival."

His tension coiling even tighter, Christian pulled his shoulders back to review posture. "Sir, I have no such plans."

Grace remained by the window, across the room, but Christian was aware she had turned to watch. He kept his gaze on a vague distance. If his father thought he meant to unseat him, Christian did not want to imagine how unpleasant his life could get.

His father rose, walking slowly around his desk, his battle-scarred fingers trailing over the brass nailheads that trimmed its edge. "I agreed to provide a dozen men in addition to ourselves: six of my choosing and six of yours. I assume you will want to take your usual *rotte*."

"If that pleases you," Christian said politely.

His father was too close to him, and closer yet when he stepped behind Christian's back. His hot breath ruffled the hair that escaped the base of his queue. With all his might,

Christian fought the defensive instincts that told him to turn around.

"Nothing about this pleases me," his father hissed, then stirred the air with what Christian presumed was a shrug. "It is a job, however, and it will pay richly. Since there was no agent in this instance, I will have our banker credit the commission to your account."

Christian bowed his head. "Thank you, sir."

He kept his gaze averted as his father moved to his side. A bead of sweat was gathering in his hair.

"Watch yourself," Gregori said, then snapped his fingers next to Christian's ear.

Christian flinched, as was intended, but only the slightest jerk. Judging it safe to leave, he bowed more deeply and backed away. His father *hmphed* and stumped to his desk.

Christian did not draw one full breath until he closed the office door behind him. Grace slipped through the panels a moment later. Her appearance startled him afresh. He had honestly forgotten she was in there.

"Golly," Grace said, an expression he was not familiar with. She was looking up at him, but he could not bring himself to look at her, not even to apologize. "Your dad's got quite a stick up his rear."

He laughed, and though it was shaky, he felt better. "That he does, Grace," he said. "That he does."

Eight

I'm coming with you," Grace said, her jaw set in the stubborn fashion Christian was growing accustomed to.

"You were with me all day," he said.

She had been, drifting to and fro in the bailey as he tested his healing back with a light practice. Grace's figure was so pretty, so womanly, that he had worried she would distract him. Instead, he had fought better than he hoped, as if he were an idiot knight with his damsel fair watching him. Idiocy aside, his performance told him he would be well enough to travel soon.

"I like being with you," Grace said. "Your company . . . feels good."

Given that he barely knew her, Christian did not want to admit how acutely he concurred with this. It was as if his whole life a piece of him had been missing, and Grace fit perfectly into the spot. That *she* had quite a few spots he wished to fit into went without saying. Would that he could plumb them now, and innocence be damned. After a day in public, they were alone again in his room. That simple difference heated him.

"You need me," she said, forcing him to wonder if she could read his mind. "You said yourself you thought this minstrel woman was dangerous."

"And, pray tell, Grace, how do you expect to aid me? No one else can see or hear you. You cannot even cry for help."

"I don't know. Maybe if you were in danger, I'd find a way. Ghosts are supposed to be able to do things. Make floorboards creak and fling pictures off of walls. Maybe I just need more practice."

"You tried *practicing* this morning." He growled the words, his earlier frustration not forgotten.

Grace's cheeks were red enough to glow. "You could have . . . taken care of the results without me."

Christian backed her against the edge of the window where they had been standing. He both reveled in and was ready to grind his teeth at the way she squirmed inside the cage of his arms. He knew exactly why she shifted. With every breath, her body declared its desire for him.

"It is *your* pleasure I crave," he said, his voice so low it rumbled in his chest. "Your pleasure bursting like a ripe, juicy fruit with mine. When you agree to touch yourself, I will no longer withhold those actions you seem so eager to watch again."

"Christian." Gasping for air, Grace laid her ghostly hands on his ribs—as though she had the power to push him off. The effect she did have was bad enough. The contact ran like effervescence through his veins, straight to the part of him that least needed it. He wanted to touch himself there, to rub the terrible itch that seemed to have taken up permanent residence in his crown.

"Grace," he responded with his jaw gritted, "if your man-

ner were not so gentle, I would swear you were a devil sent
to torment me."

"You have more experience," she said, shrinking back
as he pressed forward. "You're more comfortable with
these things."

She was blinking rapidly, nervous and excited at his
nearness. Her girlish timidity was like a flag waved before
a bull. Christian dropped his arms with a muttered curse.
He did not have the time to continue this skirmish now.

"You may come with me to the tavern," he conceded.
"But please do not speak unless we are alone."

"I'll be as quiet as a mouse," Grace promised, making a
gesture with her thumb and finger as if turning a key in her
lips. "You won't even know I'm there."

Somehow, Christian doubted that.

Grace was so excited to see a real medieval town that
she was beside herself. The streets were narrower than
she expected, the buildings taller and more substantial.
Some of the handsomer ones towered as many as six stories. Though the sun was setting, color assailed her on
every side: in the cheery frescoes on the houses' fronts, in
the people's clothes, in the charming window boxes still
abloom with bright flowers. Christian could hardly drag
her away from a pretty wooden well where women in long
skirts and head scarves were gathering.

"You would think the girl had never seen a bucket!"
Christian exclaimed softly.

Grace realized she had better keep her interest under
wraps if she wanted to conceal her true origins.

The dusty cobbled path was crowded where it circled
around the well. With no room to get out of the way, both

she and Christian sucked in their breath when a little don-key pulling a cart full of dented cooking pots clopped through her. She'd heard animals could sense ghosts, but this donkey didn't even snort.

"Shush," Christian said, though all Grace had done was try to grab his arm in surprise.

She was quiet from then on until they reached the tavern where he was meeting his father's newest client. The place was dark and smoky and low ceilinged. It didn't seem to be an hour for drinking. The only people Grace saw inside were an older man in an apron and a pretty, plump girl in a low-cut smock. Somewhere behind the bar a cricket chirped creakily.

"Is the minstrel here?" Christian asked.

The man in the apron waved to the farthest corner with-out speaking.

Now that Grace was a spirit, she saw very well in the dark. Regardless of this change, only shadows seemed to fill the place the man had indicated, as thick and inky as a movie trick. Grace and Christian weren't more than two strides away when—seemingly out of nowhere—a woman leaned forward into the firelight. Her profile was a cameo of white jade, every line and slope delicate. Such loveliness should have enchanted, but tension gripped Grace's shoul-ders, as if this female presented a personal threat to her.

In his brief account of their meeting, Christian hadn't mentioned how beautiful the minstrel was.

Her head turned toward Grace and Christian as if her neck were formed of gears and not vertebrae, an oddly robotic motion. Perhaps *she* was having trouble seeing. Her dark eyes squinted while one small crease furrowed her otherwise flawless brow. "I asked that you come alone, Christian."

Grace's intake of breath was sharp. This woman saw her? This woman knew she was with Christian? Grace tried to back away, but her arms and legs wouldn't cooperate. Some dark power was streaming out from the minstrel, and whatever it was, it wasn't a friend to Grace. For the first time since she'd died she felt like a spirit, her atoms dissolved and spread in a powerless smoke. Panic clutched her nonexistent midsection. She was going to blow away. She was going to be nothing.

Help! she thought, without much hope of answer.

Christian stepped in front of her. "I *am* alone," he said smoothly.

A second later, he truly was.

Grace's disappearance caused a far more serious jump in his pulse than the minstrel coming into view. That trick Christian had seen before; Grace abruptly ceasing to be was new. He told himself she was *somewhere*, perhaps even somewhere nearby. No doubt she had finally figured out how to make herself more invisible—and with damned good timing, as it turned out. If this minstrel was some sort of seer, Grace had best stay away from her.

In spite of this reassurance, sweat broke out beneath his arms. Christian fought not to call after or look for her.

One threat at a time was his motto.

The minstrel was under no such restriction. She snapped her gaze from one side of him to the other, then frowned at him. "I thought I saw someone there with you."

Christian shrugged. "The light is tricky at this hour."

The woman pursed her lips, slowly easing back in her chair. This time the shadows did not hide her. They seemed, in truth, to be at her beck and call.

"Sit," she said, gesturing to the stool he had used before. Her tone was part command, part silky feminine invitation. Christian knew which he was more comfortable with.

"Wine?" she offered, once he was settled.

Christian shook his head. "Might I know your name? Since you know mine."

"Nim Wei," she said. "But if you wish to call me 'mistress,' that is also acceptable."

Christian inclined his head and called her neither.

This she seemed to find amusing. A flicker of a smile twitched her mouth.

"Our itinerary," she said, sliding a map that had been hand drawn on heavy parchment across the table. It was very detailed: mountains and rivers and city names all marked in. Nim Wei tapped the edge closest to herself with a pale, shapely fingernail. Christian couldn't help noting that her fingers were almost white enough to glow. "We should cross into Savoyard territory here, at the St. Bernard Pass. The Valle D'Aosta gives us access through the Alps to Turin, from whence we can reach the old Roman road, the Via Aemilia. That will take us to Bologna. Florence, where I have business, is an easy march from there."

Christian studied the route she had traced. There would be good hunting for much of it, which would spare them carrying heavy loads of provisions—or having to "appropriate" them as they went. When they were on campaign, they often faced this necessity, but Christian did not relish it.

"Yes," Nim Wei said, following his thoughts. "And what food you cannot catch, I will pay for. I am not absolutely opposed to stealing, but I consider it shortsighted to leave a trail of angry peasants in my wake."

Christian looked up at her, the golden sparks in her eyes

momentarily transfixing him. With an effort, he shook himself. "It would be more direct to go along the coast."

Nim Wei shuddered delicately. "Too sunny, even this time of year." She leaned forward, her slender white fingers sliding over the backs of his scarred brown hands. "You should know this about me, Christian: I abhor the sun. I shall rely on you to convince the others to travel only after dark."

Her voice was sweet and smoky, her eyes like polished jet sparkling with stars. Christian's chest went tight as he stared into them. "Only after dark?"

"How else can I preserve my beautiful pallor? A woman must take her advantages where she finds them."

If she prized her feminine advantage, why had she been journeying dressed as a male minstrel? The question slid from his mind as soon as it formed. Nim Wei was stroking his hands with her fingertips, up and down, up and down, until the skin between his knuckles hummed. Christian cleared his uncomfortably thickened throat.

"How many servants do you travel with?" he croaked.

Nim Wei released his hands before he could edge them back. "None. You and your men shall provide any assistance I require."

This was hardly proper. Even if she was eccentric, a group of rough-mannered soldiers could not serve all a woman's needs. Christian opened his mouth to say so only to find he could not. He rubbed the spot between and just above his eyebrows, where something felt like it was pressing.

"Strong, too," the minstrel murmured, apropos of he knew not what. "I cannot express how that pleases me."

"Even traveling light, this route will take longer than a fortnight," Christian warned in an uncustomarily nervous rush.

Nim Wei smiled at him with closed lips. Her fingers were on the underside of his wrists now, playing as light as catkins where his veins fed into his palms. He tried not to react, but when his heart started thumping harder, her smile deepened.

"Yes," she said. "I believe that is long enough."

Christian's whole arm shook as he pushed the door to his room open. He should have reported straight to his father, but a stronger compulsion had pulled him here. That compulsion did not bear fruit. His chamber was empty. Naught but shadows and moonlight fell upon the simple shapes of his furniture.

Though he continued to stand in the doorway, there seemed no point in going in.

"Grace?" he said, soft but loud enough to hear. "Grace, if you are here, show yourself."

The silence echoed with his heartbeats. They came faster than they should have, faster than they had for his parley with Mistress Wei. Christian had almost forgotten Grace while they spoke, as if whole worlds could be lost in the swimming depths of the minstrel's eyes.

He shuddered at that thought. "*Grace*," he said more harshly.

A footfall scuffed to a halt in the passageway behind him, closer than Christian ought to have let it get.

"Christian?" Michael laid a hard, warm hand on his upper arm.

Turning, Christian tried not to be disappointed that his friend was not Grace. "I was praying."

Michael's brow wrinkled. "For grace?"

"You are always saying God's gifts are for everyone. I was feeling in extra need of virtue." Christian hitched one shoulder, disliking his awareness that he was lying. "I expect it was a waste of time."

Michael's fingers squeezed his bicep and then let go. "Your meeting with our new client troubled you."

This topic he could discuss. Christian let his back rest against the wall beside the door to his room. "Something is not right about her. She claims she 'abhors' the sun. She wants to travel only at night."

"Some women do not like to freckle."

"I am unconvinced that her reason is vanity."

"Then what?"

"I do not know. Maybe I am nervous because she is too seductive."

"You?" Michael laughed until he saw that Christian was serious. "Your father will not refuse the commission. No matter how strange this woman is, her offer is too rich."

"I know." Sighing, Christian glanced into his empty chamber, still void of any sign of his ghost.

"Charles spoke to me again tonight."

This jerked Christian's attention back. "Tell me he did not do it when others were about."

"No," Michael said, crinkling his brow to match Christian's. "Charles is rash, but he has too much wit for that. He did admit to talking to William. He said William agreed with him."

"William is too loyal to *dis*agree. Perdition take him." Christian slapped his palms in frustration against the wall behind him. "I told Charles to let it drop."

"You cannot blame him. This business with the dog made everyone realize how harsh your father has become."

"It would not serve." Christian's voice was as low as it was impassioned. The lantern at the end of the passage flickered in a draft. "My father's harshness is exactly what our clients want. *They* would not follow me if I broke away on my own, and I will not risk your lives for no better end than to have you starve."

"You think it would come to risking our lives? To your father taking arms against you?"

"Can you doubt it? You know his pride. At the least, we would have to pray we never faced his men on opposing sides of a battlefield."

Michael's blue eyes held his. "Perhaps we would fare better than you believe. Perhaps Gregori has trained you to underestimate your strengths. People respect you, Christian. There may be some among your father's men who would change allegiances to you."

"I am but twenty," Christian said. "They are veterans."

"You have been fighting since you were fifteen."

"As has my father. Michael, I value your faith in me. Believe me, I do. I think, however, that if you were in my shoes, you would not risk your men."

"Maybe not," Michael said. "But I am not the leader you are."

Christian looked away. Michael had no idea how much more admirable he was than Christian, how often Christian wished he had Michael's certainty of mind.

"I must go to my father," he said aloud. "He will want to know what the minstrel said."

Grace lay facedown on a hard surface, her head resting on her hands while an unknown pressure shoved into her back. The shove felt strange, as if it were and were not happening to her body.

"Pull," someone said.

Hands gripped her bent elbows and tugged upward. Air

whooshed involuntarily into her lungs. Sweaty fingers touched her neck.

"Still no pulse."

"Again."

Not yet, another voice said inside her head.

Not yet, Grace repeated.

She blinked, her mind losing its grip on the perceptions it had just experienced. She was sitting on the edge of Christian's monklike bed. He was there as well, lying on his back atop the blanket with his fingers woven together on his breastbone. A second earlier—or what had seemed like a second earlier—she'd been standing behind him in the dark tavern. She'd disappeared, and then she'd popped back here. Time must have passed, though. Time she couldn't account for—or Christian would still be gone.

What the hell is happening? she thought as Christian's eyes snapped open.

"Grace," he said, bolting up to stare at her. "You came back."

He flung his arms so tightly around her she had to squeak. His hard, lean cheek was squashed against her ear, his strong muscles trembling. His enthusiasm stunned her, his obvious gratitude for her return. Her throat tightened with an emotion strong enough to frighten her. *This* was what it was to be cared for. This was what it meant to matter to someone. Grace wished her reflexes were quick enough to stop him when he gripped her shoulders and held her away from him.

"Why did you leave me?" he demanded, shaking her just a bit.

"I don't know. I didn't mean to."

"You did not hear me calling you?"

Grace shook her head. "Christian," she said softly. "You're touching me."

The realization hit him, too. His face darkened in a rush, the color infusing the dramatic angles of his cheeks and jaw. Within their evening mask of stubble, his hard lips softened and then went tight. They were redder, too, the sharp points of his upper lip causing Grace to touch her tongue to her own.

"Grace," he groaned, his hold trailing down her arms. The squeeze he gave her fingers—so tight, so suggestive of pent-up longing—pulled a gush of sultry wetness out from her core.

Evidently, she was physical enough that her nose was working. The scent of her own arousal, and never mind the way Christian's nostrils flared, made her squirm with embarrassment.

Seeing this, Christian laughed shakily. "You are so gorgeous," he whispered, squeezing her hands again as his gaze raked her up and down. "I swore to myself the instant you became corporeal, I would fall on you like an animal."

"Have you changed your mind?" Grace asked, because he clearly wasn't attacking her.

This time, his laugh was silent, his dark eyes dancing with amusement. "To my amazement, I find I am simply grateful to hold your hand." He drew it to his mouth, pressing a fervent kiss to each fingertip. "Your lovely, warm little human hand."

As if this were not thrill enough, he finished with his lips soft against her palm. Grace didn't understand how such a sweet and courtly gesture could have her tingling all over. This was worse than the last time she'd taken form, when he'd kissed her so thoroughly in that stairwell. Her body was learning to need him. The place between her thighs ached with a strength that was close to pain.

"I'm not human," she gasped through her agitation. "Not really. Not anymore."

Her own words struck a blow inside her. Her mortal life was over. Flawed as it had been, perhaps she should have appreciated it more. Then again, Christian had not been there, so maybe this shadow existence, with its mysterious and unpredictable rules, ought to be cherished, too.

Her eyes were hot, the moisture that had risen to them blurring her vision. Christian didn't shy away from the emotion she was exposing. In fact, his eyes seemed brighter than normal. His shoulders straightened, a muscle tightening in his jaw as if he'd come to a decision.

"You are human to me," he said. "Human and real."

"And to think I only had to die to have someone feel that way."

He touched her cheek at her sardonic tone, a soothing stroke along its hollow. She realized she loved looking at his face. His nose was unexpectedly elegant, long and narrow, with a small bump at the bridge where it might have been broken. An equally elegant scar bisected his left eyebrow. When he spoke, his voice was soft.

"Where did you go, Grace? I have not seen you for hours."

"Hours!" Grace exclaimed. Something that might have been a memory rolled through her mind. Pressure thrust against her back, compressing her ribs and lungs, but the reason for the phantom sensation was as indistinct as fog. Oddly reluctant to unravel her recall, she shook herself. "I don't know where I went. It only seemed like seconds to me."

Christian's palms framed her cheeks in warmth. "It does not matter. Not now that you have returned."

Grace slid her hands along his forearms, loving the feel of their long, hard tendons, of their silky, ruffling black hair. Her caress was shy, but it darkened his face again.

"Would you kiss me?" she asked.

They were so close she saw his pupils swell. Christian drew a breath but hesitated. "I do not wish to frighten you."

"I don't think you will this time."

His big, lean chest moved faster, his oddly delicate lips parting. "Warn me if you think you are going to disappear."

Too impatient to speak, Grace leaned forward and kissed him.

A soft tenor cry caught inside his throat. His lips pushed against hers, parted hers, and then their tongues were sliding like wet satin over each other. He didn't rush her, but savored her, slow and deep. The taste of him was a drug, melting her, weakening her, until the curve of his long arms around her was a requirement to hold her up.

He pulled her onto his lap and groaned. His chest was her support then, matched only by the clinging, probing, devastatingly seductive kisses she didn't think she could live without. Diffidence forgotten, she strained to him, her own arms twining behind his neck. He rubbed her waist, her hip, his caresses restless and careful. She knew he didn't want to alarm her, didn't want to lose the taste and feel of this close embrace. She was sitting on his huge erection, his thighs alternately bunching and relaxing under her, as if he both wanted and feared to push that sexual part of him harder against her.

Grace was too enthralled to care. Her head fell back when his hand moved upward to mold her breast through her sheer white gown. She was making noises just like he was: small, muffled, impossible to hold in. She already knew he liked the lushness of her bosom. With a throttled cry, he tightened his fingers, his palm pressing and turning on her stone-hard nipple. The friction felt so good no force on earth could have kept her from wriggling. As she did, Christian's cock jumped beneath her. Stiff from head to toe with tension, he dragged his open, panting mouth up her neck.

"I would do more than kiss you," he said, his voice hoarse enough to burn. "If you would allow."

Grace turned in his lap and lifted his head with her hands. The look she found on his face shocked her. His expression was so intense, so naked with desire, that when his gaze searched hers, she truly thought she'd go up in flames.

"Yes," she said with what was left of her breath.

He closed his eyes—in relief, she thought—those thick black lashes dropping to his lust-flushed cheeks. Despite the reaction, despite her *permission*, he didn't push her back to fall on her. His hand found her ankle and began sliding up under her thin gown. When he reached her knee, his lashes lifted, his eyes shining like dark jewels.

With surprising gentleness, he pressed his warm lips to hers. "This is for you, Grace. Upon my honor, this time is all for you."

She didn't mean to, but she jerked as he caressed her thigh.

"Hush," he murmured, his fingertips drawing circles too near her most private flesh. "Breathe, Grace. Look into my eyes and breathe."

His expression hypnotized her, its mixture of hard need and soft concern. He looked languorous, sensual, licking his lips as his longest finger first brushed her hidden curls.

She wondered if he was thinking of kissing them.

"I shall not penetrate you tonight," he promised, his voice deliciously graveled. "Just touch you and stroke you and bring you whatever pleasure you are comfortable with. Trust me, Grace, your maidenhead is safe with me."

She gasped as one fingertip bumped her labia—and again when he pulled her hot, welling moisture up the plump meeting of those folds. He was gentle, barely touching her at all. The intimacy tickled and mortified. Though it made no sense, both reactions aroused her. The little button of her clitoris swelled, pulsing, twitching, practically stretching with its hunger for him to touch it, too. Even as her hips were trying to lift toward him, she had to fight the urge to tighten her thighs to keep him from doing more. Christian seemed to sense her struggle, ducking closer to nip her ear. The tiny bite distracted her. When the pad of his thumb joined his finger's light teasing, she knew she wanted him to overrule her more fearful side.

"I'm not sure my . . . maidenhead matters," she managed to push through her tightened throat. "Who but you would even know if I gave it up?"

Christian nuzzled the bend between her throat and shoulder, his hot breath sending shivers sliding down her spine. "If you are still feeling shy, it matters to you."

"Not so much," she groaned.

He chuckled against her breast, a sound she suspected men had been making since their days of dragging women into caves.

Without warning, he rolled them both onto their sides. He was spooning her, still wrapping her in both arms, but one hand snaked beneath her gown to caress her breasts while the other remained tucked and playing between her legs. Her awareness of his size and hardness could not have been stronger. He must have liked her softness, because he dragged his stubbled cheek in a catlike motion against the side of her face.

"You see how nice this is?" he soothed in her ear. "You feel how safe you are cradled against me? I can hardly see any of you from this position. Your modesty is perfectly preserved."

Grace rather doubted that, considering that the clever fingers of his right hand were delving with extreme direct-ness into the immodest heart of her responses. She was so wet she could hear as well as feel him exploring her. Embarrassment threatened, but his touches were too wel-come. She moaned as he took her swollen button between his thumb and finger and gently squeezed. The ache she'd been experiencing edged into pleasure, and her body tight-ened to draw it in.

When his other hand found her puckered nipple and pinched that, it felt like those fingers stroked lower parts as well. Traitor that it was, her body spilled more heat over him.

"Grace," he said, a ragged whisper that sounded awed. He shifted as if he couldn't stop himself, until his groin was jammed against her bottom, the hardness of his ridge grinding into her cheeks. Soft from many wear-ings, his hose weren't much of a barrier. She gasped, feel-ing every inch of him in length and girth. With a grunt, he started to move back, maybe fearing his intensity fright-ened her.

"No," Grace panted. "Stay close to me like that."

He froze, then rocked forward tighter yet. "As you wish. I cannot hide what pleasuring you does to me."

Obviously, he didn't mean to try. He jerked back just long and far enough to shove the clothes he wore past his hips. As soon as he pressed his body back, she felt every-thing: the pounding of his heart, his ragged breathing, his heat and sweat as she writhed helplessly in his hold. His fingers were long and hard, scarred from swordplay, but obviously not strangers to this kind of fooling around.

Her teeth bit her lower lip as one finger sank into the outermost inch of her passageway.

"Just a little," he promised, his voice gone deep. "I will just rub you a little here along with the rest. It feels nice, yes? You can almost imagine how it would be to have my prick easing into you. I would be so gentle, Grace. I would slide like silk into all this beautiful wet heat."

Grace could tell he was arousing himself as well, was picturing the action his words described. Unable to speak, but wanting him to know she was completely with him, she reached back to hold his hip. Its muscles felt amazing as he strained to her, hollowed strongly at the side from him clenching them. He gasped when she slid her hand onto his buttock. Loving that reaction, she let her fingers dig into his hardness just as they wished.

His hands contracted—on her breast, on her sex—the edge of his teeth pressing unexpectedly into her bare shoulder. The bite was almost hard enough to break skin. His chest vibrated with a growl before he forced his jaw to relax. Through it all, Grace didn't release her grip on him.

"Grace," he rasped. "You are going to be a little she-wolf someday, I think."

The compliment made her blush, but she didn't have long to do so. Her actions had encouraged his. The manipulations of his hands grew bolder, firmer, making no apologies for their incursions. He had two fingers curled an inch inside her now, and his thumb and forefinger pulled and squeezed the hood of her clitoris in a strong rhythm. He was jerking the little organ out from her body, intensifying and building the sensations, until she felt so good she wasn't sure it was normal. She knew what was coming, but this pleasure seemed too potent, like something crucial inside her was about to snap. The place his fingers pressed inside her passage was aching, though his amazing deftness wasn't focused there. Driven beyond shyness, she cupped her hand over his to help those two digits push into her harder.

She moaned at how sweetly they compressed that mysteriously sensitive wet cushion.

"Yes," Christian panted next to her ear. "Show me what you want."

Now that he knew, Christian redoubled his efforts. Grace's body began to jerk in his arms, which he wrapped around her even more securely. His hips were bucking against her, his heat a furnace, his breath broken by curses and pleasured gasps. Feeling his excitement rise heightened hers. When she tightened her thighs, it was only to trap his hand closer.

The ache of need that swelled inside her was as wonderful as it was frightening. She was mindless, speechless, every nerve coiled for an explosion she could only beg to be given with wordless cries.

Christian did not miss the nearness of her breaking point. "I'll wait for you," he ground out, his body as taut as hers. "Take your pleasure—" He groaned, momentarily unable to go on. The breath he sucked in so he could speak was huge. "Take your pleasure, and then you may give me mine."

She wanted that: wanted him in her hand, in her mouth, solid and hot and real.

The idea shot her orgasm through her like a bullet. She came with a cry of agonized pleasure. Her womb was contracting, her spine stretched back in a violent arch. The climax *owned* her, as if she'd sold her soul to it. White spots danced across her vision as she attempted to recover her power to breathe. Her skin was buzzing, the ecstasy that seized her a kind of terror. Christian's arm was too tight, the pressure on her ribs not helping her fill her lungs. She pushed at his forearm, abruptly wanting this vertiginous delight to stop. Christian didn't understand. Grunting, teeth bared against the back of her neck, he tugged her clitoris faster. Her sensation spiked, built, and then the fleshy cushion he was pressing with his other fingers gave a perversely rapturous throb. Fluid spurted hot from inside her as a second orgasm broke.

She didn't think that was supposed to happen, couldn't believe a climax was meant to be this immense.

"*Grace*," Christian snarled . . . and suddenly fell through her body onto the bed.

Despite the shock of her untimely disincorporation, Christian was too far gone not to finish what they had started. Reduced to bestial grunts of need, he gripped the corners of his narrow mattress and ground his hip bones down hard. His right hand still dripped with Grace's emissions, the shining reminder of her climax drawing yet another snarl of lust from him.

Her ghostly self tried to hug him, to soothe its hands down his bucking spine. Suddenly, she was inhabiting the same space as he was, her energy seeming to prickle and pulse in time with his. It was the most terrible of teases: that she was *in* him, rather than he in her. Worse, he could not deny that her being in him felt wondrous.

Resenting this, loving this, he surged so forcefully against the blanket that his member burned. His orgasm burst as hers had, copious and dramatic, the fiery pleasure jetting out in uncontrollable spasms.

He lay there after, felled by his own climax.

"God's blood, Grace," he panted into the covers.

"I didn't do that on purpose!" She had drawn out of him

to sit on the edge of the damp mattress, their sweat and ecstasy mingled there. The scents made his groin tighten.

"I know." He groaned, then sat up himself and raked back his hair. She stared at him, worried, her succulent lower lip caught between her teeth.

"I was too rough with you," he said gruffly.

"You weren't! You—I—" She stammered to a halt, her cheeks the color of persimmons. "I was simply . . . startled. I didn't think that was supposed to feel so good."

He growled, the sound at least two-thirds male satisfaction. Evidently, she believed her dematerializing was the equivalent of swooning at climax. "Our pleasure is supposed to feel as good as we can make it. It simply does not peak so spectacularly all the time."

"Have you ever—" Her eyes dropped to her lap, where her hands clutched each other in a fit of bashfulness. "I mean, you probably have. You're obviously very skilled at lovemaking."

"No," he said, his firmness harshening the word. "I have never felt anything that marvelous in my life."

She looked up, wide-eyed. Then her lips curved in a very pleased female smile.

"Well," she said, squirming just a bit. "That's . . . that's very nice to hear."

Something inside him melted, simply turned to sun-warmed honey and ran into a big puddle. He was lucky she was a ghost. Had she been solid, he would have rocked her in his arms like a long-lost child.

"Grace," he said. "You are going to be the death of me."

Nine

The courtyard of the Durands' fortress house hummed with orderly bustle—which Christian was both overseeing and participating in. For the most part, he and his men were doing the heavy lifting. With the exception of Hans, who was the oldest present, they were all junior to his father's handpicked half dozen. Those six men were his father's fiercest fighters; his most trusted, too, if Gregori Durand could be said to trust anyone. Some of them must have wondered why they were on this job, upon which neither the fate of countries nor important families hung. Certainly, they were not going to soil their hands stowing baggage, not when preparations for their upcoming journey entailed less hefting than usual.

Christian pulled a face to himself. *Traveling light* was a relative term. Even on a noncombative mission, there were stores to carry that could not be done without. Bandits abounded in Italia. Extra weapons were a wise precaution, bedrolls, wine to mix with the local water in those remote areas where it could not be bought. The men would carry some provisions on their backs, but a wagon and a mule to pull it was still helpful. A second cart awaited their new employer's pleasure. Nim Wei had not arrived yet, a circumstance that spurred speculation, despite her having sent word not to expect her before sunset.

"Only one extra cart?" William asked as he helped Christian swing a heavy box into the first wagon's straw padding. "Are you certain Mistress Wei is female?"

"She claims to require no more," Christian said.

Though he did his best not to show it by glancing up, he was aware of his father watching the loading from his office window on the second floor. Grace's presence on the opposite loggia was less ominous, but not without its own tension. Naturally—even flatteringly—Grace wanted to join this journey. She seemed to think that as long as she did not get too close to Nim Wei, the minstrel's strange energy would not "zap" her, as she put it. Christian was not as sanguine, but he had not found the strength to argue persuasively. In faith, the intensity with which he craved Grace dismayed him. He should have been able to do without her. Whether she would succeed in becoming corporeal again was debatable. The idea that she might and he would miss it was what was bedeviling him. If there was the least chance of it, he *had* to have her. Just as troubling was the evidence that Grace also wanted him fervently.

He *and* his ghost were going to go crazy if they could not consummate this attraction soon.

"No servants, either?" William asked, blithely unaware of what was passing through Christian's mind.

"No servants," Christian confirmed. "Mistress Wei says we men can handle her needs."

"I shall gladly *handle her needs*," Charles laughed, dropping an armload of pikes into the cart with a loud clatter. "None of you lily-livered Lancelots need bestir yourselves."

"Have a care!" one of Gregori's men snapped from the other side of the wagon. "If you break those poles, they will be of no use to us."

"You should take care I do not break *your* pole, Lavaux," Charles retorted in his customary hotheaded way.

Lavaux's face went red. The Frenchman was bigger than Charles, and older, and could probably break the slighter man in two. What he had not mastered was how to ignore Charles's sharp-tongued remarks. Wisdom, it seemed, did not come to all men with age. Lavaux had to be at least a score and ten.

"Stand down," Christian said before the man could rush Charles. For emphasis, he planted his hand on Lavaux's chest. Muscles heavy from years of fighting bunched beneath his restraining palm.

"I do not answer to you, Christian."

Christian sighed inwardly. "That is so. However, I believe you know my father's position on squabbling amongst ourselves."

Lavaux's brows lowered at Christian's nonaggressive tone. Perhaps he thought his commander's much younger son was mocking him. "You could not take me down any easier than this buffoon."

Christian smiled pleasantly. He was not afraid of Lavaux, not if it came to a hand-to-hand face-off. Because none among his father's innermost guard fought him during practice, they did not realize he knew their weaknesses— and how to exploit them. For this once, Christian let his lack of fear fill his eyes. "You are welcome to try me another time, Lavaux. For now, I propose we act like professionals."

Lavaux might be lacking a sense of humor, but he was too experienced not to read how confident Christian was. "For now," he agreed, then stalked off to other tasks.

"A fine parry," Matthaus praised from beside Christian. His pockmarked face was creased with enjoyment. "Though I confess I would relish watching you take that one apart."

Close as ever to his friend, Philippe smacked the back of Charles's orange head with the flat of his palm. "Stop causing trouble."

"Me?" Charles exclaimed.

"Yes, you." Philippe's expression was exasperated but not unfriendly. "If you do not shut that mouth of yours now and then, this trip is going to be endless."

"I am charm itself!" Charles protested. "You would be bored to tears without me."

"I shall commence weeping any moment," Philippe vowed.

Before Charles could retort, a silent ripple swept the men in the courtyard. The hair on the back of Christian's neck stood up. As if they were one unit, the soldiers turned toward the double-gated tunnel that gave access from the street to the house. All the mercenaries were standing straighter, shoulders pulled back and guts sucked in. His father had not left his window, and Christian did not think they were coming to attention. Instead, they gave the impression of males preening when a beautiful girl walks by. With a dread he did his best to conceal, Christian turned with them.

The first of the heavy house gates creaked on its hinges and then the second. No voices broke the sudden quiet, but Christian heard equine hooves. A handful of young male servants were leading Nim Wei inside. She was dressed as he had last seen her: in a fitted black velvet tunic and match-ing hose. Though she was afoot, the stallions were hers, two great black beasts with gleaming pelts and loaded panniers. Their size made her seem smaller, while their docility simply impressed. Those warhorses followed the minstrel like foals behind their dam.

She looked around as she entered, at the men, at the torches the servants were even then scampering to set alight. The serving boys' passage stirred the feather that curled black as night from her velvet cap. Male raiment notwithstanding, she was surpassingly feminine, from the curves of her hose-clad legs to the graceful tilt of her head.

"Good evening," she said, her greeting as silky as it was calm.

At least three-quarters of the men shuddered at the sound.

Christian was a bit surprised when Lavaux leaped for-ward.

"Milady," he said, offering her a bow Christian would not have guessed he knew how to make. "Please allow us to unload your steeds."

She waved him permission absently. For a heartbeat, Charles stared at Lavaux as if his rival had grown a second head, but then he moved eagerly to help. He was joined by the others, leaving only Christian unoccupied.

"Mistress Wei," he said, bowing to her as well. "My father will be down anon."

She uttered a sound that might have been a private laugh, but when he glanced up, her face was solemn.

"I am sure he shall," she said soberly.

More than anything, Christian wanted to look over his shoulder and see what Grace made of this. Surely, *she* would notice how oddly the men were acting. No matter how attractive the female they were presented with, this lot were not courtiers to dance attendance on anyone.

To Christian's perverse relief, his father did not descend any quicker than usual. He, at least, was behaving like himself.

"Mistress Wei," he said. He bowed over her white hand and kissed it, but that was not unheard of. By necessity, his father's manners were better than his men's, and—despite his bullish physique—he was capable of grace. His dark eyes were as cool as ever, something in them striking Christian as a match for their new employer's exotically glimmering orbs.

The pair of them were cold creatures, more given to calculation than passion.

"Herr Durand," Nim Wei returned.

They were holding each other's gazes while Christian watched. His father blinked first, releasing the minstrel's hand as if he had forgotten he was clasping it. Surprisingly, when Christian looked at Nim Wei, her expression implied consideration rather than triumph. She had tested Gregori somehow, and he had responded in a manner she did not expect.

"You will be ready to depart soon?" she asked. "I do not wish to waste the darkness."

"Before the next hour strikes," his father promised.

If the elder Durand thought any of this was strange, his impassive face did not reveal it.

Ten

❧

Only Christian's father and Nim Wei rode, horses being more troublesome to feed than men. His father was in the lead, surveying the road ahead for danger. Charles guided Nim Wei's second beautiful black steed beside her. The minstrel was no chatterer, but Charles was making her laugh. The sound was lovely: merry, soft, as infectious as a baby's chortle. The men walking behind the horses looked up each time the noise drifted back on the crisp night air.

As they did, shared amusement was not what moved across their expressions. To a man, the minstrel's laugh appeared to make them lustful. Bemused, Christian watched hardened soldiers surreptitiously rub their crotches, some even shoving their hands in their braies to shift members that were swelling uncomfortably. Christian began to think he should have arranged for camp followers. If all the men wanted to bed her, this trip was going to be fractious.

Lavaux, for one, resembled a thundercloud. He did not appreciate a youth like Charles stealing a march on him.

One silver lining lightened the situation. Entertained as she was by Charles, the minstrel was not insisting Christian chain himself to her saddlebow. He was free to bring up the rear as they traversed the pretty Arve Valley. Grace walked beside him in her long white gown, not troubled by the alpine cold or the distance they were covering. Christian could not determine what effect Nim Wei might be having on him. Grace was too handily taking up his attention.

Ridiculous though it was, he felt warmer with her near— not merely aware of her physically but somehow safer than he had been. This was without a doubt misleading. Thus far, Grace had demonstrated no power to act as his guardian. A distraction was what she was, a nettle to heat his already overheated blood. Refusing to respond to the growing itch as others among the company were, Christian could none-theless not bring himself to shake her off when she curled her tingling spectral fingers around his own.

He was certain he had held hands with women a time or two. He was also certain the sensation had never run through him this sweetly. The gesture reminded him of Grace's innocence, of the differences between them that had nothing to do with how many years they had lived. He knew her life had been troubled; he even wished he had been there to protect her from her father. The seriousness of her trials aside, she was still a gentle, openhearted girl. She *wanted* to be given reasons to trust. Lord help him, Christian was becoming increasingly eager to provide them. Her attachment to him was as addicting as the touch of her flesh.

He was a little disappointed when he realized she had taken his hand, at least in part, to catch his notice.

"The minstrel is doing something to your men," Grace

said, her ephemeral side nestled close to his. "I know it sounds kooky, but I think she's weaving some sort of spell."

Christian lowered his chin and spoke toward his feet. "Why do you say that?"

"My vision has been different since I died. I can see in the dark, and around her I see a sort of black energy. I noticed it in the tavern before I got zapped."

"And now?" Christian murmured.

He had been trying to hide his tension at the reminder of her disappearance. Grace must have sensed it, because she squeezed his hand. "Now the energy is like a web raying out from her. She's casting it over your men. It think it's making them"—she cleared her throat—"more *interested* than normal."

Under other circumstances, Christian would have grinned at her delicacy. Under this one, he simply nodded. He could not doubt her perceptions, though he did not know what to do about them. His father did not seem to observe anything amiss; his focus was on their surroundings. Was Gregori resistant to Nim Wei's powers, whatever they were? Was that what had surprised her earlier? Christian's father was a practical man, without much mystical bent. If Christian claimed Nim Wei was an enchantress, Gregori was liable to guffaw. Christian would have laughed at the idea himself, had his view of the spirit world not been expanded recently.

He shook himself from his musings, reluctantly releasing Grace's hand as Michael fell back to speak with him. Though Michael probably would not have felt it, Grace scooted to Christian's other side before his friend could bump into her.

"This is not good," Michael said in an undertone. "That woman is stirring up everyone."

Christian was glad someone beside himself and Grace

thought so. At least, he was glad until he took a closer look at his friend. Michael resettled the pack he wore on his shoulders as if he also was disturbed. His handsome face was disapproving, his generous lips pinched thin. Christian wondered why Mistress Wei had not set her sights on him from the first. Did not seductresses like the godly? And was not Michael's golden beauty fair enough for an angel?

But none of this was appropriate to bring up.

"She is only flirting with Charles," Christian said. "Or, rather, letting him flirt with her. The men simply are not used to having females around."

"It is more than that," Michael insisted. "She flaunts herself in that costume, worse than some bawd. Those hose are clinging to her. Everyone can see the shape of her thighs and calves."

Christian grinned in spite of himself. "I did not know you were so partial to women's legs."

"She wears her hair loose, Christian. It falls halfway down her back. She tosses it every time she laughs."

Christian's eyes widened at the heat behind his complaint. His friend was that bothered by the minstrel's *hair*?

"I cannot order her to cover it," he said mildly, hoping not to make too much of this. "And, given what she is paying, my father seems unlikely to object to her immodesty."

Michael grunted and fell silent. The tramping of booted feet mingled with the creaking of the three horses' leather. It was odd to be traveling after dark, to watch the clouds of their breath rise gray to a starry sky. Nocturnal creatures rustled through the adjoining fields, gleaning what remained of the last harvest.

To Christian's dismay, his friend was not letting the matter drop. "You could not talk to Charles? Warn him against succumbing to that siren?"

"Do you think he would listen?"

Michael's mouth twisted ruefully. "I would swive her myself, if she turned her eyes to me."

Christian did not know what to say to this. Michael almost sounded wistful, and he was not a man of casual amours. Yes, he took women but never on a brief acquaintance. Christian sometimes thought his friend would do without the act of carnal knowledge altogether, had the urges of his body permitted it.

"At least we need not fear for Matthaus and Philippe," Michael commented.

"No," Christian agreed slowly, discovering he was not as confident as Michael. Matthaus and Philippe might not be lovers of women, but who knew what havoc their strange employer was capable of wreaking?

Without looking around, he reached leftward for Grace's hand. A warm buzz of sensation told him she had accepted it.

"Just be certain *you* stay away from her," he said to both his companions.

The men made camp an hour or so before dawn on the top of a wooded slope that overlooked a flourishing farm village. When Grace asked, Christian said it was called Cluses. A river ran beside it—the Arve, according to him. Neither of the names rang any bells for her. If her angel was right, and she got another life someday, she'd pay better attention in Geography.

She noticed the men were very efficient: seeing to the horses and the mule, and warming a simple meal at a central fire as if they'd done it a thousand times. The mercenary who was in charge of cooking was one of Christian's father's men. His name was Oswald. The other men, Christian's included, treated him with respect, not joking or teasing as they did with each other. Oswald was tall and taciturn, and only had one eye. Every so often, as he sweated over his bubbling pots, he'd slide up his patch and wipe the ruined socket dry on his sleeve. It looked to Grace like the eye had been burned, but the scars didn't seem to pain or embarrass him. So many of the soldiers had them that she supposed they weren't cause for shame.

Remembering the bruises she'd expended so much energy concealing, she wondered if she'd wasted her time. Was being her father's victim any more disgraceful than a battle wound?

She chewed that question over as she wandered the camp. Christian was too busy to remind her to be cautious, but she did take care to avoid the sumptuous tent that had been pitched for Nim Wei at the center of the flat clearing— the better to protect their client, Grace supposed. The structure was round and large with a pointed top held up by a pole. Scalloped edges circled the roof, exactly as she'd pictured a king's siege tent. The temptation to sneak closer was very strong. Though the outer walls were a heavy black silk brocade, their inner lining glowed in red satin. Much of the minstrel's baggage had consisted of vibrant pillows. Some of the men were tossing them through the open flap with laughing remarks about why a woman would need so much padding, but this was probably because their employer wasn't inside yet.

To judge by their behavior, Nim Wei's male dress made her seem fast to medieval folks. Grace thought the way she acted, the way she carried herself and spoke, made her seem queenly. It didn't strike her as so farfetched to think of the minstrel weaving magic—a theory that wouldn't have occurred to her before she herself became a character from a ghost story. Even if she was mistaken about Nim Wei casting spells, this woman was used to people doing her bidding.

Considering Grace was pretty sure she *wasn't* mistaken,
Nim Wei shouldn't have fascinated her as she did.

Not wanting to be seen the way she'd been in the tavern,
Grace hugged a tree and peeked around it. Nim Wei and
the lean, orange-haired man named Charles were strolling
hand in hand up the wooded hillside to the minstrel's
sybaritic silk shelter. Charles's boots crunched through the
bracken, but Nim Wei was so light and graceful her steps
didn't make a sound.

The pair had been down to the river. Charles's bright
hair was wet, his gaudy clothing damp here and there. Nim
Wei must have ordered him to strip and wash for her. He
didn't seem to have minded it. His eyes were all for her, his
smile mischievous and broad, anticipating the pleasures
he either thought or knew she'd be offering. His fresh-
scrubbed skin was covered in ginger freckles, but both
his face and his physique were nice. Charles was tall and
strong and healthy, and Nim Wei was licking her lips as if
she enjoyed all those things. When she paused to look up at
him, the starlight seemed to strike gold sparks in her tilted
eyes. Charles gazed into them, utterly enraptured.

For one strange moment, Grace wanted to be the minstrel, wanted to know how it felt to cram so much feminine
power into one petite package. That Nim Wei might be a
witch hardly mattered, or that she had—current seduction
notwithstanding—obviously set her sights on Christian.
This interlude with Charles might even be a ploy to make
him jealous. The possibility didn't squelch Grace's interest.
To her, Nim Wei seemed enviably free of fear, not to mention consideration for opinions other than her own.

If Grace had been a woman like that, and if she hadn't
died, she really could have made something of her life.

Longing poured through her, as unexpected as it was
intense. Grace wanted her dreams back, wanted everything

she'd found in this time *and* everything she'd lost. Charles seemed the perfect reflection of her yearning as he glanced around to make sure the other men were gone, then clasped the minstrel ardently to him. Nim Wei stretched to him as he kissed her with his mouth open, wrapping him in her arms and unabashedly urging him on. Charles began to writhe in her embrace, the part of him that most desired contact pronounced enough to make Grace flush when she caught a glimpse of it. Her fingers dug into the bark of the tree that hid her, needing something to hold on to.

"Grace," said a soft voice behind her. "What did I tell you about spying?"

When she spun to Christian, his face was both amused and concerned. He reached out his hand for hers, jerking his head for her to come away with him. Grace wished she could truly feel the fingers she accepted.

"You aren't worried about your friend?" she asked. Though it seemed to her that she was walking—she could almost feel the ground—her footfalls made no more noise than Nim Wei's. "What if that woman does something to him?"

Christian strode half a minute longer before answering. They could still see the camp through the red-leafed trees but were too far from it to be heard. "I expect Charles is hoping, most heartily, that she will do quite a bit."

"But what if she has more in mind than—"

Christian placed his buzzing hand on her lips. "Charles is a grown man, and she is clearly a grown woman. Whatever her methods of luring men to her, they are both entitled to their pleasure."

"But—"

"Hush, Grace. I do not think she would truly hurt Charles, not with so many witnesses."

Still unsettled, Grace threw a look over her shoulder in

the direction from which they'd come. She hadn't gotten
the impression that Nim Wei meant Charles harm—unless
you counted the harm that could come from riding a man
just as hard as could be done.

That thought pulled hot blood to her cheeks again.

"Grace," Christian said, calling her attention back with
a low chuckle. "Stop wishing you were in Nim Wei's slip-
pers and come with me to my bedroll."

"*She* can take him," Grace said, unable to keep her
resentment in. "She can touch and hold and kiss him all
over."

Christian's breath caught and then came faster at her
words. She suspected he was trying to control his responses. She couldn't actually hear him panting, but she
could see his ribs expand. He must have realized this,
because he laughed softly at himself. "You are the witch
to be reminding me of that. You know we shall have little
privacy even if you—"

Abruptly overcome by what he wanted, he stopped
speaking and swallowed. He stared at her eyes, her mouth,
and then his gaze drifted to her breasts as if magnetized.
Grace knew their tips were pointed, just as she knew her
bosom must be trembling from the quick thumping of her
heart. Every ache she'd ever felt for him seemed to pile into
a heap between her legs. She looked down his torso to find
his erection thrusting aggressively behind the cloth at his
groin. It seemed an intimate thing to be staring at. When he
made a soft, longing sound, Grace could have wept for it.

"I wish . . ." she said.

Christian placed his hand above her heart, the gesture
tender and featherlight. He wasn't trying to hush her, but to
show her he understood.

"Yes," he said. "So do I."

*   *   *

When Christian returned to camp—with Grace in his
ghostly tow—Michael was spreading both their bedrolls
on the bare, hard ground. Michael had chosen a spot at the
edge of the main clearing, within eye- but not earshot of
the others. Two axe-headed halberds and the upper por-
tions of their armor leaned at the ready against a tree.

"William saw a lynx," Michael said, glancing up briefly.
He smoothed the doubled blankets with brisk motions. "I
warned everyone not to bed down too far away."

"Good thinking," Christian said. He eyed Michael's
actions with a dismay that he had never felt before. The
night was too cold to suggest different arrangements.
Michael was his closest and his most trusted friend. They
often slept back-to-back when on campaign. Their company
suited each other. It simply did not feel so suitable now.

"Mind you," Michael went on, plunking down on the
blankets to tug off his boots, "I am unconvinced that
Philippe and Matthaus will listen."

Christian rubbed his forehead, too aware of Grace
beside him. With an effort, he turned his thoughts to
Michael's concerns. "They will be all right, I expect. It will
be light soon, and chances are that wildcat is more interested in the local chamois goats than us."

Grunting, Michael lay down and pulled the top two
blankets up to his neck. His pack was his pillow, lumpy
though it was. "They could show some self-control."

"If they love each other, it must be difficult to have to
sneak around all the time."

Michael rolled halfway back to look at him. "If they
love each other . . . Christian, are you forgetting that what
they do is against God's law? You would think they were
Florentines!"

Christian fought a smile. Wherever one lived, the sin of sodomy always seemed to be imputed to some other town's citizens.

"This is not funny," Michael said. "There are not so many who would turn your blind eye."

"You are right. My morals are abominable."

Because he truly could not hate anyone, Michael laughed and lay down again. "Do not stand there all night, Christian. This hillside may have good sight lines, but it is freezing."

Christian shot a look at Grace, who shrugged at him. She did not know how to handle this situation any more than he did. Resigned to behaving as he normally would have, Christian dragged off his boots and squirmed in next to Michael.

"Are you armed?" Christian asked as Michael rearranged the blankets and pressed his back to his.

"My knife is under my pack, as if you did not know my habits. I claimed second watch for us, by the way."

Grace was giggling as she sat next to him in dirt that, sadly, had no chance of dirtying her. Christian glared, but her amusement did not abate.

"I'll be sleeping with *two* men," she explained between gasps for air. "I never imagined being a ghost would be this racy."

Even as he frowned, she kissed his forehead and snuggled close, on her side now with her knees bent up. The warm hum of her nearness caused his spine to relax against Michael's, who was shivering just a bit. Christian felt one of Grace's hands settle atop the bend of his waist. The heat that had been ebbing from his loins threatened to flood back.

"Behave yourself," he muttered.

"What?" Michael asked, not asleep yet.

"Nothing," Christian said impatiently. He could not look away from Grace's eyes, now mere inches away from his. They were twinkling far too brightly with dangerous ideas. It should not have been the case, but her boldness was as compelling to his lust as her innocence. He had hardened enough already for his braies to feel snug. When her palm slid from his waist to his hip, he feared he was in trouble. When she swept her thumb gently up his hip bone, he knew he was.

"I have you where I want you now," she murmured.

He couldn't even hiss her name between his teeth. Michael would have asked again what was wrong. Delight fought dread as he realized his clothes were no barrier to her spirit hand. Grace gnawed her lip as she reached through them for his throbbing erection.

"I wish I could see what I was doing," she said.

She was doing quite well blind. Her energy lapped into him, blurring their separate edges as she rubbed his shaft, until the nerves beneath the surface of his stiffened member felt like liquid sparks were sliding over them. Christian closed his eyes and fought a shudder. He did not think she could bring him to release this way; the pressure was too subtle. It felt good, though. So good the tip of his prick began to well up.

Grace wriggled closer still, her misty lips brushing his like silk. "You could touch yourself if you need more friction."

She always wanted that, and he was starting to want it for her—if only to watch how it aroused her.

Resisting temptation, he shook his head. She had left a space between their bodies where her knees bent up, and he was bracing his weight slightly forward there. His hand was clenched into a fist, submerged half in, half out of her spectral gown. He doubted he could be quiet enough for climax, not with Grace so close by. She called sounds from him he could not hold back, and—friend or not—there were sides to Christian that Michael did not need to know about.

Grace looked at his fist and then back at him. "Is that what you want? Do you think it would help?"

He did not understand what she meant . . . until she curled her own hand into a fist and, rather than continue to stroke him, punched it straight down his aching prick. Christian gasped at the immediate increase in sensation. A muscle in his thigh twitched, jerking his knee forward and into hers. Grace pulled her fist back, and that motion tingled strongly, too.

Faster, he thought, his throat tightening on a moan he could not let out. *Mary in heaven, do that faster.*

"Faster?" Grace offered.

He swore silently even as he nodded, unable to resist. She could make him spill his seed this way, maybe not quickly, but he thought she could. He only had to keep his mouth shut, and to stay leaning away from Michael when he went.

He told himself his excitement was now too high to ignore. He needed to sleep, to relax, and he could not do that while he was so hard. Her touch pushed and pulled through him as if his flesh were thick water, each time nudging him a fraction closer to ecstasy. The wave of his anticipation built by tantalizingly small degrees. His thighs were hot, his heart pumping, his prick so full in its skin it hurt. The pain was not without its pleasure. He tensed the muscles of his stomach, pulling the feelings in. When that actually worked, it took all his strength to keep his breathing even.

Grace's breathing certainly was not. Her face was so close, so real. She had three tiny freckles beside her full, parted mouth—a constellation to steer by. He saw her pink tongue glisten when she wet her lip, could almost taste it himself.

"Christian," Michael said, twisting around to shake his shoulder.

Embarrassment boiled his face, as he had not felt since he was a boy being tongue-lashed by his father before a crowd. What was he thinking, playing at this with Grace where his friend could not ignore it?

He sat up, prepared to offer an apology, though he had no idea what to say. As little as possible, hopefully.

"Something is wrong," Michael said. "Hans is walking this way."

Michael's eyes were worried but not offended. He had not been aware of what Christian was doing. He had shaken him for some other reason. Christian's thoughts took a moment to reroute themselves, the strength of his relief slowing them. Michael was no longer looking at him. He had turned to watch Hans's approach. Through the black tree trunks behind him, the eastern sky was lightening to gray.

"Sorry to disturb you," the veteran said once he was near enough. "It is Charles. He has returned from Mistress Wei, and William and I are not sure he is . . . himself."

"Who else would he be?" Michael asked.

"Come," Hans said, rather than explain.

The still pulsing remnants of Christian's arousal made rising awkward, but he ignored them. Grace rose as well, her anxious gaze on his face. *Sorry*, she mouthed when he looked at her. Christian let his fingertips brush her arm. She was just a girl playing with her budding power over men. Christian was responsible for what had almost happened in Michael's company.

"Charles is in one piece?" he asked as the veteran preceded them to the central fire.

Hans's scarred mouth grimaced. "More or less."

Christian understood what he meant soon enough. Charles was standing—or swaying—within a small circle of watchers, every one of whom had his eyebrows raised. Lavaux was there, staring daggers, and another of his father's men, a black-haired Basque whom everyone called Mace due to his artistry with that weapon. Given the racket Charles was making, Christian thought it lucky the entire company had not drawn nigh.

"I am beauteous," Charles was declaring, spinning in a wobbling circle with his arms outspread. "Beau-tee-ous."

"You are drunk," Christian said.

Charles laughed hysterically at him. "Not a drop of it. Even one. Only the sweetest swiving of my life. Thought I would swoon when my seed burst free. That wench's queinte was tight enough to crack walnuts!"

William caught him as he swayed too far and fell over.

"Sweet William," Charles cooed, trying to pat William's cheek but employing such questionable aim that he got his nose. "Always there when we need you."

"She gave him *something*," William said to Christian. "Look how pale he is. And his pupils are as big as bilberries."

"Pussy," Charles giggled. "She gave me sweet, hot, dripping wet pussy." He rubbed his neck as if it pained him, but Christian could see no wound. "Saints above, I am tired. Think someone else will have to take my turn on watch."

With a lengthy sigh, he passed out in William's arms. Lavaux and Mace exchanged glances, obviously thinking they would not mind this sort of exhaustion. Mace went so far as to rub his own neck in an echo of Charles's gesture. Beneath his fingers, a ragged scar slanted from his ear to his collarbone. The marks made Mace look as if someone had once tried to saw his head off.

The last person Christian wanted to witness Charles's peccadillo chose then to stride over. Gregori stopped on the opposite side of the fire from Christian, his feet planted wide like a standing bear. The glow from the logs cast uncanny shadows up his broad face. His thick black eyebrows looked inches high.

"What ails him?" Gregori demanded.

"Drunk, we think," William said before adding, "sir."

Christian's father grunted. It was not clear whether he believed this story. His cool eyes shifted to Christian. "You should keep your men in better order."

"Yes, sir," was the only thing he could say.

Eleven

If Nim Wei had drugged Charles, he was suffering no ill effects by the following night. In truth, he was annoyingly hale and hearty, begging seconds from Oswald's supply of bread and telling anyone who would listen that he had never felt so good in his life.

When Nim Wei requested that William lead her second mount, Christian expected Charles to take umbrage. Charles was a competitive soul—sometimes stupidly so—and Christian knew he would have relished rubbing Lavaux's nose in a repeat conquest. To Christian's surprise, Charles shrugged off Lavaux's attempts to bait him over being replaced.

"I had my hour in paradise," he said good-humoredly. "Some women are too blessed by nature to scatter their bounty on just one man."

This was not a sentiment any of them had heard Charles express . . . unless it was in regard to himself.

"What got into him?" Michael asked as the rest of them tramped more sleepily down the wooded slope to the traveler's road. The cold had hardened its ruts, but this was preferable to spring mud. Not wanting to discuss Charles's amorous adventure, Christian hiked his pack up and shook his head. Philippe walked ahead of them, his wavy brown hair ruffling in the wind where it had blown out from under his mail coif. His gray eyes looked black in the darkness— pretty eyes, Christian supposed. Creases rayed around them when he grinned over his shoulder at Michael.

"I think the more pertinent question would be: Who did Charles get into?"

Matthaus elbowed his friend affectionately for his quip, which was enough to make Michael frown.

Christian nudged Michael's arm before he could speak, his mail shirt cold even through his sleeve. "Leave it alone," he murmured. "It is their business."

He did not wait for Michael's reaction to his advice. Michael's disapproval was his own affair, and Christian's eyes were following Grace anyway. She had flitted ahead of him this evening, following their little column off to one side. He found it disconcerting to watch her walk through the occasional boulder, but pleasant to see her high spirits. It had not occurred to him that she might enjoy this journey for its own sake. He supposed she had not had the freedom to run wild when she was alive. Now and then she hesitated, checking how far back he was before darting forward in a breathless rush. Christian smiled to see it. His Grace was trying her wings.

She had plenty of room to stretch them. They were deeper in the mountains, the craggy peaks that loomed above them well streaked with snow. Here and there, stony fortified houses perched, lonely strongholds for the families who eked out an existence in these valleys. Grace seemed to like the look of the towers by moonlight. She craned her neck as they passed each one.

"At least the minstrel is leaving you alone," Michael said.

"Not bloody likely," Philippe laughed. "I think her plan is to let Charles and William present the case for her charms."

A scuffle up ahead caught Christian's eye, Lavaux and Charles testing each other's quickness as they tried to slap each other. For once, Charles was getting the better of Lavaux, which might not have been the best idea, given Lavaux's short temper and his skill with knives. Fortunately, Oswald hooked Charles's neck with an elbow and neatly yanked him away.

"You should not make me sorry I fed you," Christian heard the cook's fathoms-deep voice say.

"Never!" Charles declared. "You, dear Oswald, are a prince among men."

"You are a child," Oswald returned. "Do not make Christian ashamed of you."

This last admonition had Christian's father looking back from the height of his saddle with narrowed eyes. Christian wondered if the normally reticent Oswald recognized his blunder. Christian's good opinion was not supposed to matter to anyone.

Freedom was good, Grace decided as she hiked up her gown and bounded from rock to rock. Her balance was so much better than it had been when she was human, and her lightness allowed her to accomplish truly Olympic jumps. Her control over which things she passed through and which were solid to her was improving. Falling didn't hurt her, either, not when obstacles she wasn't paying attention to melted.

Maybe she would figure out how to fly in time.

She laughed to herself at that, propelling herself upward to land like a monkey on a frosty rock. This world Christian lived in was wide open—no highways, no suburbs filled with ticky-tacky "ranch-style" homes. Grace did miss her beloved movies, but she was having fun, maybe more than she'd had in life.

She might only have one friend here, but she wasn't alone.

She liked looking down at Christian and the other big men-at-arms. Mercenaries or not, they looked like knights in their mail and plate armor. They were in a longer, more straggling line than they'd been before, not so tightly packed on the beaten-down dirt track. To spare themselves tiring of the weight they carried on their bodies and in their packs, some of them used their halberds as walking sticks. To her eyes, Christian stood the straightest, his strides both graceful and confident. Even though they'd been interrupted, attempting to pleasure him last night had been exciting. Now that her chagrin had faded, she could hardly wait to try again. Christian would find a way they could be alone. She knew he wanted her as much as she wanted him.

That knowledge might have been the most thrilling. Grace was free to explore with him.

At the moment, she had bounded so far ahead that the group below her needed time to catch up. Grace squatted where she was and hugged her shins. Another of those funny house-towers poked up from a hill some distance ahead. Sheep or possibly cows dotted the pasture next to it. Grace squinted at them without thinking. To her amazement, the shapes sprang into focus as if she'd pressed a pair of binoculars to her eyes.

The shapes weren't cows or sheep. They were burly men, more than a dozen, lying on their bellies behind a scarp of granite that overlooked one side of the road. All were wearing leather jerkins and what looked like metal pots on their heads. They had weapons, too: clubs and crude axes. When one of the men shifted on his elbows, she saw he held a long wooden bow. Arrows bristled from a quiver that lay nearby.

Good heavens! she thought, awareness slapping her. *They're setting up an ambush.*

Christian would never see them from down below. Grace only did because she was higher. The ambushers weren't as well equipped as the mercenaries, but between the element of surprise and their sharp-tipped arrows, they might get the advantage.

She ran back to Christian, leaping down the scree like one of the local goats.

"There are men up there," she shouted, waving both arms to get his attention and then pointing. "At least a dozen setting up a trap. I saw their bows and arrows."

Christian looked where she pointed, the hand that shaded his eyes more habit than help at night. A moment later, Nim Wei looked up, too, which tugged a shiver down Grace's spine. The minstrel shouldn't have heard her, and Christian was behind her line of sight. Whatever had caught her eye, she checked her black mount so sharply that it turned in a nervous half circle. Christian's father was ahead of her, but he just snapped his reins with impatience when his big bay slowed.

"It's the horses," Grace speculated to Christian. "Hers are so pretty they must want to capture them."

"I cannot see anyone," Christian admitted under his breath. All the same, he didn't wait for her to argue him into believing.

With a decisiveness that stole her breath, he used a small hand signal to stop the men who'd glanced around at his delay.

"Philippe," he said, his voice intense but quiet. "Run ahead and warn my father that we are in danger of attack, then join William guarding Mistress Wei. Michael, see if you can climb quietly up the slope and get behind them."

"Behind who?" Michael asked.

"Bandits. I think they hide in the shadow of that outcropping."

Michael peered doubtfully upward but did as Christian asked.

"I will go with him," Charles volunteered eagerly.

Christian opened his mouth, then shrugged, probably concluding that Charles was well enough to go. In moments, Charles and Michael were clambering up the steep hillside, as silent and quick as if they weren't loaded down with weapons and plate armor. They made Grace feel a lot more humble about her gains in agility. Charles, in particular, was every bit as quick as she'd been.

The rest of the escort continued to move forward, perhaps not wanting to signal their attackers that they'd been spotted.

"Shields close," Christian said to the other men. "Be prepared to cover your heads."

The men reached for their round bucklers, which didn't look nearly big enough to Grace. In the meantime, Christian's father rode back to him. His face was a picture of annoyance.

"What shadow are you shying at, son?"

"Sir," Christian said, his chest inflating with an automatic defensive breath. "I saw figures behind that outcrop."

A whistling sound had all the men flinching.

"Arrows!" someone cried farther ahead. The mercenaries' shields went up in unison, reminding Grace of a synchronized display at a baseball game. Sadly, this game wasn't going to finish as peacefully.

The single whistle was followed by an eerie chorus, a rain of arrows now coming down. One man yelped as he was struck.

"To Mistress Wei," Gregori ordered. "Get her off her horse and form a wall around her. Do not let her ride away by herself. More brigands may be lying in wait out there."

His men scrambled to obey. With them dispatched, Gregori wheeled his horse back around to address Christian and Matthaus.

"You two. Up the hill. Hail me if you spy any more attackers concealing themselves down here." He galloped off before they could move. "Form up!" he bellowed to his men as Christian and Matthaus leaped into action.

Grace followed them, speeding ahead as soon as she was able so that she could warn them of more dangers. She didn't know how useful she was at that. All she could do was gasp when two arrows whizzed through her body. Luckily, they didn't hit their intended targets. Christian and Matthaus dropped flat beneath their trajectory, crawling onward on their bellies over the stones and grass.

When they reached the top of the hill, they found Charles and Michael struggling with the bandits who were not firing bows. At least one of the enemy was dead. Grace almost tripped over a severed arm that had rolled away from its owner. Christian's friend Michael had lost his halberd and was using his giant sword to fend off two men who were bashing at him with spiked clubs. Michael had more reach, but the clubs were sturdy. A bite-size chip had broken out of his blade.

Fighting not too far from him, Charles was roaring like a madman as he swung his halberd around. The axe at its top whistled through the air much like the bandits' arrows had. Shockingly, an arrow stuck out from the joint in the armor beneath Charles's arm. Despite this handicap, he was in better shape than Michael, who appeared to be losing steam. Charles's roar became a laugh as he decapitated a man, striking him so cleanly that the head went sailing over the scarp.

Apparently, this wasn't a common feat. Christian gaped at Charles right along with Grace. A moment later, he twisted around to meet an attacker who was trying to creep up on him from behind.

"Get him!" Grace exhorted, then plastered her lips together for fear of distracting him. Christian and the new man's hand-to-hand combat soon devolved into a wrestling match. They rolled back and forth on the ground with the bandit cursing, until Christian knocked him out with a clanging helmet to helmet butt.

"Behind you!" he panted to Matthaus, which was when Grace realized she had about as much knack for following a battle as she did for a football game—in other words, none at all. Christian was in the thick of it, but he knew what was going on around him better than she did.

She pulled back and tried to watch more comprehensively, but even then the action moved too quickly for her to sort it out. Charles caught her eye by punching a bandit in the nose with his well-articulated steel gauntlet. Though Grace was feeling pretty bloodthirsty, she flinched at the wet sound of the impact. Not surprisingly, Charles's opponent dropped to his knees and toppled. Charles finished him off by smashing his skull in with his own club.

Ergh, Grace thought in the second she had to feel horrified.

"Get the bowmen!" Charles called to his three comrades.

Grace's fog of confusion cleared. *Oh*, she thought. The men Christian and his friends had been fighting were protecting the archers, because *they* were inflicting the worst damage on the troops below.

The others knew this, evidently. They pushed up and ran after Charles. The bowmen had taken shelter within a circle of big stones, from which they were now shooting arrows in both directions. Fortunately, their aim was not as accurate while being rushed by huge armored men. Sensing this, Charles paused to snap off the end of the arrow shaft that had pierced him, after which he barreled forward with a fearless berserker's cry.

Grace covered her eyes, able to watch only through her fingers, but the fighting ended soon afterward. No doubt she should have guessed it would. The mercenaries were better armed and fought together with more coordination than the bandits. A few of the would-be horse thieves had climbed down the slope to escape, but they were no match for the trained professionals on the road. All in all, Grace doubted twenty minutes had passed from the first flight of arrows to the last bandit being sent to his presumably just reward.

As silence fell at last, Charles staggered, dropped to his mail-clad butt in the pasture, and began to laugh. He didn't seem drunk the way he had the previous night—more as if he simply didn't believe what he'd accomplished.

Far less inclined to be giddy, Christian strode heavily to him. Rather than wearing enclosed visors, which Grace imagined would have been difficult to maneuver in, the mercenaries' helmets had mail attachments to cover their mouth and nose. When Christian tugged his down, he was trickling blood in a few places.

The sight shocked her. Grace couldn't be harmed by physical attacks, but Christian certainly could. For a breathless moment, her fright was entirely selfish. Without the one person who could see her, how would she bear being stranded all alone in the past? Then she thought about losing *him*, this friend she was only beginning to know. If Christian were gone, who would look at her as if she were special? Why would it even matter if she learned to be brave? It was his opinion she valued, his courage she took as her model. Most of all, she wanted the chance to be here for him. It hadn't escaped her notice that he enjoyed the sort of kindness she offered. She didn't think her friendship was more important, but it was different than what he got from his men.

And then he wiped the blood from his cheek, the motions of his fingers absentminded and casual. The cuts he uncovered were barely seeping. Grace's lungs emptied in a rush of relief. He wasn't hurt badly.

Seeming unaware of her state, or really that she was there at all, Christian dropped his hand to his comrade's shoulder.

"Are you well?" he asked.

"Never better," Charles gasped, caught between breathlessness and humor. "I think I killed five of them."

"Six," Michael corrected, still on his feet but more winded. "You finished off one who was fighting me."

"We need to get you out of your armor," Christian said. "Have Oswald remove the rest of that arrow."

"God's teeth," Charles groaned. "I hate that part."

He tried to get up and didn't make it. A look flickered from Christian to Michael. Grace concluded Charles had not been hit in a harmless spot.

"We could call Oswald up here," Matthaus suggested, his face concerned as well.

"I swear it looks worse than it is," Charles said. "You three need not plan my funeral. I am not even bleeding much."

"We will carry you down," Christian decided. "I think I spied a broader path than the one we came up."

"Eyes like an eagle," Charles panted gleefully. "Your father will be wroth that you were right about that ambush!"

* * *

Charles's words were prophetic, though only the sharpest watchers would have been aware of this.

"To my son," Gregori toasted, lifting his goblet high, "whose sharp eyes may have saved all our lives."

He stood at the head of the supper table in the bandits' stone tower house. None of Nim Wei's guard had died, and Charles's was the only serious injury. Fired up by their easy victory, the men were enjoying the spoils of their brief battle. The wine with which they saluted Christian came from the bandits' stores, as did the side of mutton Oswald was still turning on a spit at the fire. Though Christian was grateful for the warmth of the meal and the men's approval, his father's manner provoked caution. The signs were subtle—no more than a tightness in Gregori's lips and around his eyes—but Christian knew his father resented having to acknowledge his ascendance in anything.

"To Charles," Christian returned politely, "who killed six of the enemy by his own hand."

"To me," Charles agreed with his easy laugh. William had created a makeshift camp bed for him on an extra bench, allowing him to recline near the others at the table. The wine he lifted was well watered, but he seemed well, considering he had recently had half an arrow prized out of him. He was fortunate the tips the bandits had been using were bodkin style, designed for piercing armor rather than rending flesh.

"May your fool self always prove as lucky as it did tonight," Oswald said.

"Hear! Hear!" chorused the others, with only Lavaux's contribution coming grudgingly.

"You were a beast," Mace bellowed in approval, his fist thumping his big chest. "The head you lopped off that bastard nearly hit me!"

"I aimed it thus apurpose. I knew it would not hurt your thick skull."

"Ha!" Mace barked, seeming to enjoy this riposte. "I would slap you on the back, but you would collapse."

"We have something for you, Charles," Christian's father said through the swell of laughter. "To honor your valor. Timkin found it in the lead bandit's treasure chest."

Timkin was Gregori's most effective fighter, not because he was the largest of his men, but because he was so very quick and ruthless. He spoke even less than Oswald, and rarely to anyone but Christian's father. He was often given charge of divvying up booty. Christian suspected he was honest, but even if he were not, no one dared accuse him of misconduct. Aside from Timkin's willingness to stab any fellow human being in the back, he was—from his silvered hair to the soles of his hobnailed boots—absolutely Gregori's creature.

"Timkin the Shadow" was Charles's nickname for him.

Charles's eyes widened as Timkin handed him a small object wrapped in a velvet cloth. For once, no witticism rolled from his tongue.

"Above and beyond your share," Gregori's father said.

Everyone caught their breath as Charles unwrapped his prize. It was a brooch as long as his palm, beautifully wrought and inset with smoothly polished cabochon rubies. The gold was so pure, so yellow, that it resembled butter in the firelight.

"Good Lord," Charles said as he touched one stone with his fingertip. "Saint Bernardino preserve me from gambling this away."

"The take was rich," Gregori said expansively, everything about him jovial to the eye. "These bandits were not bad thieves before they met us."

Grace made the tiniest noise. She was huddled by the fire in her thin white gown, out of Oswald's way with her arms wrapped around her shins as if she were cold. She looked small and alone sitting as she was, scarcely more than a child. Her big green eyes were on Christian's father's face, seeming to read even direr messages in Gregori's visage than Christian did. Christian's futile longing to gather her in his arms was nothing short of painful.

She had not screamed once during the battle, though he knew it had frightened her. Maybe her father had taught her not to. Maybe she would not look so shaken now if she had not held in her terror. The thought tightened his ribs oddly. He was no believer in putting one's weaknesses on display.

Sweetheart, he thought, wishing she could hear him. *I shall hold you close again as soon as I may.*

Nim Wei's smoke-and-silk voice came from the shadowed entrance opposite the fire.

"I have one more gift," she announced.

She had disappeared after the fight, somewhat to Christian's surprise. Given her taste for admiration, he had expected her to relish the men's battle-stirred concern. Also to his surprise, she seemed strained as she glided into the room. She was as graceful as ever, but her impossibly pale skin was paler, the crimson bow of her lips rolled into a line.

William rose like a puppet as she entered. The others looked as though they wanted to as well, but something prevented them. The air grew heavy with more than roasting meat as the little minstrel stopped a foot in front of William. He was breathing harder as he looked down at her, his big chest going in and out. William was pleasant looking but no beauty, and unused to being pursued by females as exquisite as Nim Wei. His desire for her, and his unsureness regarding it, were so obvious Christian felt as though he ought to turn his gaze away.

The minstrel was too worldly not to read both emotions in William's face. Though the strain did not leave her features, she smiled faintly.

"This is for you." She lifted a brass flask to him on both palms. "For throwing your body over mine when those arrows were pelting down."

"That was my job," William said, backing a step away.

Her smile deepened at his reluctance to be rewarded. She pressed the stoppered bottle into his hand and wrapped his battered warrior's fingers around it. Her skin was utterly white against his, like snow on a steer's tanned hide.

"This flask contains a special oil from Byzantium. I procured it before the fall of Constantinople. It is infused with rare herbs that speed the healing of any wound."

Christian could not have said why he thought she was lying, only that her words sounded like a claim from a fairy tale: *Wear this magic girdle, and no harm shall befall you.*

"I am not wounded," William said hoarsely. "My armor protected me."

Nim Wei rose on tiptoe to kiss his cheek, her hands bracing her weight against his broad chest. Whatever she whispered in his ear turned his face scarlet.

"Take your prize," Gregori urged him laughingly. "Or does my son train his men to be shy?"

William could not blush any harder, or he would have. Nim Wei drew back from him, amusement glittering in her slanted eyes. *Later*, Christian saw her mouth to her reluctant hero, her teeth a startling flash of white. It was the quickest of motions, but he thought she ran her tongue around her catlike incisors before her lips closed again.

She glided from the room as she had come in. The

heated glance she threw Christian on the way was so fleeting he might have imagined it. The tingle that swept his body promised him he had not. Philippe's earlier guess had hit the mark: Nim Wei was bedding Christian's men as a means toward seducing him.

His member hardened; it seemed he could not stop it. Gritting his teeth, he willed the stiffening flesh downward, not wanting to succumb to this woman any more than he had before. He was glad the men's attention was on William . . . until he realized his father was studying him.

Gregori held Christian's gaze, calculations clicking visibly through his mind. Only slowly did his eyes turn toward the darkened arch where Nim Wei had exited.

Christian jumped when Grace's ghostly fingers curled around his. Her hold was tense but steady. Appreciating her effort to convey calm, he struggled not to look at her.

"She was using her power on you," she said. "I saw it wrapping around you like a nest of snakes."

Christian rolled his lips together like Nim Wei had. Though his spine was trying to shudder, he would not allow it to.

"Let us leave here," he muttered from the side of his mouth.

Twelve

Nim Wei's grip on herself was shakier than she wanted to admit. The bandits' attack had rattled her for more than one reason. It had almost been too late to cry a warning when she read the thieves' intentions from their rapacious minds. She had allowed herself to become too fixated on Christian and her plans for him. Yes, she meant to seduce him—more than, to tell the truth—but that was no excuse for failing to use the gifts her maker had given her.

She was *upyr*, an immortal race superior to mere humans. Though she was immune to most threats, those iron-tipped arrows could have killed her if they had pierced her heart. Iron was the one metal that could harm her kind, and she was very much looking forward to humans perfecting the manufacture of weapons steel. As matters stood, she could not wear plate armor, because so much of it was impure. Worn close to her body, it damped her power. It also ruined the fit of her clothes, which possibly should not have been important, but Nim Wei chose to allow herself certain vanities. In any case, she had not expected to need the defensive services of her guard on this journey.

William had saved her from that oversight by throwing his big body over hers. She had not even bitten him, an act that intensified her influence. William had protected her because he considered it his duty. Such bravery impressed her. It could not, however, distract her from all of her questions.

She ceased pacing the chamber she had claimed for herself in the bandits' home. She had pushed its foul-smelling bed into the passage, but the room still fell short of the standards she had grown accustomed to. The stone floor was caked with dust that had not been swept in years, and the walls were not much better. As her body fell into the utter stillness only *upyr* were capable of, her power began clearing the dirt away. The dust washed away from her in a silent wave, as if she were a stone that had been thrown into its center. Because no human was there to see, Nim Wei did not rein in the effect.

The larger portion of her mind was caught up in other concerns.

How, she wondered, had Christian spied those bandits before she did? The thieves had been concealed, even to her sharp eyes. Christian could not have heard them shifting in their hiding place. Human ears were not that acute. There was something *different* about him, more than the intelligence and the passion that had attracted her in the first place.

Like his father, Christian resisted her, not simply the bespelling power of her gaze but her feminine appeal as well. In his father's case, it did not matter. Gregori Durand held no long-term appeal for her. He was smart and ruthless and cruel, and he left her perfectly indifferent. He did not have the necessary imagination to spark her lust. Already, he had reached the stage of mortal life where he felt his supremacy slip away. He could clutch harder to what power he had, but he was unlikely to garner more. The circumstance made him dangerous but not attractive. If he did not want her, she hardly cared. That his son *did* desire her but held himself apart was a thorn in her side.

Nim Wei knew her allure was formidable. Emperors had dropped to their knees before her, for no more reason than to beg a kiss from her ruby lips. Christian Durand was young and healthy, with all the appetites that implied. She sensed he did not currently have—or did not permit himself to have—sufficient outlet for his natural urges. That being so, he should have been panting for her by now. She should not have been reduced to playing games with him through his friends.

She let out a sound of annoyance, breaking her statue-like stillness to smooth her hands down her black velvet tunic front. The garment fit wondrously, clinging to the lithe, curved body that she had molded into one of her best weapons. Somewhat less elegantly, her fangs were run out and pulsing, the effect of the bloody battle and her frustration over Christian. She should have brought William back with her to this chamber instead of hoping Christian would give in. At the least, she could have fed from the big soldier. Now her hunger reminded her how frayed her discipline was. She had actually had to leave the men until their bloody injuries were patched up. Considering the centuries she had behind her, that should not have been the case. She ruled herself as she ruled her people. Not for nothing was she the queen of all the city-dwelling blood drinkers.

Prove it then, she ordered herself. *Be the queen your maker never thought you deserved to be.*

Her eyes glowed gold with anger at remembering that,

the last of her human semblance unraveling. Normally, she hid her true appearance behind her glamour, but the bit of concentration that required failed her now. Auriclus had thought her soul too cold and dark to be trusted to found a line of *upyr*. Nim Wei had founded one anyway, without his approval. She would not live off the blood of rabbits the way her sire's get did. Let the shapechangers roll in the mud and hunt with the wolves. Let them keep their precious secrets if that made them feel special. Nim Wei would not abide by anyone's morals except her own.

Her hands were fisted as she forced her overextended eyeteeth back into her gums. She would control herself by force of will if she must.

As she calmed, a wisp of awareness brushed her thoughts. Nim Wei was an excellent mind reader, a prodigy even among *upyr*. The awareness she felt was not human but equine. Her horses —those simple, loyal beasts—were calling out to her for reassurance. She had ordered them to be cared for, but clearly someone had disturbed them.

In a twinkling, she was down the stairs and at the stable to check on them. Built of stone like the house, the stable was large enough for a pair of oxen and a family of sheep. The oxen had been displaced by Nim Wei's horses, but she doubted the bandits' neighbors would be long in adopting them. Nim Wei stepped past the hulking creatures in the outer yard, aware of their sleepy eyes tracking her.

Her strides slowed to a human pace by the time she entered the hay-scented building. She stopped when she heard a voice.

It was Christian's voice, low and troubled. Her horses nickered before she made out his words.

He was standing by the stable's far wall, where her horses' saddles rested and the oxen's harnesses hung. She had a moment to absorb the beauty of his body: tall, lean, narrow of hip and very broad of shoulder, with muscles that wrapped his frame in both grace and power. His legs were long, his strong, tight ass more than worthy of a bite or two. His profile, turned slightly downward now, was an arresting combination of the cleanly cut and the viciously masculine. By any race's standards he was an attractive man. He made Nim Wei glad she was the only member of hers around.

At the sound of her horses' greeting, he turned to her. His expression was startled and then displeased. A moment later, he covered both reactions with a mask of polite calm.

Nim Wei could hardly have done better—just one of the reasons she found Christian compelling. Despite her irritation over his stubbornness, she sauntered toward him with a sense of anticipation, her hips moving with the roll and swing that had hypnotized many before him. A little chase before a capture never hurt anyone. She could not doubt he would be worth it.

"Talking to the sheep?" she asked, for no one else kept him company.

A tiny muscle ticked beside his eye. "A thousand pardons if I disturbed your mounts, Mistress Wei."

Her lips curved with enjoyment. She would parry with him if he wished. "Strangers sometimes make them uneasy, but I can see they are well enough. I notice you did not answer my question."

He stiffened, his answer clipped. "On occasion, I talk to myself."

He was lying, and she had no idea why. The realization tugged her hand back from reaching playfully for his cheek. He was alone here. She did not need to search the shadows to be convinced of that. When she was a girl—a peasant, to be precise—living her ignorant human life in the Yangtze Valley, she had been considered a sorceress.

Born with a touch of Sight, she had told fortunes and conveyed requests, most of them idiotic, to deceased ancestors. Those gifts had followed her through the change. Had there been a whisper of another soul in this stable, she would have perceived it.

Then she remembered the shadow she thought she saw beside him back in the tavern. Had that been a trick of the light, as he claimed, or was Christian somehow cloaking secrets from her?

She peered up into his eyes, pushing forcibly into his mind. He was not as easy to read as some, but she sensed his wariness of her and his worry for his friends. Beyond that was an unexpected blank region: a literal gray mist where thoughts should have been. She pressed harder, and a picture flicked across her inner vision. She saw a golden-haired man in odd black-and-white garments. An equally odd white glow rayed around his head. His arms were crossed in the universal gesture for refusal.

Nim Wei jerked her head back, blinking in surprise. Though the image lasted but a moment, she knew she had not imagined it. Unlikely though it sounded, the golden-haired man seemed to have been barring her intrusion.

"What are you hiding?" she demanded, which was unconscionably direct for her. "Who taught you these mental tricks?"

"I do not know what you mean," Christian prevaricated—or so she assumed. He bowed to her, and she lost her view of his handsome face. "If you will excuse me, I have duties to attend."

She caught his arm as he moved past her, his mail an extra hardness beneath his sleeve. "I could ask your father to change your duties to pleasing me."

He met her gaze without flinching. His eyes were every bit as dark as his father's. They were more beautiful—more vulnerable, if you looked deep enough, though in that moment, they threatened to snap with anger. *A cold anger*, Nim Wei thought. Whether Christian realized it or not, he shared his father's talent for iciness. When he spoke, his voice held just the right touch of scorn.

"I would not have thought you needed to order men to your bed."

"You have my word you would not regret being there."

He looked down at the fingers that held his arm: lovely, enticing fingers, as it happened. Nim Wei did not remove them.

"I cannot doubt you are correct," he said with no sincerity whatsoever. "But there is another who has earned your favors tonight."

"Your pulse has quickened," she said, her own picking up. "I know your member is thickening."

He did not blush, only gritted his teeth briefly. "One's body does what it does. You are a beautiful woman."

She snorted softly and released him, his diplomacy defeating her. She both minded and relished his cleverness. He was correct that she would not force him. Others perhaps, but not him. It would have violated her personal ethics to treat one of her chosen with disrespect.

On the other hand, pride demanded that she leave him with food for thought. She walked her slender fingers up the tense muscles of his chest.

"Your friend will reap the reward I am offering you."

"William is a good man. I am certain he deserves to be treated well."

Of all things, he had infused a hint of warning into his tone—as if he had the ability to prevent her from doing just as she pleased! Amused beyond her expectations, she threw back her head and laughed.

"For you," she said, "I shall make a vow: that your

friend shall leave my bower with more gifts than he came to it with."

Christian's mouth tightened, the flat, disapproving line obscuring the unusual delicacy of his lips. He did not like her promise, not even a little bit. A thrill ran down Nim Wei's spine. How she savored matching wits with him!

"If you would permit," he said with another bow, "I shall take my leave from you now."

Thirteen

Grace had fled through the wall of the stable before Nim Wei's dark aura could do whatever it did to her. She hadn't waited for Christian to urge her to save herself. Before he'd had a chance to notice the woman's arrival, her self-protective instincts had kicked in.

"My cowardly instincts," Grace muttered as—from a safe distance—she pinned her gaze to the stable's small, lantern-lit windows. Neither Nim Wei nor Christian moved into view. Because of this, squinting at the openings hard enough to give her ghostly head a headache was undeniably stupid.

Willing to be that way as long as it took, she stood beneath the only tree in the empty pasture, its branches twisted by the harsh mountain winds. Some sort of seed pods prickled but did not crack underneath her feet, reminding Grace—as if she needed reminding—that she no longer had the weight to break anything.

She wished she could have broken something. Christian and the minstrel had been in there a long time.

"It doesn't matter that she's pretty," Grace told herself.

Actually, the minstrel was beautiful. Sophisticated. Seductive. Probably expert in a thousand methods to please a man. But none of that mattered, because Christian wasn't an idiot. Christian knew the woman was dangerous.

A figure left the stable: Christian's—his tall, taut body backlit by the lantern. He turned and began to stride straight to her across the pasture. Though he had not looked around, he must have spotted her shadow beneath the tree. Grace's blood pumped faster, thicker. Something about watching him approach her excited her. His walk was slightly jerky, as if he were very determined to reach her.

Grace ran the final steps to him.

"Are you all right?" she asked at the same time he said her name.

His voice was rougher than she expected, his face twisted with fury. "If she had hurt you . . ."

His temper took her aback: the willingness to do violence his words implied. She supposed a man like Christian, a trained soldier, would do whatever it took to protect the people he cared about. The thought that he would leap to *her* defense flattered her—which stirred a little storm of shame. She shouldn't be pleased that he would be reckless with his safety. Nim Wei had advantages they didn't yet understand.

"She didn't hurt me," Grace reminded him. Christian stood a foot before her, his fists clenched tight at his sides. "She might not even know she's doing it. I might just have an allergy to her energy."

"I do not believe I care what you mean by that."

His manner was too haughty not to inspire a laugh. He'd

worn the same expression when he hadn't understood her reference to Christopher Columbus.

"I mean whatever witchy magic she's using might be inimical to ghosts."

"You are more than a ghost," he said passionately.

Maybe she was. When he reached for her, a plea twisting through the anger that lit his eyes, she felt like a woman. His palms buzzed on her shoulders, almost solid and real.

Sadly, *almost* wasn't good enough.

"St. Sebastian's arrows," he cursed, releasing his hold. "I hoped—"

She knew what he hoped. She tried to hide how her own heart sank. "Come sit with me."

He dropped down beside her beneath the twisted tree, both their backs resting on its trunk. Christian's breath heaved in a sigh she seconded. Just sitting there, with the freedom to watch his face, felt like a privilege.

"You were brave tonight," he said. "During the battle."

"Me?" Grace's eyes widened. "I was terrified. And for no good reason. *I* couldn't have been injured."

"You did not scream, and you did not flee. I have seen men do both at their first sight of real bloodshed."

"I've seen—" *Movie battles*, she began to say, but the *Sands of Iwo Jima* wasn't the same. More to the point, she didn't want to make Christian think she was crazy by explaining where she'd come from. Maybe she would someday, but for now they had enough to deal with. "I've seen pictures of battles, and I've heard stories."

"Your father taught you what violence was." Christian's gaze was steady as it searched hers. Grace read the invitation to share her burdens, but she didn't want to dwell on the shadows of her old life. Christian knew her father had hurt her. That was enough.

"I wanted to help," she said, one shoulder hunching awkwardly in a shrug. "To be an extra pair of eyes to watch for trouble. I'm afraid I wasn't very good at that."

"You warned us the bandits were there. My father himself admitted that may have saved lives."

He had turned on his hip to face her. Though she couldn't touch him, Grace loved how close they were. He had energy, too. She couldn't see it the way she saw the minstrel's, but she felt it. It was like a cloud of invisible sparkles lapping over the edges of her body. Grace hugged her knees at a delicious inward shiver. She could have sat with him like this all night.

"I had this idea," she said, finding it oddly easy to bring it up. "Maybe it's silly, but I thought my angel might have sent me here to do something. Like, if I saved your life, my soul would be yanked back to heaven."

"If that is the reason for your presence, God forgive me, but I pray you never fulfill it."

Grace caught her breath at his declaration. Come to that, Christian looked surprised himself.

"I don't want to leave, either," she confessed. "I know I should, but when I saw that blood on your face, all I could think was that I didn't want to lose you."

His lips tightened, his eyes gone bright. Heat moved through Grace's body at the ray-gun intensity of his stare. He seemed to be looking all the way inside her, to be seeing everything she felt, including things she wasn't ready to admit to herself. He was older than she was, and loads more experienced—the medieval equivalent of a good-looking college man. What would happen if he knew how deeply she cared for him? Could he be as sweet on her as she was on him? Did he really think she mattered?

It was almost a relief when he turned his profile away.

He bent one leg up and hugged it, an unthinking echo of her posture. The little scar that cut through his left eyebrow was facing her. When he filled his lungs to speak, Grace wondered what was coming.

"I told you about my brothers."

"You said they died." Her response was cautious. He'd said their deaths had made him feel like his soul was damned.

He shifted, the equivalent of her earlier shrug. "Children die. It is the way of the world. My brothers were very young when they passed. It is not wise to get attached to infants."

Christian must have felt Grace lay her hand on his sleeve. He threw a glance at her before looking away again.

"I let myself make plans for them, Grace. I let myself . . . dream of them as my companions. To play with. To teach. To keep safe from the dangers of the world. I thought a brother would be closer than a friend. I thought blood was forever."

"Your friends are *like* brothers," she pointed out gently.

He nodded at his feet. "They are. And I could lose any one of them any time. You, I do not have to lose. You have already died. You could stay with me always."

His gaze lifted to hers. To her amazement, she saw her own unsureness reflected there. She doubted he'd let many people see this far inside him. She felt afraid and exhilarated at the same time. The more he let her in, the more she wanted to do the same, but for all she knew, that yearning led to destruction.

"You might change your mind about me staying with you."

"So might you."

"I have nowhere else to go."

"Is that the only reason you want to be with me?"

"I have nowhere else to go *because* I want to be with you." Her words were nothing but the pathetic truth. She'd been so desperate for connection that she'd placed all her hopes in a complete stranger, which maybe wasn't fair. It shouldn't be Christian's job to be everything to her.

"I'm not the most convenient girlfriend," she forced herself to say.

He smiled, and the expression transformed his face—not to more beauty but to an unaccustomed boyishness.

"That is true," he agreed, "but it appears you are the *girlfriend* who suits me."

When he touched her face, it seemed perfectly natural that he could, that his fingertips skated over soft, warm flesh instead of energy. His thumb traced the cushion of her lower lip until it trembled.

"Grace," he breathed, his head descending.

Like a dream that was getting better by the second, he brushed his mouth over hers. His lips were rough from his nights outdoors, and dark stubble prickled on his cheeks. Thankful for every sign of their shared realness, Grace laid her hand on his chiseled jaw.

"Really kiss me, Christian," she said. Maybe it was wrong to be so brazen, but she couldn't seem to help herself. "I've been dreaming about you doing that again."

He made a low, hungry noise. His arms came around her, lifting her over his lap so that her knees hugged him from either side. His teeth and tongue nudged at hers. Gaining entry, he licked the sweet inner surfaces of her mouth. Grace's spine began to melt at his tenderness. She welcomed it, matched it, little sounds breaking in her throat as her lips responded naturally to his. Her moans must have been one spur too many for him. With a longing sound of his own, he angled his head leftward and speared inside.

His kiss was a claiming then, from the way his mouth

controlled hers to the breathless tightness of his embrace. He was trembling just a little. The combination of that and his male aggression sent heat sizzling through her veins. She wriggled even closer than he was holding her, her arms clutching his broad back. He was lean rather than hulking, and only now—when they clung together—was the full extent of his strength clear. A man like him could break her if he wanted, but all she felt for him was desire. Her thighs squeezed his narrow hips as she tried to rub their sexes together.

She found more hardness than she expected—and the evidence that she was the one who'd been rough. He clasped her face to push back from her.

"Grace," he gasped, a hint of pain in it. "I have not removed my hauberk."

"Remove it then," she urged. "Remove everything."

He kissed her deeply, one long stab of his tongue. The taste of him enthralled her, the sleekness and the strength. Then he tore free and groaned. "What if there is not time?"

He wasn't taking the chance of waiting for her answer. He was dressed in layers against the cold, and his hands fumbled between them, lifting his cloth outer tunic to reach the inner one made of metal rings. She realized he had to hold the hauberk up or else the heavy chain mail would fall again. With his hands occupied this way, he had to ask her for help.

"My points," he panted desperately. "Untie them."

He must have meant the ties that held his pieced trousers to the quilted linen shirt he wore closest to his skin. Grace yanked at the cords, trying not to knot them but not feeling her most coordinated then. She saw she'd been wrong to complain about the petticoats girls from her time had to wear beneath poufy skirts. Getting out of them was a cakewalk compared to this.

"Hurry," he rasped. "Please God."

The heat his body radiated was incredible, a fire that burned the fiercest where his erection bulged. Grace doubted she was much cooler, especially when her hands bumped the ridge of his trapped penis. She ached to take that thickness inside her where she'd gone liquid, but the instant she had it free, she found she wanted something else even more.

His skin was silk on her palm, his core so firm it hardly gave beneath her greedy squeeze. The head of his cock was wet where the tiny slit pierced it. As she spread the slippery drops around with her thumb, he sucked in his breath sharply. The small pleasured noise, the evidence of how sensitive he was, pushed at her deep inside. He didn't want the minstrel like his friends did; he wanted Grace. Overcome, she simply had to crawl back and bend to him.

Looking wasn't enough. His cock was too vulnerable, too hot and alive and satiny not to taste. With a hum of unbelievable enjoyment, she let her mouth sink over the plumlike crest. His stomach jerked as she surrounded it, his breath hissing out of him. When she used her tongue, the hiss came out with her name.

Flattering as that was, she didn't imagine she was an instant genius at this. Then again, being a genius hardly mattered. This part of him was suckable, lickable, the heat of blood inside his hard flesh enough to make her mouth water. She could take half of him without gagging, and the rest she gripped in one fist with the edge of her palm pressed hard into his abdomen.

The pressure and the way this tightened his sexual skin must have felt good to him. He choked back a sound as her other hand wandered: smoothing over his hip bone, dipping into his navel, lightly tugging the crisp, dark cloud of his pubic hair. Every part of him intrigued her, from the ridged muscles of his belly to the bony caps of his knees. She squeezed his thigh for no better reason than to revel in how big and strong it was.

"Grace," he moaned, his hips surging up to her, pushing more of his erection in her mouth.

It wasn't too much for her, though from the sounds he was making, he might have thought it was too little. As she sucked up and down the length she could handle, his hands clenched on the layers of cloth and metal that he was holding out of her way. The back of his head rolled with frustration against the tree. Grace didn't feel sorry about this at all. She loved that he couldn't touch her, loved that *he* was at her mercy. His thighs bunched with tension as she sank down a little more.

"Stop," he said. "Please."

"Am I doing this wrong?"

Part of her knew she wasn't, but she still adored that his groan ended on a curse. Evidently, he had decided he could hold his hauberk up with one hand, because his fingers were in her hair, pushing her gently back down on him. "You are doing it *too* right, love. I want to be inside you. I do not want to waste time we may not have on a selfishness such as this."

If he really wanted her to stop, he shouldn't have been rocking into her mouth that way, shouldn't have been moaning like she was sending him to heaven each time she drew her lips tight and sucked. The veins that rode up his shaft—swollen now, bulging—felt like an invitation for her tongue to explore.

He let her do that for one more thrust.

His fingers clamped on her nape then, pulling her off of him with a blistering oath. Grace sat back on her heels, abruptly aware of how hot and squirmy her body was.

Though it was rude, she looked at his lap where his cock was sticking up even thicker and straighter than before. She couldn't believe how arousing she found the sight of her saliva shining on his blood-darkened skin. It made her lick her lips longingly.

"Grace," Christian said sternly, drawing her gaze reluctantly to his. "Do you wish to gift me with your maidenhead: yea or nay?"

When he put it like that . . .

"Yes," she said. "Yes, I do."

H er soldierly staunchness amused him, the way she squared her shoulders and braced herself. She was readier than she knew, her cheeks flushed with excitement, her nipples little stones under her kirtle.

"Up on your knees," he ordered, immediately wanting the gown off her.

As trusting as a child, she let him pull the fine white linen over her head. Her innocence was goad enough to him, but he wished for a full moon, too, for a fire or a blaze of candles to light the bounties his hands could not sate themselves with caressing. She was a feast to touch. Her skin was velvet, her curves an intoxicating melding of full and firm. She wriggled with arousal as he smoothed his hands from her graceful shoulders to her round bottom. He would never get his fill of doing this to her, but—

"*You* need to hurry," she urged.

He gave in to his impulse to chuckle, dipping his mouth to her darkened nipple even as he did. She must have liked the feeling of him pulling at her, of him rolling her smooth, hard flesh on his tongue. Her body bucked and her fingers clutched his biceps where they were thickest. It pleased him that her fingertips were so far from meeting. He had to remind himself not to throw her to the ground like an animal.

"You are a maid," he growled, trailing kisses up her slender neck. "I need to make this good for you."

"Please make it good now." The tug of her hands on his arms increased as she scooted closer on her knees.

Considering that she was naked, this position was inspiring. His thighs were more than big enough to spread hers, and he could see exactly what their loveplay had done to her. Her red curls were spiked with moisture, the little organ of her pleasure just barely peeping out. Groaning, he used his free hand to grip her bottom, to urge all that glistening gorgeousness to his shaft.

Grace writhed against him, of course; she could not make this easy on him. The press of her warm, satiny petals against the underside of his cock sent such a throb of sensation through him that he feared he would come.

"Hold," he gasped, restraining her by the waist.

Grace's hands slipped up his neck and into his hair.

"I want you," she whispered shyly beside his mouth. "Can't you tell how much?"

He could feel how much. Her juices were running from her, warm, creamy trickles spilling onto his penile skin. Christian spread his free hand over her bottom, pushing her more directly, more purposefully onto the rigid length of his arousal. She gasped as her folds parted around him, exposing the hard little swell that was her rod of ecstasy.

"I feel you," he said, his voice a snarl from the hell pit he was no doubt bound for. "I feel how beautiful you are."

Before she could plead with him to do more than *feel*, he lifted her, sliding that soft, wet silkiness up his prick.

"Oh, God," she breathed as the quivering head of him found her warm entrance. The sensation of that nether mouth clinging to him was as sweet as her kisses.

"I will wait for you," he promised through gritted teeth. "I shall ensure you find your pleasure before I go."

He would ensure it, he swore to himself, every inch of him coiled against not exploding first. The mere idea of deflowering her wound him into a knot. To be her first, to make her his forever, spoke to the most primal part of him. Her eyes went wide as he began to press into her. Though the disparity in their sizes was obvious, he could not regret it. She was as narrow as she was hot, her tightness both bliss and torture to his pent-up desires.

"This will hurt at first," he warned her.

As if she *meant* to drive him to agonies, a fresh slick of moisture ran down his shaft.

"It feels good now," she gasped.

An alien force seemed to seize his body, his lust too fierce in that moment to be bent to his will. He had been waiting too long for this, had been thwarted too many times. With a swordsman's grunt of effort, he gripped her bottom and thrust upward at the same time. The force of his penetration slapped them together. His cock seemed to scream with pleasure as her tight sheath enveloped it. Grace made a little sound: shock, it sounded to him. He should have pulled back then; he had to be hurting her, but he truly could not force himself. He ground into her instead, as if she were a celestial mortar to his pestle.

It only took a moment before his prick was seated completely.

"Grace," he breathed against her temple. "God in heaven."

"Christian." Her trembling hand stroked his hair, the

drag of her nails on his scalp making him shiver. In truth, his whole body shook. "Please don't move yet. Please stay right there."

"I cannot pull out," he pleaded, nearly weeping with the pleasure of piercing her. "Please do not ask me to."

"Don't pull out. Stay in me."

He stayed, and groaned, and felt her inner muscles begin to undulate with signs of interest.

"You're so big," she sighed in a different tone.

Christian's hand convulsed on her bottom, causing her to twist against him deliciously.

"Christian, I can feel you all the way inside of me."

"Grace," he groaned. He wanted to thrust too badly. His body was threatening to take over for him again. "Move on me, Grace. Move on me before I cannot stop myself."

She moved, a tentative rise and fall of a finger's breadth.

"More, Grace. Use me as your body tells you to." They were so close that he felt her flush sweep across her breasts. Her body still held a hint of tension, of unsureness. More than anything, he wanted to ease that. Ruthlessly holding his needs in check, he soothed his hand gently up her spine, loving each bead of sweat dewing on her skin. "You cannot do it wrong, love. However you move will bring me pleasure."

"Promise?"

"Promise," he growled and kissed her with all the passion he did not dare express through his prick.

With his hungry tongue shoving toward her throat, she gave over. She rose five fingerbreadths, then six, and then her slow, hesitant thrusts were squeezing up and down the full length of his member. His head fell back from the kiss in order to gulp for air. She felt so good, so hot and tingling and tight. His balls were heavy, the muscles of his thighs like irons heating before a fire. He had one hand to guide her, and it was locked on her sweet bottom. His other was keeping his hauberk from blocking what they were doing. He wanted to tell her to touch herself, but he had alarmed her with that request before.

Determined to make this as good as it could be for her, he altered his hips' angle, the change strafing her clitoris along his shaft.

Grace's breath rushed against his ear. "That feels *nice*."

It was hard to speak, but he wanted to encourage her. "It should feel like when I pleasured you with my fingers, except . . . the feelings should go deeper."

"They do. Oh, Christian." Her hips rolled with inadvertent skill, a trick that nearly had his skull lifting. "You are so *thick*."

No man could hate hearing this. As susceptible as any of his brethren, Christian ground his molars together and held on by his fingernails. He had never let a woman take him this way before. He was always in control of what happened to him in bed. Giving control to her was hell and heaven wrapped into one. He was reduced to grunting, his words stolen utterly. Lost to the sensation of Grace's flesh sliding over him, he bent forward to catch her breast. His mouth was his point of action, and he would use it to good effect. Nearly starving to bring her pleasure, he ran his tongue around her nipple as he sucked it—which inspired another spine-tingling roll of her hips.

The reaction was more than he knew how to withstand. His grip on her bottom changed without his willing it. Suddenly, he was pulling more than allowing, speeding her, urging her, until at last she was going just as fast as he wished. Indeed, her pace was almost too fast. He could hardly keep his hold on the pressure swelling inside him.

Her cries were soft but thrilling, rising higher as she drew closer to her climax. If she was tender from her deflowering, it did not matter. She wanted this now. *She* was equally desperate.

Christian rose onto his knees to gain more range for his thrusts.

"Yes," Grace cried. "Oh, my God, keep going deep like that."

Christian was not certain he could have done otherwise; his body was so hell-bent on claiming hers. Their knees scuffled in the grass as each tried to intensify the other's efforts. Christian spread his thighs farther, spread her, the instinct impossible to resist. She must have liked her vulnerability. Her spine arched back, pulling her breast from him, exposing the hard churning of his cock in and out of her. He shone with her juices, his veins dark ropes beneath his wet skin. The sight was like a fuse igniting in the deepest heart of him. He took her. He had her. She was his from now on. The dam inside him was not going to hold back the flood a single heartbeat more.

"Please," he gasped. "Grace!"

Her fingernails dug into the back of his neck where she was holding on to lean back from him. She crashed down on him, loin to loin, and he went; simply gave up like a cannon whose overlarge store of powder had been kindled. He could not halt the violent eruption, only groan and succumb to it. Fire blazed from him as his seed shot free in lengthy gouts.

Grace was holding him when he at last ceased shaking. Both her arms were around him, and his head lay on her shoulder. He was almost peaceful, almost perfectly content. His spent prick slid slowly out of her.

"Perdition take it," he said, the curse slurred from the fullness of his release. "You did not finish."

"It doesn't matter. I'm glad you did."

"The hell you say!"

She laughed softly and kissed his hair.

"Grace, this is not how the love act is supposed to be."

"I expect it was a lot better than most girls get."

"That is not good enough for you." He cupped her face to show how much he meant it. She was smiling, her features soft and relaxed. It amazed him that she was not angry, humbled him in a way. She deserved the best of everything.

Her smile stretched into a grin at his expression. With only a hint of shyness, she took one of his hands, drawing it seductively down her front. Nerves he had thought exhausted began to rouse.

"Finish me now," she said huskily.

He should have known he would not get the chance to redeem himself. Grace stiffened on his lap. Before he could blink, what had been beautiful, warm flesh had turned to smoke in his arms. He could not find it in him to be grateful that she had not disappeared from his sight as well.

"Damn it, Grace."

"One of your friends is coming this way. Philippe, I think. You had better straighten your clothes."

She was correct, but Christian did not have to like it. He set himself to rights, cursing. Her gown had magically rematerialized on her, an annoyance he decided he would think about later.

He got to his feet hastily.

"There you are," Philippe said once he was close enough to be heard. "Matthaus and I have been looking for you this past half hour. We feared the minstrel had decided to make a meal of you *and* William."

Though it was dark, Christian thought he saw Philippe's cheeks darken.

Grace snuffled out a laugh behind him. "I guess he doesn't hate that idea."

Christian prayed his own face would not grow hot. Leaving Philippe and Matthaus to their own affairs was not the same as knowing Philippe was imagining things about him. He cleared his throat to cover his embarrassment.

"I am well," he said. "Though I thank you for your concern." He drew in a breath as something beyond his own situation occurred to him. "How fares William?"

"Happily, I should imagine." Philippe's eyebrows wagged. "He has not returned from Mistress Wei's chamber."

Christian cast his gaze toward the star-dusted sky. "Charles left her tent close to dawn."

"He did," Philippe said, seeming unsure why Christian thought this worthy of mentioning.

Christian was not sure himself, just a feeling tightening his gut. Nim Wei had promised to leave William with more gifts than when he came to her, but what exactly did she mean by that? More than giving him a flask of oil, he presumed. His mind slid to a new thought. Charles's performance during the battle had been impressive, perhaps unnaturally so. Was his time with Nim Wei somehow linked to that?

He turned his eyes again to Philippe. "I shall sleep in the barn tonight. Someone should guard Mistress Wei's horses, just in case. If you see William before I do, bring him directly to speak with me. It does not matter if he is tired, this is important."

"As you wish," Philippe said. "Shall I tell Michael where you are as well?"

"Yes," he said. "He and I will take second watch again. And Philippe? If it is possible, keep William away from my father and his followers."

Philippe did not ask why he wanted this, but only nodded, as obedient to his captain as Gregori's men were to him.

"I shall do my best," he promised.

Fourteen

William was not as giddy as Charles had been after his time with the minstrel, but then his nature was not as giddy to begin with. Christian still had to slap him to alertness before he could question him. Though Michael's golden eyebrows shot up at the action, he did not object.

Per Christian's request, Michael was the only . . . well, the only *living* witness to this interrogation. Christian could tell his best friend was uneasy with the honor—or at least concerned. Then again, perhaps it was the topic of Nim Wei's seductive powers that had the former novice's hackles up. Michael looked uncharacteristically slight sitting next to William on a bale of hay, his long legs stretched and stacked at the ankles, his hard arms folded over his chest. William, the comrade who dwarfed him, was hunched sleepily forward with his forearms propped on his knees. Too tightly wound to sit, Christian paced the stable floor in front of them.

Grace sat in the shadows by the tack, silently observing. Though he could not see her from his position, his awareness of her presence was a quiet warmth in his mind. Grace lent him a steadiness he had not known he lacked before he met her.

It seemed no amount of interrupted coitus could change that.

"I told you," William said wearily. "Mistress Wei did naught to harm me."

"Are you certain you remember everything she did?"

At Christian's question, William sagged back against the rail of the sheep pen. "I doubt I could forget it. It was . . ." His eyes unfocused as he traveled back, the softness of his expression sending a prickle down Christian's spine. William looked beatific. "Swiving her was wondrous. No doubt you and Michael are accustomed to women being eager to bed you, but I have never known one who was that hungry for me. Mistress Wei pulled things from me, capacities for pleasure I did not know I possessed. I am surprised you did not hear me shouting myself hoarse. Repeatedly, as it were."

The state of William's muscles supported his claim. His hulking shoulders were relaxed, his huge boots sprawled wide on the dirt and straw of the floor.

"How repeatedly?" Michael craned around to ask.

The question was reluctant, not to mention intrusive, but William did not take offense. The grin that stretched his mouth was as foolishly prideful as one of Charles's. "Six times. In scarcely more than an hour. I did not know I could rise that often. And if I look exhausted, I assure you, that is the sole reason why."

Though Christian was aware that Michael's wide eyes had turned to him, and that his palms were rubbing nervously down his thighs, Christian kept his attention on William.

"She did not offer you food or drink? Anything that did not taste as it should?"

"She did not drug me, Christian," William insisted. "All she did was wring out my balls. Perhaps you should let her do that for you, if this is how you behave when you go without."

Christian blinked at him, any impulse to deny that he was *going without* dying in his breast. William's tone was sharper than was his wont, and he was famed for his steady humor. He had never, that Christian could recall, lost his temper with him. Christian would have let the matter drop, had he not noticed William rubbing his throat just then. Charles had done that, too, though the skin both stroked was perfectly unmarked.

Christian did not believe in coincidence. The minstrel had to be doing something to the men once they were alone, something more than wrapping them in her energy as Grace described, and definitely more than just wringing out their balls.

"Did she say anything?" Christian pressed with renewed vigor. "A chant or a ritual? Maybe she lit a candle or spilled some blood."

At the mention of blood, William's face went lax. His eyes were absolutely empty, as if he had gone deep inside himself. The blankness seemed a strange reaction. Horror or disgust would have made more sense. Michael thought so, too. He sat up straighter and shot a look at Christian.

"For the love of heaven," William burst out, exactly as if the odd pause had not happened. "What are you suggesting?"

His hand had remained on his throat while he had his fugue. It fell now as Christian watched.

"I am suggesting nothing," he said. "Only that we have no reason to trust Nim Wei. Perhaps we would all do well to keep our distance from her."

"Good luck with that," William snorted. "Mistress Wei is hard to say no to."

His eyes were drifting shut again as he spoke. Always quick with a kindness, Michael laid a gentle hand on his broad shoulder.

"Lie down at least," he advised. "You will get a crick if you sleep like that."

William did not hear him. He was already out, so much so that when Christian and Michael tried to move him he was dead weight. This was no common occurrence for someone trained to awaken at the snap of a twig.

"Something *is* going on," Michael acknowledged once they were done dragging William to a more comfortable resting spot.

Christian could no longer doubt this himself. He looked down at William's deeply sleeping body. Their colleague had curled on his side beneath the blanket Michael had drawn over him. His face was peaceful in the gray dawn light. He might have been a farmer's son instead of a mercenary; the strain of a life of soldiering had been that thoroughly erased. Was this peace what Nim Wei meant by leaving him with a gift, and if it were, did Christian have the right to start a witch hunt?

"She *could* be drugging all of us," Michael said slowly. "Something tasteless in the wine, perhaps. That would explain why she did not need to give William more. Or she might be working a spell. One does hear tales of such things. I admit—" He cleared his throat. "I admit I am reluctant to blame anyone for my personal weaknesses but myself."

Christian supposed Michael would consider it a weakness to be attracted to a beautiful woman. Christian did not share this belief. Beautiful women might be a distraction or an inconvenience. Grace could certainly be both.

Desiring her as much as he did might even be a sign of poor judgment. Not weakness, though. He shifted uncomfortably, abruptly unsure of this. Then he shook his head at himself. Had he not just been thinking that her company steadied him? If wanting her were a weakness, so be it. He was a man. God had made him and his desires. If the Creator disapproved of them, He should castigate himself.

"We will watch William on the road tonight," Christian said. "Perhaps the evening after his carnal adventure will reveal more to us."

"We can but hope," Michael said dryly. He jerked his thumb toward the stable's outer yard, where the oxen were dozing. "Going to stretch my legs for a few minutes."

His tone suggested he intended more than to take a piss, which made Christian wonder just how bothered Michael was by the minstrel's charms. Bothered enough to need a bit of privacy? But that was not Christian's business. And chances were, it was best Michael not ignore his body's demands right now. Mistress Wei seemed to have a nose for sniffing out the susceptible.

"Watch your back," was all he said to Michael, at which his friend nodded.

Grace waited until he left to walk up to Christian's side.

"Your friend believes you," she said.

Her clear green eyes were on the open door, the intelligence in them keener than Christian had given her credit for. She might be young compared to him, but her life had not wholly sheltered her. How could it when her father's violence had ended it? More importantly, Grace seemed to have seen the world beyond her brutal doorstep. She understood the workings of human minds.

Appreciating this more than he expected, Christian stroked the gleaming hair he could not quite touch. The weak morning light made its long waves seem darker, like rubies cast in shadow. He noticed her nose turned up a bit at the end, as if an angel had pressed its finger against the clay. The sharpness suited her occasionally tart humor.

"Michael believes something," he said aloud. "That will have to suffice for now."

"He believes *you*," she said firmly. "He trusts your judgment."

"That may be, but I do not think I want to test how far his trust stretches."

Grace cracked a smile. "Not to witches and ghosts?"

"Maybe to witches, and possibly to ghosts, but not to *my* seeing them."

"Maybe I can learn to make him see me."

She was only half teasing. The protest that should have sprung to his lips did not. Christian had thought he wanted to keep Grace as his secret. He still did—mostly. Given his monkish past, Michael might consider Grace as dangerous as Mistress Wei. But if they were able to meet . . . If his closest friend could allow himself to become acquainted with this extraordinary young woman . . .

A pinching ache tightened Christian's chest.

They would like each other; he was convinced of it.

Fifteen

Why not allow Lavaux to lead your second mount to-night?" Gregori suggested to Mistress Wei. "He is excel-lent with animals."

Christian's head jerked up from buckling his shin greaves in place. His hips were resting on a boulder beside the road. All around him, Nim Wei's little train of hired men were similarly hooking into light armor. Though Greg-ori's manner had been offhand, Christian's weren't the only eyes that snapped upward.

"If Lavaux is good with animals, my mother was a goat," Charles muttered next to him. "Your father must think any man who leads Nim Wei's horse will end up playing her stallion."

This had been the minstrel's pattern thus far: first Charles and then William going to her two nights running. She had selected no companion the following night, and then Charles had done the honors a second time. Hans had walked her mount after that, though he claimed not to have been bedded. *Woman only wanted to play chess*, he had said upon emerging from her sumptuous tent. *Beat me in a dozen moves, damn her eyes.*

Christian was not certain he believed the gruff veteran. Hans had remained with the minstrel nearly as long as the other men. He had come out seeming absentminded rather than drunk, but he, too, had taken up Charles's and William's habit of caressing their necks. Christian wondered if the gesture was due to some philter she had them drink. Did the feeling linger in their throats after they lost the memory of quaffing it? Or perhaps it related to a carnal practice Christian was unable to imagine. Something about the gesture struck him as sexual.

"I wonder why my father wants her to take Lavaux."

"That is easy," Charles said. "She has favored only your men till now. It makes it look as if his are less desirable."

Christian supposed this could be the reason; some of those who had not been chosen were beginning to grumble. Unfortunately, this seemed too simple a motivation for Christian's sire. He thought it more likely that Gregori wanted to puzzle out what Nim Wei was doing, and hoped Lavaux would serve as his informant.

If this was true, would his father fare better than Christian had? William's behavior had not cleared up the mystery. Though he mentioned his battle bruises had healed quickly, he had performed no great feats of valor. Christian thought he might have been a bit haler than usual. His appetite was hearty, and the other night he had carried two large wine butts up a slope without help. The problem was, William was so strong already that this was unexceptional. Overall, William had seemed both quiet and happy, whistling softly to himself as they tramped through the mountain-shadowed Valle D'Aosta.

Being calm and happy was benign enough, and yet it
disturbed Christian. If Nim Wei were poisoning his men,
what could be more ominous than her venom tasting sweet
to them?

But maybe he was too suspicious. Any man might
whistle, if he had been blessed with two lengthy trysts in a
woman's arms.

Christian's thoughts of a woman's arms were enough
to conjure Grace to his side. She had slept near him and
Michael in the stable, close enough to look at but not to
touch. When he and Michael woke to take watch, she
had still been visible, curled like a semitransparent kitten
within a heap of hay. Her transparency alarmed him, but
she had not faded further over time. Sleep, it seemed, did
not steal her from him. It took some other power to do that.

"I could watch Hans tonight," she offered now. "Let you
know if something seems wrong with him."

He looked at her, taking in the calm intelligence in her
face. She was making his concerns her own, before he
could ask her to. Heat flashed behind his eyes. Nodding
curtly, he turned his gaze to Nim Wei. She had accepted
Gregori's suggestion. Lavaux was helping her swing into
her saddle by forming his hands into a stirrup. Small as the
minstrel was, she needed the boost. Still clad in her black
velvet tunic and hose, which were as snug and neat as the
first time he saw them, she rode astride like a man—one
more example of her disregard for convention.

The black steed calmed beneath her when she bent to
stroke its neck, the beast as firmly under her influence as
the men. Christian had already observed that she was an
expert horsewoman, but he suspected something other
than satisfaction with her skill was behind the corners of
her red, red lips turning up.

She wore the same tiny smile Hans did when he knew

he was going to beat his opponent in a chess game. Apparently, Christian's refusal of her advances weighed as nothing with her. She exhibited no doubt that the ultimate victory would be hers.

A goose walked over his grave as Grace sidled closer to him.

"She isn't bespelling this one," she murmured. "She doesn't seem interested in seducing your father's man."

As if he had heard her, Charles broke into a laugh. "Lavaux fails again," he chortled under his breath. He elbowed Christian to indicate what he meant. "See, she calls Philippe forward. She is inviting him to ride on her second horse, instead of letting it rest today. Lavaux's face has gone so red he looks as though he will burst."

Christian could read the tableaux as easily as Charles: Lavaux stiffly objecting, Nim Wei politely putting him off. Philippe appeared entertained by this, not outrageously so but enough that Lavaux could discern it. Lavaux's fellow Frenchman seemed neither afraid nor overly eager to be in the minstrel's proximity, which Christian took as a heartening sign.

Charles saw it differently. Finished buckling on his lower armor, he stood and tested it with a shake of his knees. "Let us pray Matthaus is not the jealous type."

Christian held his tongue as Nim Wei's infectious laugh drifted back to them. She was amused by something Philippe said, and he was looking just a mite flattered to have his wit recognized. Charles took note of the expression, too.

"If anyone can straighten out that bent nail, it is Mistress Wei." He seemed undisturbed by the idea, though he had never indicated disapproval for Matthaus and Philippe's clandestine bond.

"You do not mind if Philippe takes your place?"

Charles shrugged. "Some women are too blessed by nature to scatter their bounty on just one man."

It was, to the word, exactly what he had said before.

"You speak as if she controlled your mouth," Christian said.

Grace snapped her fingers. "She's hypnotizing them," she exclaimed—which he assumed meant the selfsame thing.

Charles tucked his orange hair more securely beneath his coif. "I am just being sensible. You would, too, if you knew the ecstasy she offered. You have only to say *yes* to her once."

He sounded like himself and not a puppet. If Christian had not known how competitive Charles was, he would have thought nothing was amiss.

But maybe he should say *yes*. Maybe that was the path to discovering Mistress Wei's strategy.

"No, Christian," Grace said, clearly having read what just crossed his face. "If an experienced older man like Hans can't remember what she did to him, why do you think you would?"

Christian looked at her, belatedly realizing she thought he would bed Nim Wei.

"I would not go that far," he said, which caused Charles to snort and ask, "Since when?"

Ignoring him, Grace wrinkled up her nose. "I don't care about that. If I was sure you could do it safely, I wouldn't stand in your way."

She did not meet his gaze when she said this. Christian rolled his lips together to hide his smile. His Grace was lying . . . at least about not caring.

Nim Wei was making progress. Though Christian was not the soldier who rode beside her, he was walking close enough to eavesdrop. Even better, his annoyance radiated out from him in waves. Long centuries of practice at deception hid any sign that she was aware of him. Inside, though, her queenly nature exulted. At last, she had found the trigger that would drive Christian to action.

"The proper love object," Philippe was saying, his smile for her surprisingly sly, "is always unattainable. That which is easily won cannot be strongly desired."

He was continuing their conversation on courtly love, a choice of topic she found amusing, considering. Philippe might pretend a willingness to pay court to her, but a single pass through his vulnerable mortal mind told her where his true interests lay. Nim Wei turned her own coy smile back on him.

"If strength of appetite is your standard for *fin' amors*, I can think of many circumstances that would whet it. For instance"—she drew one suggestive finger along the pommel of her saddle—"that which is forbidden often adds savor."

She gave her companion credit for not blushing. "Some poets say if love is consummated, it is not true."

Nim Wei threw back her head and laughed, the sound echoing off the gray mountains. "Such fainting fellows are invariably unable to hold up their end of the bargain. I say, true love is heartier fare. True love is the dish humans kill for, the feast that makes heroes of ordinary men."

"Not honor?"

"It is my experience that honor is mostly pride. Men seek it because they worship public opinion. Virtue is much the same. The virgin with her thighs locked together merely dreads getting caught."

Philippe brushed a wavy lock of hair from his face. He truly was a lovely creature, with his natural elegance and his unknowingly naive youth. Add to that his warrior's strength, and Nim Wei would have no trouble enjoying him.

"You are too young to be so cynical," he said.

Because—in that moment—she liked him, she allowed her smile to soften. "I am old enough to know that love, however true it seems, always fades with time. Its bonds are easier to break than its most avid followers conceive."

Her pity unsettled him. Philippe looked away, the clatter of the horses' hooves filling the silence that had opened in their repartee.

"Why live, if not for love?" he asked.

"Because you wish to. Because an enemy can be as interesting as a friend. To live for love makes one a pawn of forces beyond one's power to control."

He met her gaze, no guard or pretense shadowing his own. "You do not wish to be loved?"

Without willing it, her fingers tightened on her reins. As if it were a curse, Edmund Fitz Clare's visage rose in her mind, still handsome in his white-haired old age. *I would rather rot in the ground than let you change me*, he had declared from his deathbed. *Your dark soul shall never taint me or mine.* Brave words, given that another *upyr* stood ready to transform him. Naturally, Lucius—his savior—had been one of her sire's rabbit-loving shapechangers.

Edmund had not been worthy of the promise Nim Wei kept by coming back to him.

The horse missed a step beneath her, and Nim Wei forced her hands to relax. "I wish to be intrigued," she said light as air. "I wish to meet my equal on the battlefield and in bed."

"On the *battlefield*," Philippe repeated with a soft male laugh.

Nim Wei lifted her brows at his condescension. "Never doubt a woman can fight."

Her compassion had evaporated beneath the burn of her memories. She pushed her power at him, through his soft gray eyes and into his human veins. He did not have the wherewithal to resist. He shifted in his saddle as his flesh began to react, swelling, stiffening, until the discomfort of his erection drew a flush up into his face. Nim Wei could see his color darkening, of course. Her eyes were as sharp at night as a cat's.

"And so the appetite betrays the heart," she murmured, too low to be heard by anyone but him.

He jerked his head away, breaking the connection. Nim Wei let him do it, satisfied she had made her point. Behind her, Christian's gaze was a red-hot auger boring into her neck. He did not know what she had done, only that he disapproved of it.

You know how to stop me, she thought.

He would not hear that, either. Their bond was not yet established, nor would she force it. And perhaps she did not want him to stop her, not so early in the game. These men of Durand's were a toothsome bushel of fruit. She could take a bite of any one of them she wished.

Grace grew more uneasy as the night's march wore on. As far as she could tell, Hans was fine, telling bawdy jokes to his neighbors that had them roaring so hard with laughter a few were crying. No, it was the front of their little column where the storm seemed to brew—with Nim Wei and Philippe and Christian, with Lavaux and the silver-haired man named Timkin whose pale, dead eyes gave her the willies. Gregori Durand led them all in solitary splendor, sitting like a king on his big bay horse, his cool eyes surveying the snow-capped peaks around them for new dangers.

From what Grace could see, the dangers came from within.

By the second hour, Matthaus had fallen to the rear to march beside Hans. Nim Wei and Philippe were no longer flirting, but that tension coiled between them a child could see. Their horses walked close together, and their lower legs were brushing. Even from the back of the line, Grace read disquiet in Philippe's expression as he stole looks at the minstrel.

If Grace had been in Matthaus's boots, she wouldn't have wanted to watch, either. She'd seen this man alone with his lover. She knew how much they cared for each other. She realized she was getting caught up in more than Christian's fate—which was stupid, even for her. Had he been aware that she existed, Matthaus wouldn't have wanted her knowing what she did. He was more of a stranger to her than the popular kids at school.

None of this discouraged her sympathy. Though Matthaus could not feel it, Grace rubbed his arm. "It's not Philippe's fault," she whispered. "The minstrel is using her power on him."

Matthaus might have sensed something, because he shivered. His rough-skinned face lifted to the sky. "Why is it that moonfall always makes the night seem colder?"

"Our eyes are dreamers," Oswald, the one-eyed cook, answered from the row up ahead. "They mistake the moon's fire for the real article."

"Why, Oswald, you are a poet!" Charles exclaimed.

Oswald rewarded him by clouting his head. Charles danced away, laughing, and pretended to clout him back.

"Disrespectful ass," Oswald growled.

"*Your* fires warm men inside and out," William offered diplomatically.

"His fires are not the only ones," Mace quipped.

As if they were hooked onto a single guide rope, the men's eyes rose and fastened on Nim Wei. Seen from behind in the saddle, her torso was a delicate hourglass, her black hair falling straight down her swaying back.

"She could warm me," Mace said. "Forsooth, she is welcome to burn me to cinders."

A few of the mercenaries made noises of agreement, but their joking didn't sound humorous. To Grace, they seemed wolfish, ready to break into snarls at the least excuse. For the first time she wondered if Nim Wei knew what she was doing. If her admirers got out of hand, could she really control these rough-mannered men? Wasn't she worried she might be hurt?

"She is a bitch," Matthaus muttered.

"Better a bitch than a cold fish," Mace observed.

His mild words broke the tension, though Grace didn't think they improved the mood. That remained strained right up until they made camp.

Christian's father chose a ruined castle as their stopping place for the day. Its crumbling fortifications offered protection against the wind, as well as providing a perch for the guards to watch for uninvited intruders. Nim Wei's tent went up behind the soundest of the ancient walls. She disappeared inside it while the men broke their fast. Grace had noticed the minstrel didn't like eating with the soldiers. Not that it mattered. No one could forget she was there. Nights were long now. Full dark would not lift for hours, and she was burning candles inside the black enclosure. Their glow allowed the red of the inner lining to penetrate. Within that somewhat hellish illumination, Nim Wei's moving shadow was indistinct.

Grace knew all the mercenaries were asking who she would pick tonight.

With the gifts she had at her disposal, Nim Wei knew how to gauge the nuances of danger to a fraction of a degree. The hunger of the men-at-arms was just as she liked, their lust a sweet perfume to her *upyr* nose. Judging it time to bring out another of her weapons, Nim Wei retrieved her lute from the padded sack in which it traveled. Her minstrel role was more than a disguise. The instrument she carried to the central fire was well exercised.

"Shall I play for you?" she asked as the men looked up.

A few cast glances toward Gregori, who—petty tyrant that he was—sat higher than the others on an upended barrel. He had finished eating, and a metal cup rested on his thigh. Nim Wei suspected its contents were mild. The elder Durand preferred to keep his faculties in firm rein. A quick rummage through the men's minds also told her he was no aficionado of the musical arts.

Personal preferences aside, he could not fail to note the hopeful looks the men sent his way.

"Just this once," he said indulgently. "I am sure your discipline will hold up under the pleasure."

"You are too kind," Nim Wei said, inclining her head to hide her amusement. This was hardly the most gracious acceptance he could have made.

Someone snickered at his faux pas—the carrot-haired boy—though she doubted any ears but hers caught the sound.

"Here," Charles said, leaping up. "Allow me to offer you my seat."

His seat was a section of fallen log. The man he had

been sharing it with, the hulking giant with the vicious scar on his neck, jumped up a beat later. He seemed too stunned by her appearance to step aside for her. His mouth hung open while through his mind ran thoughts so unabashedly erotic they actually intrigued her.

He must have a great deal of stamina if he planned to do all of them.

"Mace," Charles hissed. "Spread your cloak over the log for Mistress Wei."

Mace spread it, then jerked away like a poorly operated string puppet. The ever courtly Charles led her to the now-padded seat. The wool was pleasantly warm from the human who had been wearing it.

"Thank you, Charles," she said, flashing a smile that temporarily dazzled him.

He recovered enough to bow. "I am, as ever, your servant."

She sat the rounded body of the lute in her lap, making a show of tuning the pearwood pegs. They did not truly need the adjustment. Contact with her energy swiftly returned the instrument to its ideal state, including the precise tension for each of its eleven strings. Nim Wei used her fingertips to test them, having embraced the recent fashion for plucking notes by hand instead of using a quill plectrum. The new technique provided her a challenge, allowing her to play more intricate harmonies.

"Shall you sing, Mistress Wei?" the unctuous blade named Lavaux inquired.

"Not tonight." She offered him a smile that did not mollify him. "I should not like to overwhelm an audience unaccustomed to much music."

Clear in her intent, she ignored the murmurs of disappointment. Played unencumbered by any story, music spoke to deeper levels than the mind's normal awareness. It stirred emotion, tugged memory, carrying her thrall past the most obstinate barriers. Stone vibrated for sound, after all, though it stood against battering rams.

She enjoyed the silence that fell like a blanket as she began.

Accustomed to improvising, she did not play a tune they would recognize, but a complex twining of melodies and rhythms her immortal fingers never lost track of. Here were children laughing, there a woman sighing on her pillow. Men marched to battle, fought with a clashing sound. Nim Wei sent her listeners the images she wished them to see. The mercenaries barely breathed in their desire to catch every note. Even Christian's father, the music hater, had leaned forward. When she smiled at him from beneath her lashes, he shook himself and frowned.

As for Durand's stubborn son, he was hardening. Nim Wei could almost taste the hunger in Christian's flesh. His lips were parted, his breath coming shallowly.

She was tempted to test how far she could push him. Her body longed for his tonight. But it was too soon. She wanted him more willing and less coerced, and that balance was delicate.

She let her fingers dance freely, her left hand sliding up and down the frets as her right plucked skeins of magic from the catgut strings. She had no trouble performing many tasks at once, maintaining her human semblance being but one of them. The music only occupied a portion of her mind. The others she filled with thoughts of sex, of beautiful bodies writhing together by candlelight—male bodies in particular. Her hook perfectly baited, she turned her gaze to Philippe.

She had not given him her full thrall before. Philippe rocked back as if the force behind her eyes were solid, as if his entire body felt the shock of her attention.

He was sitting on a block of stone that had, once upon a

time, formed part of the castle walls. Chances were, Nim Wei had been many centuries old when it fell. Naturally, Philippe was not aware of that. To him, she appeared younger than he was. Her body was slight and girlish, the signs of her youth triggering lifelong habits of protection. Her forwardness offended and confused him, with confusion being the stronger of his reactions.

How could he respond to her as he did? Why did his body burn to know hers as it had for only one person in his life? Oh, he had wanted men before Matthaus, but only his current lover made fornication seem like an act he could not live without.

And then—as Nim Wei let her song soften—Philippe remembered. There had been a girl when he was young, a townsman's daughter whose face he had watched, whose hands had fascinated his boyish self. What if . . .

He became aware of the distance between his stony seat and the rest of the company. In their different variants of envy, the other mercenaries had drawn slightly back from him. Across the popping fire, Matthaus sat between Christian and Charles, nervously rubbing one elbow. He was not looking at Philippe or the minstrel. He was looking at the ground as if he were ashamed.

Philippe regretted that. Matthaus's eyes were the color of Spanish sherry, a striking contrast to his dark hair. Philippe loved the times he was free to stare into them.

But this was not where Nim Wei wanted his thoughts to go.

You could end both your shame, she whispered to his mind, *if you let Mistress Wei seduce you. She is even prettier than that girl you watched. She is small and sweet and as clean as a mountain stream. It would feel so good to empty your lust in her. You never quite get enough with Matthaus. With her, you could sate yourself.*

Philippe's thoughts took over, as she hoped they would. He would not have to hide that he had been with the minstrel, would not have to face the speculation and the embarrassment. He shifted on his cold seat, aware that his prick had swollen inside his braies, so full and hard that it was hurting. Maybe he had been wrong about his true nature. Maybe Matthaus had as well. Maybe they could live normal lives.

Nim Wei had observed too much of human predilections to believe the chance of that was anything but slim. Many mortals were flexible in their desires, but she did not think Philippe was among them. Since it served her purpose to let him fool himself, she stood up and smiled gently, briefly, into each of the lifted faces in her audience.

"I can see some of you are tired," she said, her words sufficient to provoke yawns. "Perhaps I have played enough music for one night."

The mutters of protest were halfhearted. Nim Wei held her lute by the neck and bowed. "Gentlemen, you have my thanks."

She slipped silently away from the fire, an ability inherent to the most powerful *upyr*. Her feet did not crackle among the weeds, nor her infrequent breath fog the chilly air. To her ears, the footfalls that followed her were as loud as arquebuses firing iron balls. They were not, however, as dangerous.

Philippe was coming after her to her tent. She did not need to turn to be sure. The turbulence of his and the others' thoughts made it obvious.

Sixteen

With his garments scattered around his feet on her sea of colorful silk pillows, Nim Wei's partner for the evening was becomingly vulnerable. His arms hung by his naked sides, where she had ordered them to stay. Periodically, his fingers curled into his palms, struggling against the urge to fist the throb and ache of his hugely erect member.

From his mind, she read how often his situation with his secret lover had forced him to resort to that method for relief.

Not tonight, though. Tonight she had forbidden him to touch himself. As a result, his unruly soldier was deeply pink and frustrated. He must have had occasion to work outdoors in his underclothes. His shaft rose from a strip of paleness where his braies had protected him. By contrast, the sun had kissed the rest of him golden brown—a phenomena she never failed to find exotic. Her kind did not bake themselves. At best, the poisonous effects of sunshine inebriated them. At worst, the result was incineration.

Nim Wei was seeking a different sort of fire tonight.

Although Philippe's coloring entertained her, she was pleased to see few scars marred his mortal beauty: a puckered knife wound on his left thigh, a whip stripe on his right buttock—the latter probably thanks to Gregori's discipline. More marks would have been a shame, as would an overplus of hairiness. Nim Wei liked to see the morsels she had chosen. Philippe's muscles could have been sculpted by an artist's chisel, their strength and conformation marvelously pronounced.

She circled her unexpected treasure, enjoying the visual feast but also aware of how little of the night remained. She had more resilience than most *upyr*. She did not positively have to slumber when dawn broke, but the urge to do so was very strong.

Best not to waste the darkness eating him with her eyes.

Perhaps Philippe thought so, too.

"What do you wish of me?" he asked huskily. He wet his lips—part lust, part anxiety. Though his prick stood high enough to shudder with eagerness, he truly did not know what to do with her. When it came to women, he was virginal.

She touched his thickly muscled arm, delighted to inspire a shiver of pleasure. She waited to answer until he opened his eyes again. Then she stared into his smoke-colored irises.

"I want you to desire me. I want you to take me swiftly and with great force. I will show you what to do, and you will adore it. Once you have come, if I tell you I wish it, you will want to start over just as much as before. I will warn you when the last time must be. No matter how much pleasure you have experienced, you will crave that climax the most. Achieving it will feel like reaching paradise. It will satisfy you as nothing has in your life."

Philippe took to her thrall like a duck to water. His eyes were starry, his pupils huge. A sound of pain came from his throat when he tried to speak. Each word she uttered had impelled his arousal a measure higher, until clear drops of excitement squeezed from his tip to roll over his corona. He swallowed and tried again.

"I want that," he said in a ragged voice. "I want to take you like that, but—"

"But?" she prompted, her eyebrows flicking up in surprise.

"Please do not ask me to kiss you."

She could have forced him to want that, too, but it seemed childish. Let him save that intimacy for his lover, if it soothed his sense of loyalty. She drew the back of her left hand's fingers up the brown column of his throat. She knew her skin was cooler than he was used to. Her normal temperature was lower than a human's, at least until her arousal was at full sail. Philippe's jugular throbbed hard and quick at the place she stopped.

How it had amused her to hear Christian pondering why his friends stroked their necks! An *upyr's* bite was indeed a sexual act, strongly—and irresistibly—orgasmic for both parties. Had Philippe known this, he would not have worried about his performance, even in the face of her worldliness.

She could have reassured him, but she enjoyed the way he watched her like a sparrow stalked by a cat. Since his nervousness did not lessen his arousal, she could not repent causing it. She was a predator, after all.

Why wouldn't she like having prey who both dreaded and desired her pounce?

"I will only kiss you here," she said, her knuckles caressing his racing pulse. "Not on your mouth. And I swear to you, my kiss will be the sweetest you ever felt."

He groaned at the unfulfilled promise of her words. "Must I stand frozen here forever?"

"You will not try to touch yourself if I let you move? You will allow my body to be the sole source of your release?"

"Yes," he moaned. "Please."

"Very well," she said. "I give you permission to begin our congress now."

Her words snapped the chain that held him. He fell on her like a Viking, his weight dragging her ungracefully to the floor. The cushions that broke their plummet were firm and rectangular, ideal for copulating on. She doubted Philippe noticed. He was too busy yanking her hose down her legs. They were made in the newer fashion, sewn together at front and back. Beneath them, per her current preference, her pubis was as bare as a young maiden's.

No arcane unguent had done this, only her *upyr* power. Exquisite though her body naturally was, she could play with its characteristics in subtle ways.

"So smooth," he said, palming her mound in fascination. "So white."

She surmised that her flesh was glowing; her glamour had a tendency to fray when she was aroused. Not that its marble glister mattered now. Philippe was firmly under her spell, and she could thrall any inappropriate memories from him later—just as she could order him not to resent her coupling with other men. She did not care that he was uninterested in stripping her further. His knees worked between hers, wedging hers apart eagerly. Her body heat increased at the evidence of his excitement, however involuntary it might be. That excitement was no less potent for being artificially induced. Supported on one elbow,

Philippe gripped his stiffened prick and steered it, bumping her but not going in.

He gasped with pleasure at even that awkward touch.

"Here," she said, reaching down for him. "Allow me."

The instant she had him placed, he plunged in.

"Christ's blood," he swore at the relief of finally having heat and tightness around his cock. "Lord help me, I must do that again."

If the Lord was going to help him, Nim Wei would attend church.

True to her instruction, Philippe took her swiftly and with great force. Nothing lacked in the fervency of his thrusts. Sensation was sensation and, stripped of his personal inhibitions, he could not help but enjoy her snug clasp on him. Her strength intensified the friction, her control of muscles mortal women barely knew they had. His desperate grunts as he shoved through her internal grip were music, his speed impressive for a human. The only skill he fell short on was knowing how far back he could pull. He was bucking in and out so wildly, Nim Wei had to hold his hips to keep him secure.

His wildness took another toll. They had not been driving at each other long before he lost his hold on his lust. A sudden pressure in his balls filled him with alarm. His peak was rising sooner than he expected and much more powerfully. He feared he was going to make a fool of himself. . ."

"Christ," he cried, unable to stop it. "Oh, sweet Lord . . ."

He gasped for air and stiffened, his hips locked deep as his body clenched with his orgasm. His hot human energy flooded into her along with his seed, triggering an echo of his ecstasy in her. All signs indicated his climax was ferocious. Nim Wei noticed his eyes were actually rolling back.

He must have been longing for this sort of total abandonment. It took some time for his spine to go slack again.

"Saints above," he panted, sagging down on her. "That was wondrous."

She stroked his laudably muscled back while he regained his strength. Thanks to the backwash of his pleasure, her fangs were fully extended within her mouth, her hunger not intolerable but rising. Fortunately, she did not think he would keep her waiting long for another round. After a bit of heavy breathing, his hands found her hips and squeezed. His cock twitched inside her, beginning to thicken as his fingers pushed a little shyly beneath the smooth, taut muscles of her bottom.

Nim Wei was not about to discourage his initiative. She could tell he especially admired this part of her. He was thinking that her skin was velvet, that her buttocks were deliciously small and firm. Guessing exactly why he might like this, she laughed silently to herself.

Even when one's partner was bewitched, one could benefit from being built like a boy.

"Would you like to take me from behind?" she asked.

The twitch inside her passage became a thump, as if his member were kicking her.

"Yes," she said, plucking the hope from his thoughts. "I *do* mean from behind in the ass."

"Could I?" he breathed, an innocent being offered his heart's desire. "Would you order me to do that?"

"I might want to hold your arm while you did it. I might want to . . . kiss you there."

"Whatever you wish," he said without hesitation. "Anything to experience those heights again."

The queen in her could not let him have his way at once. She ran her tongue around her sharp eyeteeth. "I want you to yearn for this intensely."

"I do. I swear."

"Enough to do it just as hard as before?"

"Harder," he promised roughly, his face abashed. "My balls are aching. I want to stuff myself in you there."

"You could not hurt me," she told him, divining at least one source of his shame. "No matter how hard you went. I am stronger than you can imagine."

He had pulled himself from her queinte in preparation, his erection pulsing thick and hot and wet on her inner thigh. His heart beat so hard to pump blood to this lower organ that the entire surface of his body shook. His prick had been large before, but now it looked positively bloated. The shaft was much broader than the glans, as if his member had been designed to facilitate this precise entry. Nim Wei curled her hand over the uppermost portion of his penis, enclosing those tapering inches in her slim white fingers.

Philippe closed his eyes in erotic pain, the delicate folds around his lids puckering. He liked the clasp of her slender hand, mute reminder of the girl he had once desired. This, however, was not the only complicated thrill pushing him.

"I would like to use all my strength on you," he confessed. "To fuck you so hard that both of us long to scream." His voice sank low with embarrassment. "I have never dared to truly let loose before."

Oh, he was enchanting, his admission more than she had compelled from him.

"I would allow it," she conceded, gracious ruler that she was. Her lover jerked, ready to commence then and there. She held his chest off with the flat of her palm. Afraid he had miscalculated, his pretty eyes locked onto hers anxiously. He had no idea how easy he was making it to thrall him. "I would allow your dearest wish more than once, Philippe. In fact, if you like, I would allow you to pretend I am someone else."

Her permission let a tiger out of its cage. His face flushed red an instant before he hauled her up and maneuvered her onto all fours.

Here was the confidence he had been missing. Here was the dominance. All she could do was ride out his frenzy; he was beyond controlling as he took her in the place of his male lover. His groan of entry did not have time to fade before it turned into grunts of force. She was fortunate she enjoyed this act, and that he was built for it, because he went at it wholeheartedly. Though he did not regard the sensitive places a mortal female would wish him to, he *was* skilled, each surging thrust finding other, highly pleasurable tingling spots. *Upyr* bodies were designed to make the most of any stimulation. Nim Wei's fangs soon throbbed in their sockets, and she could not help but think Matthaus a lucky man. When Philippe's breath began to whine from him in warning of another impending peak, she knew she wanted to go with him.

She only needed one arm to brace their weights, so this time she bit him when he climaxed, her teeth penetrating the tightly corded muscles of his forearm. He came again instantly, his prick jamming deeper as the subsequent orgasm swamped his first. Each time she pulled his heated blood down her throat, his nerves fired explosively. Though his release kept jetting, he was so hard inside her he felt like stone.

"God," he growled against the back of her neck. "How can I keep doing that?"

He could keep spasming until he fainted, if she commanded it. She could not, however, not if she wanted to finish this safely before dawn. Her head was heavy from its approach, or maybe from the intense pleasure of drinking him. She let go of his forearm so she could speak.

Before she could, he yanked her upright onto his lap,

still facing away from him. Nim Wei could not help squirming. She felt as if she were sitting on a hot poker.

"Order me, Mistress Wei," he demanded. "I want to sodomize you again."

Her eyes widened at his imperious tone, and his use of her name. This was more than her thrall talking. For whatever reason—perhaps because she had told him he need not fear for her physically—he was finding real satisfaction in this encounter, enough that he wanted more. Indeed, this level of participation might weigh on him afterward, but she shrugged off the wisp of concern. If he felt guilty, that would only goad Christian more. As long as his remorse did not affect her, Philippe's conscience was his affair.

"This will be your last release," she warned him. "I order you make it good."

He made it so good she nearly screamed. She would have if her mouth had not been buried in the sweaty bend of his arm, sucking his salty skin there but not biting. She had ordered him to want this climax the most. From the way he was pounding into her and groaning, he did. She read from his mind that his balls were aching, but he did not go over; he had known too much pleasuring already. Instead, the coil of need in his groin simply wound tighter. Faster he went, and more forceful, until his prick was virtually jabbing her.

The thoughts of their watchers from around the camp, moved to lechery by the sight of her and Philippe's silhouettes, began to brush hers. Thankful for the candles that cast their frenzied shadows against the walls, Nim Wei drank in the mercenaries' envy like fine French wine. For his part, Philippe was aware of no needs apart from his own, those that drove him fierce enough to blot out the world. Belatedly, she realized he could not come again unless she bit him. He was gasping out helpless pleas, truly in savage pain. Loving his struggle, she held off and held off and then—when she herself could not bear it—she drove her fangs in again.

He roared as the gargantuan summit crashed over him: no words, no names of pretend partners, only a shout of relief so violent she was certain he would be hoarse. Over and over, he shot his seed into her until not a drop remained.

He collapsed back onto a pile of pillows when she disengaged shakily from him. Unable to rise just yet, which was rather an accomplishment on his part, she turned on her hip to observe him.

His lips were curved, his eyelids fallen, every muscle on his hard frame relaxed. The beatific glow would pass, as would his weariness. Though he had earned the right to sleep, she could not give it to him. A hint of pale yellow was tinging the sky outside, and she needed to be alone. Walls of silk were not enough for her peace of mind. Considering what they had witnessed, others among the company might try to come to her. Because of this, she had wards to set and a shallow resting place to dig. Too practical to spare her partner, she slapped Philippe's cheeks to bring him around. His satisfaction-glazed eyes looked up at her blearily.

"Heed me well," she said, steadying his face in her hands. "These are the events I wish you to forget . . ."

Seventeen

Philippe's culminating roar was unmistakable, making a mockery of the separation between the minstrel's tent and the dying fire. The logs had burned down to embers, a last few orange cinders floating up into the dark gray sky. It was by these embers that Matthaus and Christian sat—Grace, too, though Matthaus was unaware of that. Left alone by the others, the pair had been pretending to enjoy Christian's small brandy stash. Or Christian had been pretending. Matthaus held his cup morosely, its contents untasted as he rested the tin on his thigh.

Matthaus was not given to emotional outbursts. Even when Philippe's voice rang out, his sole response was a wince.

Christian felt helpless to comfort him. He could not even admit he thought Matthaus needed it. Since no one was supposed to know Matthaus loved Philippe, Matthaus was denied the ordinary jilted man's expressions of discontent.

He handed his cup to Christian as the last carnal sounds were swallowed by the wind's rushing.

"Thank you for the drink," he said, his gaze on a cluster of pines that huddled in the opposite direction from the scene of his cuckolding. "I think I shall take a walk."

"Matthaus—" Christian said, but the other man waved him off. The further away he got, the more the line of his shoulders slumped.

"Should I follow him?" Grace asked.

Christian's throat was too tight to answer. He would not have said he was a romantic, but Philippe's betrayal of Matthaus incensed him. How *could* it have been this easy for Mistress Wei to separate the pair? They risked so much to be together, she should not have been able to snap her fingers—or strum her lute, as the case might be—and have her way. That she had done so frightened him, and that angered him as well.

"Fie!" he said, jumping to his feet with his need to take action. "This is just a game to her, but to them, it is everything." He looked down at Grace, who was sitting tailor-style on the ground. "I have to confront her. This cannot be allowed to stand."

"Christian—"

Grace's fear eased his own. Her, at least, he could reassure.

"I know," he said, stroking her phantom hair with his fingertips. "I will be careful."

He reached Nim Wei's tent just as Philippe was stumbling out. Despite his unsteadiness, Philippe grabbed Christian's arm and steered him away. Christian resisted, a scrabbling noise from inside having caught his ear.

"Let go of me," he hissed sharply to Philippe.

"Christian," Philippe scolded. "It is not right for you to seek entry here. Mistress Wei did not invite you."

"Mistress Wei has done little but *invite* me since the night we met."

"You may not pass," Philippe insisted.

Christian cursed him, wrenching free of his hold to reach for the closed tent flap. The moment he touched the heavy silk, an ice-cold tingle rolled up his arm. His mind went briefly but completely blank. His hand fell back to his side. What was he doing here? He knew he ought to remember, but he could not.

He turned to Philippe, whose face was unnaturally wan—ghostlike, he would have said before he met Grace; *she* had plenty of color. With sad and heavy eyes, Matthaus's lover gazed back at him.

"Tomorrow night is soon enough to speak to her," he said.

His words shoved Christian's memory back. *That* was why he had come here: to confront Mistress Wei.

"You do not look happy," he blurted out. "Did she do something different to you than she did to William and Charles?"

Philippe's chest deflated with his slow exhale. "I am well, Christian. In truth, I have never been so satisfied in my life."

"Again I say: You do not appear satisfied."

Philippe grimaced but did not argue. His boot toed a hole between two brown tufts of grass. "Mistress Wei rests. I must resign myself to carrying my burdens."

Burdens sounded like a problem Christian needed to address. He rubbed his right hand, the one that had touched the black tent flap. It still felt cold, as if tiny feathers of frost were crawling along his bones. When he looked at his hand, it was normal—probably just icy from this chill break of day. He did not think much time had passed since Philippe's exit, but within Nim Wei's shelter, her candles no longer burned. The tent gave the impression of being dead, as if no living soul were in there. Assuredly, calling to her now was pointless.

With that decision, Christian's cramped hand relaxed. Philippe was right. Tomorrow night was soon enough to beard the lioness.

In fact, now that he thought about it, maybe he should drop the matter entirely.

In the end, Grace decided Matthaus deserved his privacy, even from a ghost. She searched the camp until she found the spot Michael had chosen to bed down, where Christian would probably turn up once his errand was done. The place was out of the wind, behind a low length of ruined wall. Michael had the blankets pulled tensely to his ears, but he was sleeping. Like the rest of the soldiers, he was used to cold weather.

Wishing she could warm him, Grace sat on the ground nearby to wait for Christian. When he appeared, the sun was rising behind him, and his figure seemed very tall. She could not see his expression, but his strides were relaxed.

"It is I," he announced to Michael as he dropped down.

Michael grunted, evidently all the sign Christian needed that he wouldn't be mistaken for an attacker. He lay down spine to spine with the other man, tugged the blanket to him until he had half of it, and smiled sleepily at Grace.

She lay down facing him, her hands cushioning her cheek as she enjoyed the simple pleasure of gazing back at him. Her heart quieted inside her. This was her Christian. This was her friend. Their heads were perfectly aligned, and his dark eyes were warm. His lashes were a thick frame of inky spikes. As if he liked staring at her, too, his smile deepened. The dimple she hardly ever saw sprang to life on his stubbled cheek.

Michael must have sensed his friend was happy. He relaxed behind him and began to snore.

Judging it safe to speak, Grace asked the question she'd been waiting to be able to. "It went well? Nim Wei agreed to leave Philippe alone?"

Christian's smile erased itself, his straight black eyebrows drawing together in bafflement. A shiver gripped Grace's neck.

"You talked to her, didn't you? You're the one who said that what she did couldn't stand."

Christian pressed two fingers into his furrowed forehead. "I did not speak to her. It seemed unwise to wake her after she slept. Philippe was well. He . . . he said he had never been so satisfied in his life."

"You couldn't have believed that!"

"I did," he said. He had the haughty manner he sometimes got when he wasn't really sure of himself. "I would rather sleep now. Tomorrow night will be soon enough to talk to her, assuming I choose to do so at all. I am no longer certain what that would accomplish."

Grace's eyes felt as big as saucers. "Christian, what did she do to you?"

"Nothing. I told you, I decided not to disturb her." He closed his eyes, seeming determined to shut her out. "Please be quiet. I need to rest."

Grace's mouth fell open. A little squeak came out, but Christian did not relent. Somehow, without even seeing him, Nim Wei had put a spell on him.

She had to do something about it. Of all the people in the camp, only Grace was unaffected by Nim Wei's magic. All right, the zapping thing was an effect, but it didn't compromise her judgment. Plus, she'd come back the last time Nim Wei's energy sent her away. There was no concrete reason to think she wouldn't recover if she was zapped again.

I have to get to that tent. See if I can find clues.

The stomach she didn't really have tightened with dismay. Christian was sleeping now, his breathing deep and even. Grace rolled to her feet and smoothed her light nightgown.

Ghost or not, she wouldn't have minded her own suit of armor then.

You'll just look outside her tent, she told herself. *If that feels okay, you can peek inside.*

The eastern sky was bright as she walked through the slumbering camp, but in the west line after line of clouds massed over the big mountains. Grace wasn't solid, and her nose wasn't functional, but that western sky looked like it smelled of snow. It occurred to her that, no matter what century the calendar was turned to, a cloud was always a cloud. A million castles could crumble, and that would remain the truth.

The idea kept her metaphoric feet on the ground. She was hardly shaking when she reached the dull black sheen of Nim Wei's infamous bower. The guy ropes creaked in the wind, but nothing looked in danger of blowing over. Grace crept closer to the door. The tent was silent. Nothing buzzed or prickled at her. Maybe the minstrel's magic energy slept with her. Still not ready to let down her guard, Grace studied the column of Chinese characters that were embroidered on the entry flap. Naturally, she had no idea what they said.

For a good time, call Nim Wei? she thought.

That made her laugh, which made her feel better. This was just a tent. It wasn't going to bite her. Christian faced far worse every time he went into battle. Today it was her job to protect him.

Something flashed at the bottom of the door flap, catching the corner of her eye—a piece of metal, she thought. Grace crouched down for a closer look. No, there was no metal. In fact, there was nothing shiny here at all.

Then she turned her head and caught the flash again.

Her shoulders rippled with nervousness. Whatever the effect was, she couldn't see it if she looked at it directly. She tried squinting the way she had when the distant bandits had abruptly sprung into view. That didn't work, but when she blurred her eyes, crossing them to lose their focus, images appeared.

Runes—or something like runes—marched around the hem of the minstrel's tent. They had not been sewn there. The primitive little figures looked like they'd been drawn in glimmering golden light. Grace saw stick people with bows and arrows, a shield, a tree, a crescent moon with a teardrop dangling from its tip. Every third or fourth figure seemed to be a dagger, which suggested that this message wasn't welcoming visitors. The writing ran up the seams of the tent as well, all the way to the peak of its scalloped roof.

Literally ran, as it happened. Some of the writing seemed to be moving.

Grace would have examined that effect more closely, except that crossing her eyes so long was giving her a headache.

"Bleh," she said, shaking her head and coming to her feet.

She plunked her fists on her waist and considered her options. *In or out, Grace. Fight or flee.*

But maybe thinking too hard about this wasn't a good idea. She drew a deep breath, willed her teeth not to chatter, and stepped *through* the black silk wall.

Her nerves were jittering like crazy, but absolutely nothing happened. The diameter inside the tent was about the length of a four-door car. It was dim, thanks to the double layer of the walls. Grace could just make out a floor heaped with pillows and a number of unlit candles sitting in glass votives. What she didn't see was any sign of Nim Wei.

She has to be here, Grace thought, though in truth she was relieved not to find her. On the other hand, given the fuss she'd made about not going out in daylight, where else would she be sleeping?

She looked up, but the minstrel wasn't hanging from the roof peak like a spider.

Down then, Grace thought, turning her attention to the floor. The pillows in its center weren't high enough to hide a body, but did they seem more disturbed? Grace walked there, wishing she could kick them out of her way and see what was underneath. If she could just focus her body the same way she had her eyes . . .

Or unfocus it, as it were. Maybe the trick was not trying too hard.

Too bad she had no idea how to do that.

I'm not kicking you, she thought to the nearest pillow. *I'm not, I'm not, I'm not!*

She swung her foot like a soccer player, but it only went through the thing.

"Shucks," she said. This was so frustrating.

She thought about how important her success could be to Christian and the others. Regardless of what they were meant to do, the glowing spells on the walls pretty much proved Nim Wei was a witch.

Grace sincerely doubted she was Glinda the Good.

I ought to have power, too. I'm just as much of an uncanny being.

If she could embrace what she had become, be glad of it instead of afraid or sorry, maybe she'd get somewhere.

She was what she was now. There wasn't any fighting it. She *wasn't* sorry she had met Christian. Learning to help him was absolutely a good thing.

Her hands and feet began to tingle.

Oh, boy, she thought, kneeling down before the effect could pass.

She batted away one pillow and then two more. She could see the dirt of the floor now, could feel it under her naked toes. It was smoother than she expected. Someone had cleared every rock and blade of grass from it, a task that should have taken quite a while on this icy ground. A tangle of glowing runes covered the spot she'd bared, forming the shape of a small body: Nim Wei's body, Grace couldn't help thinking. The way the symbols looked, the way they *felt*, reminded her of dogs snarling.

Stay away, they seemed to say, *or I might bite you*.

Grace pulled her right hand against her breast. She wanted to know what was under this strange protection, but the only way to find out seemed to be digging. She was solid enough to do it. She just wasn't sure she dared.

Only an idiot would, she berated herself. Sometimes fear was a good thing.

She placed her palm on the ground instead. The runes glowed brighter, seeming to swell bigger and rise to her. Grace's vision shimmered. Gritting her teeth, she pressed more determinedly on the dirt . . . which suddenly became transparent.

Grace could see Nim Wei. She was lying on her back a foot beneath the surface, as white as marble and as beautiful as a painted doll. She was asleep, thank God, and appeared unaware of Grace. She looked different than when she was awake, almost as if she glowed. Calling her Sleeping Beauty didn't cover it. Grace had never seen a human being this gorgeous. Nim Wei's thick-lashed eyes were closed, her arms stretched peacefully at her sides. Her skin was so perfect it didn't seem to have pores.

Part of Grace didn't ever want to look away from her.

She jerked back with a gasp of belated shock. Did witches really sleep underground? Most of what she knew about them came from decorations at Halloween. Since Nim Wei didn't wear a pointed hat or fly on a broomstick, what she knew was probably baloney. Grace wished she'd been taught real folklore in school. As it turned out, that would have been more useful than "duck and cover."

Shaken to her core, she stood up and retreated from the minstrel's odd resting spot. Her skin felt cold, like a film of ice was crystallizing over it. When she looked down, she gasped louder than before. The runes weren't on the ground anymore. They were crawling over her!

"Stop it," she hissed, trying to slap them off. Her panic accomplished nothing. The glowing symbols weren't bugs she could swat away, and they definitely didn't follow her orders. More swarmed down the walls and headed straight for her. Grace hadn't been imagining before. The runes *were* making a growling noise, one that was almost too low to hear, like a distant motorcycle gang. No less terrified because of their lack of volume, Grace edged hastily toward the door.

"Fine," she said. "I'm leaving."

And then she *did* leave, as if a cosmic hot-rodder had popped her clutch and laid down rubber.

Eighteen

Grace's atoms felt like they were vibrating in their shells. She'd been flung back to the grassy amphitheater. Pretty though it was, she'd rather not have been there. Her angel was lounging on his back on the painted stage, one knee up and both hands clasped on his lean sternum. The giant screen behind him twinkled at the edges but was otherwise invisible. Beneath the brilliant sunshine, on the green distant hills, the Hollywood sign gleamed white.

She'd half forgotten this place while she was away— as if it were a land from a dream. She'd half forgotten her angel, too, though she might be able to chalk that up to him being good at ignoring her.

"You!" she huffed when he just lay there in his stupid tuxedo.

He turned his head to her and blinked. "Grace. What are you doing here?"

"What am *I* doing here? Why are *you* sleeping on the job? I've been calling for you like crazy."

He sat up and straightened his fancy jacket. "You wouldn't have heard me if I'd answered. You've been Immersed."

"Whatever that means," Grace muttered.

He smiled, and she really couldn't imagine how she'd forgotten someone this beautiful. His eyes were a true sky blue, his golden hair as shiny as a wedding ring. He seemed familiar, as if she'd met him in real life and ought to remember it. She tried to tug the memory to the top of her brain, but even as she did, it skittered away.

Impatient with everything around her, Grace plunked her hands on her hips. "Send me back," she demanded.

Her angel hopped off the stage and strolled to her, his infuriating smile intact. "Like being a ghost that much, do you? You should learn to raise your standards. Your Father wants more for you than crumbs."

"Maybe they're good crumbs," she snapped.

Her angel laughed outright and took her face in his hands. "All is well, Grace. Ask your questions now."

His touch radiated love into her, as if that emotion were an element as basic as oxygen. He wasn't angry with her impatience. He wasn't going to slap her around. He adored her just as much as when she was a good girl. Hot tears welled up into Grace's eyes. She wished she knew how to love like this.

"You do," the angel murmured. "I promise you."

"I don't know what to do," she confessed, "how I'm supposed to help Christian."

"Nothing is required of you on that score."

"Maybe nothing is required, but what if I'd like to? How can I learn to control my powers when I'm back there?"

Her angel brushed a lock of hair from her cheek. "There are countless ways to achieve your goals, some of which you've already stumbled on. You must have noticed you're making progress."

"Not enough!"

"Your impatience slows you. When you feel it, it is your personal signal that you do not believe you'll succeed."

"Then help me believe. Wave your wings and make it happen."

Her angel shook his shining head. "That was never meant to be my job. It is up to you to convince yourself."

"Figures." Grace sighed and crossed her arms, taking a moment to stare up at the perfect sky. As she did, a gorgeous red and emerald parrot curved across it. Was it a real bird, or a symbol from her unconscious? The fact that she could ask the question suggested she wasn't as irritated as she thought. Already, the peaceful atmosphere of this place was sinking into her. When the angel rubbed her shoulders, his hands felt like they belonged there.

Here, with him, she could believe they were the same kind of being.

"I envy you," he said. "All those adventures ahead of you on the earthly plane."

Grace widened her eyes at him in surprise. He didn't look envious. He looked calmly ebullient.

"My sort feel envy differently," he explained. "We don't mind desiring things. We know any dream we have can come true in time."

His mention of time brought her out of her daze.

"I need to go back," she said gently, not wanting to insult him. "Before I get too comfortable here."

Her angel grinned at her as he adjusted his white bow tie.

"As thou wilt, milady," he said, and snapped his long, manicured fingers.

Nineteen

Cripes, Grace thought as her brain rattled in her skull for the second time. She was back with Christian, who—to judge by his snores—hadn't realized she'd left.

Well, really, she thought. *Play the hero and nobody notices.*

She laughed a little at herself, too grateful to be back to mind. She was solid, which was nice, so she wriggled down next to Christian, snuggling into his front with a happy sigh. His arm came around her and then his leg. Either he was dreaming about her, or he wasn't completely out. The hump that dug into her belly was pretty hard.

"Mm," he said, his hips working up and down as if he itched. "Grace."

Grace edged her leg between his. That felt so good she had to give his thigh a scissoring squeeze. Christian's hand slapped onto her bottom.

"*Grace*," he said, his eyes open now.

"Wait," she gasped as he began pulling up her gown.

He stopped, but his expression wasn't pleasant, and his hold on her rear anatomy remained firm. She got the feeling he would rather have rolled her underneath him *before* he could reconsider if that were a good idea.

"I need to talk to you," she said. "It's important."

His glare grew darker, almost as dark as his voice. "I want you, Grace, and you are wet. This had best be good."

She was certain she was blushing, but she couldn't worry about that. "You trust me, right? You know I wouldn't lie to you."

"I trust you," he agreed, a bit of growl in it.

His long fingers tightened, pushing the cloth of her gown into the wetness he had mentioned. Grace squirmed for more than one reason.

"Nim Wei *is* a witch," she said in a rush. "Or something a lot like one. I snuck into her tent after you fell asleep."

"By yourself?" Christian was aghast. "After what happened last time?"

Grace spread her hands on his chest, wishing she could calm his angrily pounding heart as easily as her angel had calmed her. "I had to. I could tell she'd bespelled you."

"You are not speaking sense. How could she bespell me when I did not go near her?"

Christian's body jerked forward as Michael shoved it with his elbow. "Christian," he grumbled. "You are talking in your sleep again."

"Sorry," Christian said, his glare for Grace undiminished. "Must have drunk too much brandy. I will rise now and walk it off."

He yanked Grace bodily up with him, pulling her after him through a gap in the crumbling wall. She could feel his tension in the fingers that wrapped her wrist, could see it in the stiff steps he took. He stopped when they reached the weedy ruins of a small chapel. The far wall was mostly standing and still formed a point at the top. Since she had lungs now, Grace was breathless from keeping up with him.

"I had to spy on her," she said before he could start his scold. "I couldn't be a coward when your safety was at stake."

"What about *your* safety? Do you know what it would do to me if I lost you?"

"Christian." She caressed his arm as she touched it. To her relief, he let her, catching her hand in his when she reached it.

"Grace . . ."

"Just listen. Nim Wei wove some sort of spell into the fabric of her tent. I don't imagine you could see it, but my eyes are different now. It was meant to keep people out, to convince them they didn't want to go in. I think that's why you didn't confront her the way you planned. I know you would have otherwise. You were very angry about what she did to Philippe and Matthaus."

"Not nearly as angry as I am at you." He pulled her hand to his mouth and kissed it hard enough to sting. It would have been nice to shut up then, but Grace knew she hadn't said all she needed to.

"I saw her, Christian. She had . . . buried herself underneath the ground. I pressed my palm to the runes that protected her, and somehow my eyes saw through the dirt. It was very strange. She wasn't breathing. She looked almost like she was dead. I'm not . . ." Grace hesitated. "Christian, I'm not sure she's human."

"People say witches make pacts with the devil. Do you think she might have sold her soul?"

"I don't know. Before all this happened, I wouldn't have said witches existed."

Christian dropped his hold on her hand. He paced a distance away from her and then returned. He was such a physical man she supposed it helped him think if he moved around. "You are certain I was enchanted?"

"I promise you, you weren't acting like yourself."

Christian tapped his fist against his mouth. "When I touched her tent flap, I did feel curiously cold."

"So did I, right before I saw her magic symbols crawling over me."

"Crawling over you . . . Grace!"

"I got them off me," Grace said, deciding she wasn't going to mention the part about being zapped again. "And I came straight here as soon as I could."

Christian's lips were pressed so tightly together their edges were livid. She watched him struggle with his anger before he spoke. "I will not have you risking yourself like that. Not for my sake."

"But I love you," Grace said.

She knew how true the words were when tears sprang stingingly to her eyes. The feeling of having said them was extraordinary. Like floating, though she knew she was physical. All her life she'd been wishing someone would love her, and here she was loving someone else. She felt twice the size she'd been a second ago—free in ways that made absolutely no sense to her.

Of course, she hadn't planned on blurting it out. And Christian certainly didn't react like her true love did in her fantasies.

"Love is for idiots," he said. "And you are not an idiot."

It was, in its way, a compliment—just not one she could accept.

"Apparently I am."

Christian's face twisted and went red. She knew he was going to argue.

"I am," she repeated, something about the ridiculousness

of having to debate this calming her. "I left the waiting room to heaven so I could be with you. I seem to like you no matter what you do. I feel good when I'm with you. And I'm much more attracted to you than I've been to anyone before."

"Attraction is not love," he said stubbornly.

"Can't it be a sign of it?"

Christian snorted and crossed his arms. "I do not want you to be in love with me."

"And now I know you're lying. You always get snooty when you're not sure of yourself."

"Snooty!"

Grace smiled angelically at him. "Maybe you're afraid you love me back."

He opened his mouth to deny it. A second later, calculation narrowed his eyes. "If I said I did love you, would you promise to take more care?"

"I don't think so. True love doesn't come with strings."

His expression was such a war of outrage, confusion, and concealed male pleasure that she burst out laughing.

"Cease your caterwauling," he said, grabbing her shoulders and shaking her.

"I love you," she teased, still laughing. "I. Love. You."

He cursed and then crashed his mouth on hers with a groan. "Grace," he said, his interest in kissing her garbling it. "You must keep safe!"

Maybe she would have gotten him to admit that he felt the same. Maybe they simply would have made love. Either would have pleased her, but when she broke free to tease him some more, she saw someone approaching over his shoulder.

"Lavaux," she said warningly.

"God's teeth," Christian hissed between his own. "I swear, I am going to kill that clay-brained puttock."

Grace assumed *this* was not a compliment.

"Christian," Lavaux said as he turned. His smirk alone was enough to put Grace's hackles up. "I had heard you talked to yourself, but I did not credit it."

"Who else should I talk to?" Christian returned coolly. "It is a conversation with someone I trust."

Lavaux was smart enough to flush at the implied insult but not to counter it. He jutted his chin pridefully. "I am on patrol."

"Then perhaps you should get back to it."

Lavaux frowned. "She does not take you either, Durand." Who "she" was didn't need an explanation.

"Would that she did not want to," Christian muttered under his breath.

Grace guessed Lavaux didn't understand that, because he shot Christian a suspicious look before he stalked away scowling. Probably he'd planned on the exchange going differently—withering Christian with his wit or some such thing. He should have known he wasn't in Christian's league, not as far as poker faces went. Christian had picked up that skill from Lavaux's commander.

Once the Frenchman was gone, Christian tipped his head back to stare at the all-gray sky. Grace had been right about the snow. A few light flurries were floating down. They melted on Christian's nose and cheeks, but somehow avoided hers, even when she tried to catch them. It gave her a peculiar feeling, as if—even in her physical form—she weren't able to change the fate of one snowflake.

"I cannot turn to Michael for help with this," Christian said.

Grace looked at him. He seemed to have forgotten they'd been kissing. His expression was sad and serious. "I didn't know you were hoping to."

"When you first came here, I considered asking him if

he knew a ritual to banish you. He studied to be a monk for a time." When she said nothing, he reached out to rub her arm. "Looking back, I do not think that is the sort of knowledge he acquired. I also do not think he knows any prayers to safekeep the men from Nim Wei's magic. If he knew them, he would use them, and he has admitted he is attracted to her himself."

Grace had deduced all this, but hadn't wanted to say.

Christian slid his hand to hers and hooked their palms together. "I cannot go to my father. Either he will laugh and call me a milk-livered cur, or he will believe me—which might be worse. I fear he would find a way to use Mistress Wei's powers to benefit himself." He shook his head at the thought of it.

Grace squeezed his fingers. "I doubt the minstrel would be easy to take advantage of."

"No," Christian said, "but she might pretend." He compressed his forehead between the thumb and fingers of his other hand. "I do not know what to do, Grace. I have no evidence that the threat she poses is lethal. I cannot kill a woman over a seduction."

Not having known this option was on the table, Grace fought a kick of shock. Christian sure had a different set of standards. "Assuming she *is* killable," she said.

"Assuming she is. Quite possibly, the moment I was near her, I would forget I intended to kill her." Christian's body twitched as if he wanted to resume pacing. His hold on Grace's hand kept him where he was. "I do not like being helpless to protect my men. I do not like it at all."

Grace hardly needed to be told that. She stepped to him and laid her head on his shoulder. Christian had a second of hesitation, and then both his arms wrapped her close. His chest was hard, but she found its warmth comforting.

"It will be all right," she said. "Some solution will come to us."

He kissed her hair, not believing that any more than she did. Her cheek lifted and fell with his heavy sigh. His hold on her loosened reluctantly.

"Lavaux's interruption proves we are not private here. I think we had best return to camp."

Grace didn't mind sleeping in his embrace, even if Michael's nearness meant not trying to make love. When she opened her eyes the following night, making love proved really impossible. Though Christian's usual waking arousal had returned, Grace was—once again—her ephemeral ghostly self.

An impression of wrongness snapped open Nim Wei's eyes at the break of dusk. Even in sleep, her aura kept the dirt at a slight distance, and it did not fall in her face. Without moving any more, she reached out with her senses. Her tent was empty, her protective rune-spell quiet above her.

Quiet now, at least. Someone had disturbed it, someone who had also disarranged her pillows. Nim Wei should have woken the moment whoever it was breached her wards. For that matter, the person should have left a trace she could pick up now.

Nothing remained of the intruder: not scent, not energy.

Unaccustomed to being thwarted, Nim Wei twisted uneasily in the ground. First there were those blank areas in Christian's head and now this. Did she have a rival sorcerer among the soldiers? Was it possible for anyone to hide from her so well? Unlike most *upyr*, who relied strictly on their inborn powers, Nim Wei collected magic. It had interested her since she was human. She had never, however, run across a mortal who could do this.

The mystery irked her as much as Christian's resistance to her seduction. For a moment, she considered abandoning her goal. Humans crawled upon the earth in legions. With patience, she would find others equally passionate and interesting—and quite likely more grateful for her attention.

Her hands made a negating motion. *No*, she thought. She was queen. If she could not devise a path around these obstacles, she did not deserve the name.

One fact was indisputable. Desirable though winning Christian was, she would have to proceed cautiously from now on.

Twenty

Whatever Christian expected would happen next, it was not that Mistress Wei would stop bedding anyone. They passed Turin without her enjoying another tryst, and Piacenza and Parma. Once out of the northern mountains, the weather grew milder. Bands of pilgrims were traversing the Via Aemilia, the old travelers' road to Rome, in ample enough numbers that their campfires lit the mercenaries' nocturnal way. Normally suspicious of soldiers they had not hired themselves, the pilgrims seemed to find Nim Wei and her escort irresistible. More than once, her party was invited to join a meal, so that she could play her lute for them.

Christian doubted this fascination boded well for the pilgrims' hopes of piling up merit. They most certainly were not entertaining angels unaware.

Anywise, they never stayed with the groups for long, and the minstrel never seemed reluctant to part from those who had feted her. Indeed, Christian did not think she was interested in them at all. She was getting something else from the interaction. He simply had not figured out what it was.

Christian became her choice to lead her second horse. Night after night, she only requested him. At first, she tried to draw him into conversation, but Christian was no great talker, and he had no wish to be charmed—naturally or otherwise. She left him alone after a few rebuffs, ignoring his father's gracious suggestions that one of his men accompany her. Christian did not press her to choose another; he was relieved no one else was at risk from her influence. He did not sense her trying to use it on him, a conclusion Grace concurred with. The worst the minstrel did was stare at him broodingly—unblinking, it seemed to him. Her attention made him uneasy. Had she been less adept at obtaining any partner she wished, he would have said she had a tendre for him.

She had no reason to develop one. He was as cool with her as he knew how to be. Still she watched him: when he helped pitch her tent, when he ate his food, when he stripped to his braies to wash in a reed-lined stream. Kept under such close surveillance and, given that they were not in the hinterlands anymore, Grace and Christian scarcely had a moment to themselves.

His need to be with her grew unbearable. Even her companionship was denied him while he walked with Nim Wei. He had been wrong to scorn the sorts of release they had managed when Grace was only in spirit form. He craved the touch of her soft, warm flesh, but any relief—no matter how imperfect—would have been welcome. Christian was hard and aching far too often, a circumstance he suspected Nim Wei was aware of.

If she chose to push him with her witchcraft, he did not know how he would resist.

He was not the only one whose humors were unbalanced. In Modena, in a piazza outside the church that housed San Geminiano's holy bones, William—of all people—got into a knife fight with Lavaux. The smaller man had been insane to provoke the scuffle. Though William performed no song-worthy deeds of arms, he had enough sheer size to over-whelm any quickness Lavaux could call upon. Lavaux was fortunate William's temperament was not as bloodthirsty as his own. He had given William a few slashes, but William could easily have killed him. Gregori might still do so. The pair's lack of discipline had earned them all a request from the town's rulers to take themselves and their trouble out-side the walls.

Fortunately, not for nothing was this area called the "fruit bowl" of Italia. They set up camp in the orchard of a villa some distance into the gentle hills. Nim Wei had bribed the laconic *vignerolo* to allow them to stay. The vines of the country retreat were brown, the lemon and orange trees past their prime. The gardens were likely beautiful in summer, but the absent owner might have been in residence then.

Christian doubted the minstrel's florins would have spo-ken as persuasively to a rich man's purse. Gregori's men were not the sort of guests princes coveted.

Such were his sardonic thoughts as he knelt before Wil-liam to clean and bind his wounds. William sat on a bat-tered stool that had been forgotten under the dead vines.

"You know, William," Michael said, standing above them both, "I expect this sort of behavior from Charles but not you."

"It was a mortal insult," William said stubbornly. His

eyes were turned to the clear black sky, refusing to watch Christian's treatment of the shallow gash on his calf. "I had to defend the honor in question."

"The honor in question being that of a fornicator and Mother Mary knows what else."

Christian had set a lamp to see by on the arbor's stacked stone wall. Grace perched beside it, swinging her pretty legs, though only he knew that. He loved having her close by, more than he cared to admit. William must have had his own partiality. At Michael's accusation, the big man's eyes flashed sharply.

"Lavaux did not insult Mistress Wei, though I would have been happy to bash that varlet on her behalf." He winced when Christian tightened the bandages, finally looking at him. "You should have used the oil she gave me after the battle with the bandits. I do not know what was in it, but it made my bruises heal wondrously."

This was too much for Michael. "We are not using some potion that whore gave you!"

William turned slowly back to him. "You are my friend," he said, "but call her that again, and I will demand an apology."

"Peace," Christian said before Michael could retort. "We are all friends here. We must exercise respect for our differences. If we do not, you know well there are jackals who will feed on our weaknesses."

"Forgive me, William," Michael said, stiff but chastened. "I did not mean to . . . belittle your affections."

Quicker to release a grudge than he was to form one, William smiled at him. "I hear Lavaux has been ordered to scrub Oswald's pots for the next sennight."

"That is all?" Christian asked, startled. "He provokes a fight in public, and my father does not have him whipped?"

William shrugged. "We are on a job. Perhaps your father does not want him unable to perform."

This was how a man like William would think, but not necessarily Gregori Durand. Lavaux would loathe scrubbing pots, but as a punishment, it was barely a slap. Could there have been some reason his father wanted Lavaux to attack William?

"What are you thinking, Christian?" William asked.

Christian met his simple, honest stare. "I am thinking my father is not really angry. I am thinking we had best not let any of his men draw us."

William cocked his head before nodding. "Charles believes they are jealous because Mistress Wei shows them no favor."

"Maybe," Christian said. "And maybe my father plays a deeper game than any of us realize."

"A game for what?" Michael asked.

"Power," William answered. "That is always the prize men like Christian's father want."

Finished patching him up, Christian came to his feet and laid his hand on William's strong shoulder. Whatever Nim Wei had done to William, she had not changed his faithful nature. The words Christian spoke came without his planning them.

"I am glad you are mine," he said. "I am glad I do not have men like Lavaux and Timkin following me."

"We are glad to *be* yours," William said with a laugh for his earnestness. "That is why we follow you." He pushed up from the stool with a weary groan. "Now, if you will excuse me, I would be glad to sleep."

Together, Michael and Christian watched him disappear into the night. Michael rubbed his upper lip with the knuckle of one finger. "What *do* you suppose he and Lavaux fought about?"

Christian could hazard a guess. Lately, Matthaus and Philippe had not been speaking to one another, the rift between the former intimates painful to observe. Once or twice, Christian had seen Matthaus's eyes tear up as he stared at nothing sadder than a distant line of cypress trees. Knowing the reason for his emotion, Christian had looked away. How much Lavaux knew or guessed Christian could not say, but his character was not one to ignore a vulnerability. Like a blowfly, his instinct was to attack the wound. He had been gibing at Matthaus for days now, saying he must be pining over some lost damsel.

Was her bosom snowy? he had taunted. *Did her pudendum smell of cherries or day-old fish?*

If Lavaux had worse calumnies to share concerning Matthaus's romantic habits, William might have felt honor bound to defend his friend . . . even if he believed them.

"They could not have fought about Matthaus," Michael said, stealing the thought if not the attitude from his mind.

"I think it possible," Christian said mildly.

Michael turned on his heel to stare at him. Christian expected another lecture about sins against God and nature, but this was not his friend's main concern.

"You have been different of late," he said.

One of Christian's eyebrows quirked. "Different?"

"Your temper has been softer. And there is all this talking to yourself. I wish you would tell me what troubles you."

"You are the one who warned me against letting myself grow cold."

"I know." Michael watched his eyes steadily. "Would that I believed it was I who inspired this change."

Christian fought the heating of his face. Though he did not mean to do it, the haughtiness Grace had pointed out earlier thinned his voice. "I do not think I understand your complaint."

"You used to trust me with everything."

"I trust you with my life," he said, genuinely shocked.

"Your life but not your secrets." Michael dropped his head and laughed softly. "I am acting like a woman spurned. No wonder people sometimes say the same of us as they do of Matthaus and Philippe."

"Michael—"

"No, Christian. Keep your secrets if you wish. Every friendship has an occasional parting of the ways."

"We are not parting ways! Michael, you are the dearest friend of my heart. Upon my honor, were it not for your decency, I would have turned into my sire years ago."

Michael patted his cheek lightly. Christian knew both their eyes were shining. "I would lay down my life for you, Christian. Your affection saved me when I thought my heavenly Father had turned his back."

"If God would turn his back on *you*, He does not deserve children."

Michael smiled, one bright tear spilling over even as he turned away. "I shall bed down on my own today. Your perpetual mumbling keeps me awake, and the air is more than warm enough."

Christian could not bring himself to call Michael back. From the corner of his eye, he saw Grace waiting on the wall, her eyes turned down, her hands folded in her lap. Though he owed his friend more than could be counted, his body sang at the prospect of being alone with her.

Maybe Michael was right. Maybe they had come to a parting of the ways.

Christian stood looking into the darkness after his friend. Even seen from behind, he looked torn. Grace slid off the wall carefully.

"Are you sure you don't want to tell Michael about me?"

"He will judge this," Christian said without turning. "He will judge you."

"But maybe someone else should know the truth about Mistress Wei."

"I cannot prove our suspicions."

Grace stepped to his side. Christian's profile was harshly beautiful in the lamplight. "He'd hear you out. He's your friend."

Christian's narrow lips grew thinner as he compressed them. "He is my friend whether he knows about you or not. You are my lover. I . . . care about you."

He sounded afraid to make the admission. Moved more than she could say, she brushed her ghostly hand down his back. When his eyes came to hers, the lines of his face were strained.

"You are my love," he said hoarsely. "And he could not prevent Mistress Wei from doing as she pleases any more than I can."

"I don't like hearing you talk that way. We can't just give up on stopping her."

Grace's cheek tingled where he cupped it. His smile was crooked but gentle. "I shall not give up. And I do not rule out ever telling Michael about you. If there is a compelling reason, I will do it."

His gaze cut behind her. Grace thought someone might be coming, but then Christian strode past her and snuffed the lamp. Hidden from other eyes by the darkness, he turned to her. The lack of illumination didn't prevent her from seeing the ridge swelling at his groin. A slash of white caught her unnaturally keen vision. The linen of his braies was showing. The seam between his hose had parted for his erection.

"Grace," he said, his voice even rougher now. "Let us not waste this time alone."

Her breath snagged with excitement. "I don't have the power to touch you tonight."

"I do not care," he said rashly, though she knew he did. "It has been too long. I am going mad from not sharing any pleasure at all with you."

"I don't want to disappoint you."

"Trust me, Grace. That would be impossible."

He dug into his clothing, drawing out his hardness and stroking it. He was trying not to rush, but it looked like that was a struggle. His fist moved tightly, slowly, up the thick, pulsing length of flesh. Groaning, he closed his eyes for one moment. His index finger circled the spot where his rim split into two wings. The crease there must have been sensitive. Watching him, wishing her own finger were doing that, flames seemed to lick wet heat between Grace's legs.

When their gazes met, the heat became summery.

"Be in me," he rasped. "Move in me the way you did with your fist that night when Michael was sleeping."

He leaned back against a post of the arbor, his hips cocked forward from his pelvis, his spine undulating against the weathered wood. He was sex in motion, a big, beautiful male shoved to this exhibitionism by his own hunger. Lured like a moth, Grace came to him and pushed inside.

Joining with him was like being showered by sparks, electricity bursting in flowers from inside of her. When she moved, the sensation thickened—for him as well, apparently.

"Grace," he whispered. "I can feel that."

She tried to pull the feelings tighter, stronger, needing this as much as he did. Her gown had melted away. She was bathing naked within the pool of his energy. Currents and waves moved through her from her humming scalp to her curling toes. Maybe her imagination was very vivid, but she thought she felt his fist moving on his cock.

"Touch yourself," he said. "I cannot last much longer. I want you to finish yourself with me."

No matter how shy she was, she couldn't deny him now. She touched herself, tentatively at first, and then with a moan of need. It always startled her how real she felt to herself. The flesh between her labia was slick, the little bud on which her pleasure centered painfully swollen.

Running her fingers over it just increased the ache.

"Harder," Christian ordered. He panted, his body writhing around hers. "You need to rub yourself harder. I can feel what your hands are doing."

"I can feel what yours are," she gasped.

He arched his head back on the post and groaned, his boots digging into the earth to brace. "Can you feel how much I long to be inside you? How much I wish I were swiving you?"

Knowing every pleasure was shared with him, she worked her fingers faster. He jerked when she curled one inside her sheath.

"Grace."

It was a cry that demanded her to respond. "Your balls are heavy, Christian, but they feel like they've tightened, too."

"They are full," he confirmed, sounding strangled. "Because I have not enjoyed release in so long. Zounds, Grace, I could come a river for you."

When she palmed her breast, a spike of excitement surged through his cock. His body twisted like an eel. Every movement intensified what she was feeling, as if his molecules were rubbing hers.

"Pinch your nipple, Grace. Pray you, do that for me."

She did it and he grunted with approval, pumping

himself faster. He was tugging his cock out hard from his abdomen, wrenching it with a force that astonished her. It felt good to him, and to her. His sensations folded over her own—his hot, rigid shaft, her aching clitoris, the wetness that ran so freely from both of them. When pressure tightened in her groin, she wasn't sure whose it was.

"Hurry," he whispered. "Love, I cannot . . . hold on."

She came when he cupped his second hand hard against his balls, as if that grip squeezed her, too. Fluid seemed to spurt from her, all thought blanking out in a blaze of bright white delight. This was stronger than any release she had known before, the pleasure stabbing and sharp. As strong as it was, she—or maybe he—knew it wasn't enough. To have experienced each other's touch and then have it snatched away was torture. The longing forged a tighter bond between them, maybe in compensation for what they'd been denied. Her own name echoed inside her head.

Grace, he thought. *I love you.*

The words were sunshine on the long winter of her soul. How much she'd needed to hear them embarrassed her. Fearing he'd sense her weakness through their mental connection, she pulled slowly free of him.

Christian wasn't trembling like she was. Christian was flushed and relaxed and absolutely gorgeous from his orgasm. She could see he must have needed it. His ejaculation had formed a large dark spot on the earth beneath him, and the weather-silvered arbor pole seemed to be holding most of his weight. Despite his obvious languor, what shone from his eyes wasn't satisfaction.

"I want to hold you," he said, his warrior's chest going in and out as he caught his breath. "Just once, I want to hold you in my arms until all our lusts are spent."

Twenty-one

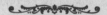

Mistress Wei asked us to remain with her while she conducts business in Florence."

Having calmly dropped this cannonball, Christian's father stopped walking. His expression unrevealing, he squinted across the stone-flagged expanse of the Piazza Maggiore. The day was bright, and most of Bologna's residents were home enjoying their afternoon siesta. The nearest witness was a skinny dog dozing in the sun. Gregori and Christian had all the privacy they could require, which probably explained why Christian had been invited on this father–son perambulation along the city's shadowy arcades.

The tidings Gregori had waited for this moment to deliver were not welcome. Christian had been clinging to the idea that this situation with the minstrel had a foreseeable endpoint.

"I thought Mistress Wei only wanted an escort *to* Florence.

I thought she could not predict how long she would stay there."

His father grunted, meaty palms pressed into the small of his back so that he could stretch. Christian suspected the popping sounds his spine made betrayed his age more than he liked. He grimaced, straightened, then shot a cool and somehow mocking look at Christian.

"Mistress Wei is a woman. Women change their minds. And perhaps she has grown fond of certain members of our company."

Christian knew there was no safe response to that. His father had made it clear he disapproved of Christian resisting their employer's overtures. Not that Gregori would have approved of him giving in. Sometimes there was no winning with his father. Judging silence was the only viable approach, Christian clasped his hands behind himself. If he could have erased all thoughts from his head, thus precluding them from showing, he would have done that as well.

"I am of a mind to accept her," Gregori announced to the crystalline blue sky. "The money she will pay would make a nice addition to our coffers." Again, he shot that cool, laughing look at Christian. "No comment, son? No maidenly protests that you cannot bear her attentions a moment more?"

"You have observed for yourself the effect she has on the men."

"We are not here for the comfort of the men."

Christian knew this was true. He also knew he could not risk his friends in the manner Gregori was proposing. Despite the coolness of the shadows beneath the square's arcade, sweat was gathering at his hairline. Christian did not wish to draw this line in the sand, but he knew his father would keep pushing until he did.

"We will not stay," he said quietly. "Once Mistress Wei is safely in Florence, we will go home."

"*We*," his father repeated, too proud to make it a question.

"My men and I."

"*Your* men."

Christian turned to his father. He was conscious of the inch or so he had on Gregori, though this did not make him feel more secure. His father resented being looked down on. "You know which men are mine as well as I do."

His father narrowed his dark eyes, the hardness of his soul starkly evident. No joviality hid his nature in that moment, no courtly manners or sham learning. Christian clenched his fists behind his back, willing himself not to quail.

"You would break with me," his father said, "over a woman whose feet you ought to kiss for wanting to bed you."

Christian said nothing. There was no argument, no explanation he could have offered that would have improved his position. Gregori might even be aware that Nim Wei was dangerous. What he would never believe was that she was a danger *he* needed to be careful of.

After what felt like forever, Gregori shifted his gaze back to the sunny piazza. The huge facade of San Petronio cast knife-blade shadows across the way, its brick the same terra-cotta red as Bologna's signature rooftops. The sheer size of the basilica, the way it dominated its neighbors, made it seem like an echo of his father's will bearing down on him.

"We will see," said his father. "We will see what you decide when it comes to the choosing point."

Christian knew what he would decide, knew what he *had* to. Whether strategy or fear kept that knowledge locked inside him, he did not want to contemplate.

* * *

Grace had been trailing Christian through the Italian city at a discreet distance. When she was alive, she wouldn't have wanted people seeing her interactions with her father, and she had just been a girl. Though Christian wasn't that much older, his responsibilities were a man's. If he felt afraid or intimidated, Grace knew it was better that she not see. Her sympathy wouldn't in any way be what he wanted, nor her assurances that she thought he was a hundred times the man Gregori was.

When he walked away from his father to veer toward her, she pretended to be staring up the hulking front of the piazza's church. She didn't find the building particularly attractive, though its size impressed. She'd seen football stadiums that were smaller.

Christian stopped beside her, not turning his head but causing her arm to tingle where his touched it. His deep, deliberate breathing told her how carefully he was composing himself.

"San Petronio," he said, nodding at the church. "He was a bishop in the fifth century."

As interesting as it was to think of history having history, Grace really couldn't get excited about this.

"What did your father say?" she asked.

Christian squeezed the fingers of his hands together, as close to wringing them as a man could get.

"Nim Wei wants us to stay with her in Florence. My father claims he will accept." Christian swallowed, the sheen of sweat on his face more than the autumn sun could be blamed for. "I told him if he did, I would take my men and go home."

Grace touched his sleeve. His hand came up to cover hers as well as it could. The sparks his palm was shooting into her ghostly fingers felt nervous. When he turned his eyes to hers, they were hollow.

"Grace, it was as if my father wanted me to defy him, as if he wanted the excuse to do something terrible."

"The minstrel won't let him," Grace said, hoping this was true. "Her interest in you might be uncomfortable, but she won't want to see you hurt."

Christian shook his head at his feet. "My father can be . . . persuasive, and Christ only knows what she really wants."

"You told your father what you had to," Grace assured him.

"I told him what he pushed me to," he corrected. "And I fear I might have made things worse."

When Gregori Durand requested a private meeting, away from his men-at-arms, Nim Wei was not about to let him choose the venue. That would have been tantamount to accepting a fox's invitation into its den. Nim Wei might be a lioness by comparison, but foxes had their wiles. Simply on principle, she set the time and place.

Consequently, she awaited Gregori at the home of one of her few human friends. Vincenzo was abed, as befitted his advanced age, but he had put his study and his servants at her disposal.

The room was small but handsomely appointed, with slanted shelves that extended along the intricately painted right and leftward walls. Illuminated manuscripts bound in leather rested on these supports. The texts ranged from Greek to Latin to Hebrew, and Nim Wei had procured many of them—from the ground where they had been buried in some cases. She did not share Vincenzo's passion for their contents. Long experience had taught her modern problems could not be solved by antique outlooks. The most successful members of any species changed with the times. Nim Wei had, however, enjoyed the quest to recover these ancient volumes, just as she enjoyed her numerous meetings with her old friend.

Her only regret was that Vincenzo had never wanted her to change him, even when he grew too old to enjoy more energetic sports than poring over musty tomes. According to him, no sensible person wanted to live forever.

Considering how he had looked tonight, he was going to prove that soon.

Nim Wei touched the hourglass on the shelf nearest to his hearth. How quickly the sands of mortal life ran out, and how lusty and handsome her friend had been when he was just a student at Bologna's famous university. He had called her the cleverest woman in Christendom—and the most beautiful. Many were the nights she had exhausted him with lovemaking, only to spend the hours till dawn sleepily arguing philosophy. She had loved Vincenzo's enthusiasms, foolish though most of them seemed to her. Sometimes she thought she needed that from humans as much as blood. Without their excitement to spark her own, would she find immortality a burden?

She blinked a wash of pink from her vision and shook herself. These were dreary thoughts for a queen to have, no doubt the result of seeing her once-young friend after a long absence. Nim Wei was a phoenix. Her joy in life always rose again. She would not be here tonight if she were not still engaged by the adventure.

When a soft rap sounded on the study door, Nim Wei was perfectly composed.

"Enter," she called, and the servant brought Gregori in.

Christian's father wore an outfit she had not seen him in before, more merchant than soldier. The loose, tabard-like outer garment was dark blue velvet with black cuffs and broad lapels. Striped black-and-white sleeves puffed through the tabard's slashes, with sober black hose to encase his legs. His round cap was red, the single burst of bright color. Naturally, his sword was strapped at his hip. Beneath his shirt, his chain mail hauberk peeked.

All steel began as iron, created by the heat and pressure of working that metal over charcoal. Since mail armor was processed less than plate, its iron content was high. Coupled with Gregori's resistance to her will, the hauberk would probably preclude her from thralling him at all tonight.

Resigned to relying on her wits, Nim Wei waited until Vincenzo's servant set down his wine tray and left.

Gregori refused her offer to fill his goblet. Because it required a considerable amount of alcohol to impair her, Nim Wei poured a cup for herself.

"Now," she said, once she had wet her palate with the soft red wine. "Care to tell me what this is about?"

Gregori looked surprised that she remained standing. Prevented by custom from sitting himself, he straightened the cuffs of his full blue sleeves. "I believe we can be useful to each other."

"Are we not already?"

Gregori's brows lowered at her refusal to provide him an opening, but Nim Wei was not about to kiss his hindquarters. She pursed her lips at him—a subtle, teasing gesture that had his mouth narrowing.

Now, she thought, *the gloves will come off.*

"I do not know what sort of enchantress you are," he said more bluntly, "and I do not care. What matters is that I have seen the marvels you can perform: the way you charm all who meet you and your uncanny effect on the soldiers who share your bed."

"Pleasing soldiers in bed is hardly an uncanny talent."

"You please them so well they stagger. And then you fortify them unnaturally."

Nim Wei's normally lazy heart rate picked up slightly. She was not frightened, merely interested and alert. Mystic that she was, she sensed an opportunity approaching.

"Do tell," she said, sipping casually at her wine.

Gregori's face tightened with the anger he was fighting. He did not relish his pronouncements being treated dismissively. His enunciation turned very crisp. "After you bedded them, Charles excelled in battle as he never had before, Hans stopped complaining about his aching joints, and William outdid any previous demonstrations of muscular power. Anyone who watched closely could have observed these changes."

Gregori, of course, was the closest watcher of all.

"I noticed no difference in William," she said. "Did not your man Lavaux pink him in that knife fight?"

Gregori's fist smashed down on the surface of Vincenzo's desk, causing the ink-stained quills that lay there to roll away.

"That is only because whatever you did to William wore off! And do not insult me by denying it. I promise you do not want me as an enemy."

Nim Wei knew her smile would infuriate him. She made it small but obvious. "My only possible interest is your value as my friend, and as yet you have made no arguments for that."

Gregori opened his mouth to snap at her, then drew a calming breath. He had a temper, but he did not like losing it. "I want you to bed my men. I want you to revitalize them as you did Christian's."

This was an interesting request, though apart from a slight widening of her eyes, Nim Wei did not let her reaction show. "Even if I could *revitalize* them, as you put it, I fail to see how that would serve me—unless you are suggesting they cannot defend me otherwise?"

Gregori's jaw worked for a moment before he spoke. "My men are more than capable, Mistress Wei. The problem lies with my son. As you may have noticed, he is stubborn. He has been trying to slip his leash. Use your"—he waved his hand vaguely—"use your magic to strengthen my men, and I will pit them against his in a test of arms. When my son is suitably humbled by his defeat, I will deliver him to you, to do with as you please for an entire night."

Nim Wei did not need a great deal of breath, but this proposition stole what she had. She saw she had underestimated Gregori's determination to hold on to his dominance.

"You would risk your son's life?" she asked.

"He risks it with his defiance. I would simply be returning him to his proper place."

Beneath your thumb, you mean, she thought with an inner snort.

"I am aware that you desire him," Gregori went on, smooth as olive oil. He slid a sly glance at her. "If he were injured, he would be that much easier to control."

The depth of the insult shocked. Nim Wei felt as if her insides were frosting over. Yes, she was a law unto herself, but this went beyond the bounds even for her. If all she wanted was to bed Christian, she could have accomplished it long ago. She wanted to make the boy her next blood companion, wanted to offer him the priceless gift of immortality. Her personal code demanded that she treat him with more respect than ordinary humans. He had to choose her, had to *want* the change for his own. And here Gregori, his father, was offering to deliver Christian to her with all the care of a pig trussed up for slaughter.

Fortunately, none of her thoughts leaked onto her face. She stared into Gregori's eyes without blinking.

"I shall consider your proposal carefully," she said.

Gregori held her gaze, undaunted by her coolness. "He is threatening to take his men and leave once we reach Florence."

For one slow heartbeat, temptation beckoned. Her conversations with Philippe had perhaps been too much on target. That which seemed unattainable did indeed whet the appetite. Christian was a prize, more than he himself realized. Proud, fiery, but with a personal discipline that kept his sharp mind ascendant over his passions. He was a match for her. More ambitious than Vincenzo. Harder than Edmund Fitz Clare. In truth, Christian was a man she could come to love. The future would taste sweet with him at her side.

Then the frost inside her thickened. She was better than this. Neither love nor lust ruled her. If she had to lose her chance to change Christian, better that than to lose herself. Offended by her twinge of weakness as much as by Gregori's belief that she was so small, Nim Wei inclined her head regally.

"You may leave," she said. "You have given me much to think about."

"Do not think too long," he countered. "Florence is not that far away."

Twenty-two

A second traveler's road, its origins as Roman as the Via Aemilia, led from Bologna to Florence through the Futa Pass. Every stride they took down it intensified Christian's dread. His time to find a solution was running out. If none came to him, he and his father would have to clash.

The gloom of their surroundings did not lighten his mood. They were in the Apennines, both dwarfed and hemmed in on either side by a forest of firs that rose a hundred feet in the air. Rain had been falling since before sunset, never pleasant for a troop of men in armor. With the wetness, everything they wore chafed them. Christian's boots clung to the mud each time he lifted them, and he did not envy the men guiding the wagons. Forced to labor harder than usual, the aroma of the group was pungent. The smell of slowly rusting mail did not allay it, nor the ever-present clouds of pine. For the past hour, Nim Wei—who had once again requested his attendance on her second horse—had been pressing a scented pomander to her button of a nose. Though she sat as straight as ever in the saddle, she seemed weary—not a look Christian had seen on her before.

He rubbed her second horse's damp black withers, far more comfortable offering the animal his sympathy.

"Your men have stopped joking," Nim Wei observed, breaking a long silence. "Tonight they only grunt at each other."

Christian glanced at her, but her attention was directed forward where Charles and William led the way with lanterns. It occurred to him that she was lonely, that she truly minded him refusing her. Disconcerted by the idea, he ran his hand down the horse's nose.

"It is the weather," he said, hearing his own stiffness. "It lowers everyone's spirits."

The stallion tossed his head, tack jingling with annoyance that Christian had stopped petting him. When Christian resumed, he felt rather than saw Nim Wei look at him.

"You are always kind to Balthazar," she said.

It was a comment he did not know how to answer. Was she wishing he would be kind to her, or perhaps complaining that he was not? It cost Christian nothing to be kind to a beast. Being kind to her might spill out a different kettle of fish.

She is a witch, he reminded himself. *A dangerous, uncanny being.* The seeming vulnerability she was displaying could be her version of a crocodile weeping.

He slid another glance at her, long enough to notice that the rain had not dampened her waist-length hair. Instead, the droplets beaded up and then rolled down her straight black tresses like dew on a spider's web. Her clothes and her saddle were dry as well. For that matter, so was her mount's ebony mane. One wave of gooseflesh

chased another across his skin. The minstrel was not wet.
Nature itself avoided her.

Perhaps he made a sound of horror. Perhaps she stole
his thoughts from his mind with her witch's power. All he
knew was that her head rotated toward him with an odd
smoothness. The reflection of the bobbing lanterns glinted
like sparks of hellfire in her pupils. Some force seemed to
push at a spot between and just above his brows. If Grace
had been near him, he would have said the pressure was a
ghost's fingertips.

"You will come to my tent tonight," she said in a smoky
purr. She raised her pale, small palm to forestall the protest
he drew breath for. "I wish to speak to you on a matter of
importance. You have my oath that I shall not"—here, her
rosebud of a mouth twisted—"impose on you."

Christian was not certain what her oath was worth. The
horses' hooves sucked at the muddy road, reminding him
he needed to answer. He may have waited too long. The
minstrel looked away, the spectral nudge fading from his
forehead as she shifted her slender fingers on bone-dry
reins.

"As you wish," he acceded . . . but not because he wanted to.

They nailed their blankets to the trees, creating makeshift
lean-tos against the wet weather. Christian waited until
Grace slept beneath his before picking his way between the
rain-blackened tree trunks to Nim Wei's tent. He wondered
if he were wrong to keep the minstrel's summons to himself, but there were simply too many reasons not to involve
Grace.

His heart pounded in his chest as he reached the
entrance to her shelter. Dozens of candles burned inside,

the red black glow no balm to his nerves. The foreign characters on her door flap stood out sharply. He assumed the invisible writing Grace had mentioned remained. If he touched it, would it bespell him again? Was he already spelled to come here alone? Unsure of anything, he cleared his throat and waited to be let in.

She came to the door quickly, lifting the silken flap and standing aside to admit him. Christian ducked inside. Entering her bower was like being transported to a distant land. The color and the pattern and the luxury of her appointments were so different from what he was used to. A chess table and two low chairs with tasseled cushions had been set in the center of her floor pillows.

He wondered if she would burrow into the ground beneath that table at break of day.

"Do you play?" she asked politely.

He shook his head, fighting a shudder at the idea of sitting above her resting place. "Chess is more Hans's game than mine."

"Well, no matter," she said, though he sensed she was disappointed. She stepped around to where he could see her.

His mouth went dry.

She had changed out of her habitual black velvet tunic and matching hose. Silk enfolded her instead: sheer, complicated, wrapped layers of green and yellow and blue, embroidered with gleaming thread he knew had to be real gold. In some places, the thread formed dragons; in others, giant chrysanthemums, but it was the fit of the semi-transparent cloth that had his blood heating helplessly. The exotic material robed her from neck to ankle, clinging to every gentle curve she had. She was feminine and mysterious, as much shadow as she was flesh, her delicacy calling to instincts he doubted any male could have ignored.

For a heartbeat, he could only gape at her naked toes. They were tiny, with perfect, clipped nails that twinkled like clear crystal.

He felt disloyal to Grace for reacting, which startled him. He could not remember being ashamed on a woman's behalf before. Though he did not speak, Nim Wei seemed to divine his thoughts.

"Thank you for appreciating my effort," she said dryly.

As uncomfortable with her thanks as he was with his arousal, he pulled his gaze away and his thoughts together. He noticed her tent was untouched by the dripping weather, just as she and her horse had been.

"Would you like a glass of wine?" she inquired.

Again he shook his head, wondering if he should take heart at being able to say no. Surely she was capable of forcing him to any action she chose. He swallowed as he met her eyes.

"I am able to force you," she said. "But I will not."

His mind took a moment to absorb the significance of her words. He had not been mistaken. She could read his thoughts, and yet she seemed not to be aware of Grace in them. That was a puzzle he did not dare mull too hard over, lest the minstrel discover what he would rather not have her know.

When he spoke, his voice was hoarser than he wanted it to be. "You are admitting you are a witch."

She was silent. Golden lights that did not quite match the flickering candles flashed in her eyes. Christian had the unnerving sensation that he was falling into her irises. The feeling stopped when she dropped her eyelashes.

"Forgive me," she said. "Old habits. You are harder to thrall than some, and so something in me must try. Your guards are . . . different." She looked up at him again, her eyes simply eyes this time. He did not have a chance to sort out what she might mean. "I am not a witch. I belong to a race of creatures called *upyr*. I am the queen of all our kind who live in cities."

"The queen," he repeated, because he still was not following. "Of the *upyr*."

"Sometimes soldiers call us death angels. We have been known to put an end to those left wounded on battlefields."

"Forgive me, Mistress Wei, if I do not take you for an angel."

His candor might have been unwise, but a smile tugged the corners of her mouth upward. "No," she agreed, "I am no angel, but if I dropped my glamour, you would understand why they thought I was."

"Why are you telling me this?"

Her smile remained, though a hint of sadness entered her eyes. "Your father came to me. He believes me a witch as well. I suppose that is the monster your church puts most frequently in your minds. Gregori was under the impression that by sleeping with your men, I imbued them with extra power; true, as far as it goes. He proposed a deal. If I gave *his* men that power, he would pit them against yours in some contest. Once you were—and I quote—'suitably humbled,' he would turn you over to me for a night, to do with as I pleased."

A number of responses warred inside him, not the least of which related to his father's utter disregard for his safety. Overwhelmed, he found himself blinking rapidly.

"Did you accept his offer?" he asked.

Nim Wei closed the distance between them, her hands landing gently on his pounding chest. Her touch was cooler than it should have been, not that he had the presence of mind to do more than register the fact.

"I did not accept," she said firmly. "It is your friendship I wish to court—more than friendship, if it comes to that. That is why I am laying my cards so frankly on the table. I can open new worlds to you, Christian, can offer you power and security you scarcely know how to conceive of. Never again would you have to worry for the safety of those who rely on you. Never again would you be helpless to protect them. Once I change you into what I am, it would be the simplest matter for you to crush threats like your father."

Christian had not thought his heart could beat faster. Nim Wei was a devil at midnight, whispering temptations into his ear. A peculiar sort of terror filled him, not so much for her as for the darkness he had always known lay inside himself. This was his oldest desire. From the first of his brothers' deaths to the day he recognized what his father was, this had been what he wanted.

How large a step was it from killer-for-hire to patricide?

"I do not understand what you are saying," he rasped numbly.

Her hands slid from his chest as she took two steps back from him. By some mysterious process, the tight wrappings of her gown allowed her to move freely.

"Watch," she said. "See the nature that could be yours."

He watched, and she began to glow. At first, she simply looked a little paler, but soon the shimmering radiance was unmistakable. It shone through her skin, through her clothes, until her very bones appeared to burn with the white gold light. The effect *was* like a halo, and she the dark-haired angel who stood within. Christian knew his mouth had fallen open with awe.

"*Not* an angel," she said softly. "An immortal blood-drinker."

He shuddered with sudden understanding. "That is why the men rubbed their necks. You bit them!"

She inclined her head, her features so lovely, so perfect

his heart should have been breaking. "The neck is among our favorite spots to feed."

"How do you make yourself glow like that?"

"I always glow. The trick lies in hiding it." She seemed pleased by his interest, though Christian was not certain his questions sprang from anything more than shock. He jerked when her glow snapped off. Apparently, hiding her light was not difficult for her.

"I can recover from almost any wound I suffer," she continued, "a power I am able to share with mortals to a certain extent. The healing oil I gave William was infused with my blood."

She bent to the chessboard and plucked off a pawn, which she displayed to Christian cradled in her palm. The piece was polished bronze. One by one she curled her white fingers over it. She did not wince as she compressed the fist she had made. A crunching noise issued from her grip. Christian expected the pawn to be broken, but when her fingers opened, nothing remained in her palm except a little heap of brown dust. Even after all he had witnessed, Christian could not contain his sharp intake of breath.

"As you can see, I am very strong. You have surmised already that I can read minds and influence humans. I am better at that than most *upyr*, but we all have a gift for it. I will never grow old, never be less beautiful than I am. I can run faster than my horses, and could leap across the Coliseum in one bound. I absorb knowledge very quickly: languages, music, whatever interests me. All these gifts I am prepared to lay at your feet."

Christian's head was spinning, believing and refusing to at the same time.

"Why?" he asked. "Why me?"

She almost came to him. Her muscles tightened to do it and then relaxed. Her arms fell to her sides instead, her right hand swiping the remnants of the pulverized bronze chess piece on her silk-covered hip.

"You are what I love," she said. "The kind of human. The kind of man. You live life as fiercely as I do, but you rule your passions. You would not waste the opportunity I am offering you."

"You drink blood."

Nim Wei's expression grew more guarded. "Yes."

"You cannot live without it."

"Not for very long."

Christian bit his lip. The minstrel could have been a painted statue, standing there so still with her dark gaze fixed carefully on his face. He realized he had wanted her to deny the facts of her existence, that he would have preferred she make this terrible temptation less horrific.

"I am not a godly man," he burst out, "but even I believe saying yes to you would damn me!"

She flinched back as if he had struck her, this woman who did not move unless she wished to. Her stone white cheeks drained paler.

"Forgive me," he said, fearing he was not in control of his tongue even as he tried to undo his misstep. "Mistress Wei, I am sure you mean to do me honor, but you would turn me into a fiend."

She laughed, a short, harsh sound that ended with her spinning halfway away from him. Her mouth struggled for a moment before smoothing into a perfect bow that showed nothing.

"You are entitled to your beliefs, of course," she said coolly. "That I think them provincial is only meaningful to me."

"My soul is dark enough," he said more gently. "I simply—"

Her hand snapped up and something hit his body: a cool, rippling force like invisible water. The energy coiled around his throat. For a heartbeat, his vocal cords would not move. When he recovered enough to speak, he had the sense not to try.

"Say no more," she commanded, her tone full-fledged icy now. "I comprehend your attitude perfectly. My gift is far too tainted to offer a paragon such as you."

He certainly had the urge to deny this, but he feared she would just silence him again. With his lips pressed tightly together, he bowed to her, as deeply and respectfully as he could. The skin along his spine was twitching, his scalp and palms prickling with cold sweat. He wanted to dry his hands on his hose, but knew he had better not. She let him retreat, let him fumble out the black tent flap and into the dripping night.

He could breathe then, but the fresh pine-scented air was not much comfort. Nor did he feel better as he forced his quivering legs to carry him away. The ground was matted with needles from the tall fir trees, making it less of a morass. Maybe he would be grateful for that later.

Grace had been right. Nim Wei was not human. She was something worse than they had imagined, and what she wanted from Christian was no less than his soul. Too late, he realized he should have stalled her, should have pretended he might say yes.

In refusing, he had fallen into a deeper pit than before.

Nim Wei's aura boiled around her like stinging wasps. Was this to be her life forever? Rejected by her maker? By Edmund? By Vincenzo, if it came to that? The human scholar had loved her, but not enough to be changed.

No one she loved truly loved her back.

Her right middle finger snapped from the force with

which she was fisting it. The pain cleared her head. She relaxed her hands, pulled the joint straight, and did her best not to grimace as the bone crackled whole again.

She breathed deeply in and out until her heart rate calmed to what would have been slow for a strong human.

She was making too much of this. She did not love Christian. She merely found him interesting. On the other hand, why should she tolerate his disrespect? Who was he to act morally superior to her? He killed for money—and would have killed for less. She had known that since her first wander through his head.

Her toes were curling among her cushions, so she forced them to relax as well. Still, her long hair writhed in the angry wind of her energy. She ran her palms along it until every lock was smooth. Aware that revenge would also make her feel better, she contemplated it. Her pulse slowed more. She was queen. She was beauty and power personified.

She knew how to respect herself even if some did not.

Gee willikers," Grace exclaimed when Christian finished telling her what had happened. "I should have guessed she was a vampire. I mean, a person has to be a little crazy to believe it, but still!"

Christian shifted on the fallen log he was sitting on, its dampness making Grace thankful for her ghostly state. While the next watch was eating breakfast, she and Christian had walked away from camp. It was misty but not raining, the water simply dripping off the tall trees. Still at the weather's mercy, Christian mopped off the latest splash that had hit his face.

"I do not know this word: *vampire*. Mistress Wei called herself *upyr*."

"*Upyr.* Vampire. I know Bram Stoker hasn't been born yet, but what's the difference if they've got fangs?"

"She did not have fangs. And why are you speaking of people who have not been born?"

Grace waved her hand. "Never mind that now. If she's biting people, she must have those special incisors. She probably didn't flash them because she thought it would spoil her attempt to seduce you into evil. She *is* afraid of the sun, and she *did* try to impose her will on you when you stared into her eyes. You shouldn't do that anymore, by the way. It gives vampires extra power over you."

"You seem . . . excited by all this," Christian said disapprovingly.

Grace stopped walking back and forth in front of him. She supposed she was a little bouncy, but didn't he understand how crazy cool this was? Grace was pretty sure she would have been excited even when she was a scared human.

"She's a *vampire*, Christian. That's like discovering fairies are real."

"Or ghosts?" he suggested wryly. "Or perhaps angels?"

Grace's brain gave a little hiccup. She'd almost forgotten her angel again.

"Right," she said. "But lots of people believe in ghosts, while most folks think vampires are made up. We could stake her in her sleep, maybe—except I can't hold one, and her magic keeps everyone else away." She rubbed her chin thoughtfully. "Maybe we could find a bunch of garlic and try to poison her with that. This is Italy, after all."

Christian made a dubious expression. "Garlic?"

"All the stories from my, um, town say they don't like it, though I guess that could be a myth. Your friend Michael wears a cross around his neck, and the minstrel still succeeded in attracting him." She met Christian's perplexed eyes. She had to admit she got a kick out of knowing more about this than him. "The symbols of Christianity are supposed to repel vampires. And silver bullets. Or maybe that's werewolves. Geez, I wonder if they're real, too."

"Pray you, let us not borrow trouble," Christian advised.

Grace's thoughts were jumping all over the place with exhilaration, but she saw his point. With a conscious effort, she reined in her attention. "You said she couldn't read about me from inside your mind."

"It appears not," he said. "Thank the Almighty."

Grace thought this was lucky, too, but strange . . . unless she and Nim Wei had repelling power over each other.

"It would kind of be a shame to kill her," she said.

"Grace! How can you want her to remain alive?"

She saw she had truly shocked him. "Well, she tried to do the right thing by warning you about your father."

"I harbor no illusions about how long her defense of me will last, now that I have spurned her."

Grace plunked down beside him on the tree trunk. "I guess she'd know you were lying if you pretended to change your mind."

Christian patted her buzzing thigh. "I think I must warn the others what she might do."

He didn't look happy about the prospect. "Are you afraid they won't believe you?"

"I would not believe me if I were them. Especially given how strangely I have been acting."

Grace twisted to face him more squarely. "You have to try, Christian."

"I know." He smiled and drew one finger around her ephemeral cheek. His eyes shone with more fondness than she had ever seen in her life. She could tell he liked having her to talk things over with. In spite of everything, a glow of happiness washed through her. It was truly wonderful to be someone's confidant. Christian let his hand drop reluctantly. "Matthaus may believe me. And Michael. She has not . . . fed from either of them."

Grace laid her palm on his arm. "Your men might have an easier time believing you if you show them something else supernatural, if you explain why they keep catching you talking to yourself."

"But, Grace, your powers are not under your control."

"I'll think of a way," she promised, determined to. "You and your friends' safety is important."

Twenty-three

Christian was a private person, and sharing this business with others was not comfortable for him. Though the men were too well trained to ask immediate questions, he was grateful for Michael's help gathering them—some from sleep and some from patrol. As unobtrusively as they could, they came together in the same green mossy clearing he and Grace had used earlier. Only Hans was missing from their number. Their stores being low, he had gone off with Mace, Christian's father's man, to hunt wild goats. Christian wished none of his *rotte* were absent, but he could not magically bring Hans here.

True to his expectations, Michael was the most skeptical of his listeners. Then again, as Christian's closest friend, perhaps he simply was the most comfortable airing his doubts. Now that Christian had laid out the worst of it, Michael raked both hands through his golden hair, pushing forward from the tree on which his weight had been braced.

"You want us to believe a ghost told you Mistress Wei is—what was the word—a *vampire*?"

"Mistress Wei told me herself. Grace merely confirmed it."

"Grace." Michael shook his head as if Christian had given a snake a name. "And how is it you are certain that this spirit is not evil?"

This was a fair question. Christian strove to answer it reasonably. "She warned us about the bandits. And she has been nothing but kind to me."

"*Kind*," Michael repeated with a roll of his sky blue eyes. "That would explain a number of things."

Charles snickered, stopping abruptly when Michael and Christian both shot a glare at him. The jest Christian suspected involved St. Onan died unspoken.

Matthaus spared Charles their reproval by clearing his throat. His rough-skinned face looked gaunt in the gray daylight. Like the rest of the men-at-arms, he was standing with his back to a tree. Philippe was next to him but not close enough to touch. The look Philippe sent his lover was so careful it hurt to see.

"If Mistress Wei has the powers you claim," Matthaus said, just as carefully *not* looking at Philippe, "it would account for other . . . changes in people's behavior. Both Charles and William were stronger after they went to her, and I do remember Hans rubbing his throat afterward."

Philippe uttered a soft, pained sound. Matthaus's body tensed, but he did not look up from his study of the damp ground.

"Forgive me," Charles broke in, his tone not the least bit apologetic. His cheeks were so red with anger his freckles blurred together. "But I remember everything Mistress Wei did to me. I swear on my ballocks, she did not drink my blood."

"Nor mine," William seconded, though not as heatedly. Because he seemed less resistant, Christian addressed him.

"She has the power to make you forget. She did it to me as well, when I went to—" He hesitated, then pushed ahead—because what did Philippe and Matthaus's secret matter compared to the other troubles they were facing? His men had their suspicions even if they did not speak of them openly. "When I went to confront the vampire about seducing Philippe against his will, she made me forget why I had come there. I never would have remembered had Grace not reminded me."

"Is she here now?" Philippe asked, his face almost as flushed as Charles's. Christian knew he was pretending very hard not to be embarrassed. "Not that I distrust you, Christian, but can she prove her existence to the rest of us?"

"She is going to try," Christian said at a nod from her. She had been watching, in her usual quiet way, from the edge of the men's circle. "Grace is still learning to control her abilities. You might have to wait a minute or two."

Grace stepped to the center of the clearing, closed her eyes, and tried to ignore her stage fright. She'd spent a lot of her life working at being invisible. Attention was not enjoyable when you'd had her father. She knew she had to release all memory of that now, and all anxiety that she'd fail. Her angel had warned her impatience stood in her way . . . or maybe he'd warned her it was a sign that she didn't have enough faith in herself.

Either way, she had plenty of reasons to be convinced

that this world held magic. She was a ghost who'd met a
vampire and an angel. She'd traveled through time and
found someone wonderful to love her. That was a miracle
by itself, just like how fully her heart had opened to love
him back.

Hadn't her angel said it was her job to talk herself into
believing? His words seemed like a dream now, but hadn't
he said that bit by bit she could do it?

I'm not afraid, she told herself, each thought calming
her a fraction more. *I'm relaxed and patient and I'm doing
this because I love Christian. I can let the others see me,
too. They couldn't hurt me even if they wanted to.*

Out of the blue, like a blessing flung from her troubled
past, a scene from the movie *Sunset Boulevard* came to
her, where Norma Desmond glides down her staircase
toward the crowd of waiting reporters. Norma was a mad,
bad murderess, about to be sent to jail, but both the actress
and the character had been fearless. No one who'd seen
the moment would forget it, not as long as film and eyes
to watch it existed. *I'm ready for my close-up*, Norma had
said.

Grace was ready for hers—more than, to tell the truth.

She felt the hum in her bones that said her energy was
rising, the subtle increase in the weight of the air. Her nose
wrinkled as she began to pick up a scent, like a pack of
dogs that had not washed in too long.

Almost there, she thought, resisting the urge to open her
eyes. *They'll see me any moment now.*

A sudden, concerted clanking startled her eyelids
up. As one, all the armored men but Christian had taken a
step away. Their mouths formed a silent chorus of match-
ing *O*s.

"Hey," she said, waving at them a little embarrassedly.

Only William jerked his hand to wave in return, either

too surprised or too polite not to acknowledge her. The rest were busy crossing themselves.

"It's okay," she said. "Really. I'm on your side."

"I can hear her," Michael said wonderingly. "Though I do not fully comprehend her words."

"The people from her town speak strangely," Christian said. "You will grow accustomed to it with time."

"You—I—" Michael shook his head. "Old friend, you must pardon me. I see why you were reluctant to confide this."

"Can she hear us?" Charles asked Christian in a loud whisper.

"I can," Grace said, which spun the orange-haired man around.

"Tell us everything," Charles said, taking a stride to her. He stopped a second later, not daring to close the whole distance, though he quivered with eagerness. Grace fought her instinct to retreat from him. "How did you die? Where do you come from? Can you communicate with other dead people? Do prayers and indulgences really help sinful souls progress to heaven? Are all friendly spirits as fair as you?"

"Charles!" Christian remonstrated as Grace broke into a laugh. "Grace is not here to satisfy your idle curiosity."

"Can you help defend us?" Michael asked. "Do you have heaven's ear?"

His manner was unexpectedly tentative, though something in his expression was as hungry as Charles's. Grace remembered he'd studied to be a monk. Did he believe that, because he'd given up his calling, heaven wouldn't lend its ear to him?

"I'm sorry," she said, her laughter fading as her compassion rose. "I'm afraid I don't know much more than you do. I only got a peek at the afterlife before I came here."

"Of course," Michael said with a small head bow. "Forgive me. I did not mean to be intrusive."

"You weren't," Grace assured him, not wanting this sensitive, handsome man, this friend of Christian, to be uncomfortable with her. Of all the mercenaries, he was the one she most felt as if she knew. Unfortunately, she didn't think the reverse was true. He seemed less confident with her than he was with Christian alone— maybe because she was a ghost, or possibly because he didn't spend much time with females.

"Can you spy for us?" William asked, more practical than either Michael or Charles. "Could you let us know what Gregori's men are plotting without them seeing you?"

"She can spy for us," Christian said. "But not on the minstrel. The vampire's energy is inimical to Grace."

"What of the minstrel's power to discern our thoughts?" Matthaus asked. "Will Mistress Wei not uncover our strategy—once we have one, of course."

Christian began to answer again, used to being in charge. He stopped himself, then gave Grace a little bow that said she should proceed. Though she liked it, his deference increased her shyness.

She had a feeling this was harder than meeting a boyfriend's folks.

"I think Nim Wei's power is stronger closer up," she said. "It affects me more anyway. And it helps not to meet her eyes. Vampires can bespell you with their gazes."

William drew in a breath to ask another question, but Philippe interrupted him.

"Hsst," he said, immediately causing the others to fall silent. "Someone comes."

"*Grace*," Christian said, low and urgent.

For a second, she thought she wouldn't be able to disappear in time. That, however, was an easier process for her. Even as her panic receded, she felt the air lighten on her skin.

She must have blinked out, because Charles muttered, "Mary save us," under his breath.

"Christian!" called a voice she wasn't familiar with.

"Timkin," Michael hissed in a tone someone else might have used to say *bastard*.

A thin, silver-haired man appeared through the trees, his heavy boots snapping a pair of fir twigs as he came to a halt. Grace recognized him then, especially his ice-pale eyes. She simply hadn't heard him speak before. His shark-like gaze took in the group, some of whom Grace knew were supposed to be patrolling. Grace was impressed that Christian didn't shiver when Timkin's attention settled on him.

"We have been searching for you," he said, his voice no more revealing than his expression. "Hans has suffered an accident."

All of Christian's men had straightened when Timkin first showed up. Now a ripple of horror swept over them, as if they were one person.

"What sort of *accident*?" William growled.

Grace couldn't help shuddering at the dangerous light in the big man's eyes, but Timkin remained unmoved.

"Come," he said, already turning away. "Your father and Mace are with him."

Grace didn't follow. Her concern for Christian's friend aside, she didn't want to accidentally appear in front of the others. To her surprise, Michael also hung back for a moment. She knew *he* couldn't see her. When he spoke, it wasn't quite to her face.

"You had better not harm my friend," he said, his jaw

clenched with his intensity. "Whether you be devil or angel, for that I would seek vengeance in hell itself."

Christian was not running, merely striding very fast, but his heart pounded the same as if he galloped. Though Timkin led the way as swiftly, his breathing was not labored.

"How far?" Christian demanded.

Timkin stopped and pointed.

Christian saw the pair at the bottom of a slope. Hans was on his back on the ground, unmoving, and his head lay in Mace's lap. They were near a stream, the earth around them torn up in violent clods. Two other men stood nearby: Lavaux and Christian's father, but Christian barely noticed them. Tears were running down Mace's face, causing the brutal scar that crossed his neck to glisten even at this distance.

"God's teeth," Christian said, breaking into a run. He could not have said what kept him from stumbling on rocks and roots: perhaps a lifetime of having to function in the thick of danger. When he was close enough to see clearly, he cursed again. Hans's gut was ravaged, his intestines bloody and exposed. The veteran turned his head to him.

"Christian," he said weakly.

Christian's first thought was that Hans was as good as dead. His second was that someone must rouse Nim Wei. She had said she could share her healing gift with humans. Maybe, if she could be woken, she could save Hans.

Christian's body acted independently of his mind. His legs gave way, dropping him to his knees beside Mace. Shaking like a leaf, he reached out to touch Hans's weathered face.

"Hans," he said, his voice as broken as a child's. *"Hans."*

Hans's eyes glittered up at him. "Sorry, son," he rasped. "Wanted . . . to stay with you longer."

Then he was gone, as if a pair of fingers had snapped. His eyes went blank, and his body sagged. Christian's throat felt like it was both on fire and spasming. The hardest thing he had ever done was choke back his sob.

"It was a boar," Mace said, his voice as raw as Christian knew his would be. "I could not move fast enough to block it. It ran at us from nowhere."

The stream chuckled over the rocks inside it, mingling with the sound of Christian's harsh breathing. His hands were fisted on his thighs. He looked up, not wanting to see his own white knuckles, not wanting to know why the ground beneath his knees was stained dark. Hans's death was a terrible stench in his nose.

His gaze stopped on Lavaux's face. His father's man was looking down at Hans's body, unaware of Christian's eyes on him. Something in the set of his lips was at once sly and pleased.

Rage exploded in Christian's head. He launched himself straight over Hans's corpse, barreling the smaller man backward. Lavaux did not have a chance to defend himself. Christian's hands were on his throat before they hit the ground.

"What did you do?" Christian demanded, slamming Lavaux's skull down into the squelching mud. "I know you are behind this!"

"I did nothing!" Lavaux protested. "A wild pig gored him."

"You worked on an estate before you signed on with my father. You were a gamekeeper!"

Lavaux's face was purple from lack of air. "I kept deer and grouse," he choked. "No man can control a boar."

Christian growled and squeezed his neck harder. Hands grabbed his wrists, forced his wrapped fingers to uncurl.

"Christian," Michael snapped, joining William in hauling him off his victim. "Now is not the time for this."

Weakness fell on him like a wall. Suddenly, William and Michael had to support him. Lavaux had regained his feet and was dragging one sleeve across his mud-splashed face. Christian's father had Lavaux by the elbow, though Lavaux was not trying to get away. Evidently, he knew better than to give Christian another chance at him right now. Unlike William, Gregori's son would show no mercy. A snort broke from Christian's nose, his scorn for Lavaux's cowardice causing anger to flare in the other man's slitted eyes.

"You will regret this," Lavaux promised. "Sooner than you may believe."

Christian did not think he imagined Gregori's hold on Lavaux's arm tightening warningly.

"Go, son," his father said, his face showing nothing but what it ought. "All of us need to mourn this loss."

They did not wait to bury Hans. It was not practical to carry a dead body, so Christian's men dug a grave in the forest and put him to rest in it. Charles fashioned the cross that surmounted it. It was nicer than might have been expected. Charles was clever at carpentry.

Christian stood staring at the marker after the others left. Their group would not journey on tonight, no matter what Nim Wei preferred.

No one interrupted him. He was alone with the lengthening shadows, with the birdsong and the crickets and the rustle of the autumn wind through the pine needles. He remembered the day Hans expressed his willingness to fight under Christian's young captaincy. Before that day, the men had obeyed him. After, they began to respect. He had never thanked Hans for his trust, but he doubted Hans would have wanted thanks. If the older man had not been a friend, Christian would have said he was a kind of father. *Could* a father be a friend? Christian shook his head to himself. Maybe other men's sons could fathom such wonders.

"Christian."

Grace's soft voice was so close he started. She had crept up on him like the ghost she was. Her hand rubbed a gentle tingle into his upper arm, her eyes searching his until he had to turn his away. She seemed to understand what he was feeling. Her hold squeezed once and released.

"Your father's men are talking about what happened. Mace and Oswald the cook are wondering if your father could have put Lavaux up to this. The others say it would have been impossible to know the opportunity would arise, but it's hard to tell what they really believe inside."

Christian nodded. Maybe later this would seem important. He dug the toe of his boot into the recently tamped-down earth. He could not smell Hans now, only damp soil and decaying leaves.

"I know you probably aren't comfortable with my sympathy . . ." Grace began.

Christian stiffened without thinking, and she stopped speaking. He looked at her profile. She was gazing out at the trees, clearly trying to seem composed. Despite the attempt, the pleat between her eyebrows betrayed her concern for him.

She is still with me, he reminded himself. So many he loved were.

"I value your kindness," he said stiffly.

She slid a sidelong glance at him, her smile a bittersweet twitching of her lips. "I value yours," she said.

Her hand curled around his, not solid but still warm. The touch loosened something inside of him.

"I wanted to call the minstrel," he confessed. "When I saw Hans dying, all I could think was maybe she could save him."

"I'm sure that's natural."

"It frightened me. How strong can my principles be if they crumble so easily?"

Grace stepped in front of him, both hands holding his now. His eyes burned at the conviction her face conveyed. "Nothing about losing a friend is easy."

Christian sighed and let his forehead pretend to rest on hers. His longing to embrace her was an alarming clutch in his throat.

"I saw Matthaus and Philippe walk off together," she said. "I think hearing what Nim Wei did is helping Matthaus forgive him."

"That is good," Christian said, though he could not truly feel the sensation of gratitude. "Someone should find happiness in all this."

Grace's ghostly arms slid around his back.

"I love you," she said.

He could not answer, but this time he knew he did not have to.

In the days that followed, Grace wished she knew how to help Christian. He ate, he slept, he fulfilled his duties like a sleepwalker. Somewhat to her relief—though the change also made her nervous—Nim Wei no longer tried to talk to him. Hans's death lay like a pall over all of them, the mystery that swirled around it causing even Gregori's men to snipe at each other. Lavaux was shunned and Timkin avoided, while Christian's father was handled with more than the usual kid gloves.

It gave Grace hope to see it. Hans had been well liked. Maybe Gregori's men would turn against him, and this would end peaceably.

And then, just as the tension looked like it might ease, Nim Wei asked Lavaux to her tent. He emerged, hours later, smug and swaggering. Regardless of their suspicions about their leader, Gregori's men weren't going to refuse her if she invited them. Her enchantments were hardly needed. She was female, and beautiful, and they'd spent too long resenting her partiality to Christian.

The other side's ascendancy seemed to wake Christian up.

He called his men together as he had the day Hans died. Grace watched him meet each pair of waiting eyes in turn.

"We make a stand," he said quietly. "Whatever my father starts, we finish."

"Agreed," said Michael.

"Agreed," said Matthaus.

Philippe smiled at his lover.

"What about Mace and Oswald?" Charles asked.

"Win them to our side if you can," Christian said. "If you cannot . . ."

When he shrugged, everyone seemed to know what he meant.

"And Mistress Wei?" William asked cautiously.

Christian's jaw muscle ticked grimly. "She is making her bed. For the sake of Hans's memory, she will have to face the consequences of her choice."

Twenty-four

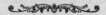

They reached the village of Fiesole, north of Florence, amidst a stretch of beautiful weather. Clear and sunny, the air felt more like spring than autumn to Grace—or it did when she managed to materialize a bit. Between her bouts of spying, and encouraged by her success at turning visible, she was working on becoming solid more reliably. The spying was going better than the materializing, though saying that was good would be stretching it.

In public, Gregori's men hid Nim Wei's effect on them. In private, when they didn't know Grace was watching, she could tell they were stronger. Lavaux and another man— Jürgen, she thought he was called—had been practicing knife fights at lightning speed. Forsaking his namesake weapon, Mace had swung a spiked iron ball on a chain with no more effort than if it were a feather. Maybe most impressive, Oswald the one-eyed cook accidentally tore off a goat's head with his bare hands. Christian's men were also training, which meant no one was sleeping much. The difference was that Gregori's men looked like daisies and Christian's, at best, seemed grim.

Christian's father should have been delighted, but whenever Grace invisibly crossed his path, his manner was brooding.

"That would be my doing," Charles had said, laughing softly when she brought it up. "I have almost convinced Mace and Oswald that Gregori would order them killed as readily as he did Hans."

"Do not push them too hard," Michael warned him. "Mace and Oswald are no one's fools."

"I am subtlety itself," Charles said. "And it helps that I am not lying. Gregori *would* kill them if it suited his purposes."

Grace tried to ignore how ragged Christian's fighters looked. She made sure he slept, humming songs from *South Pacific* when he collapsed in her arms at last. His favorite was the wistful serenade "Bali Ha'i." Interestingly, the tune to "I'm Gonna Wash That Man Right Outta My Hair" did absolutely nothing for him.

He slept this morning as she trailed Gregori and his group of six up a hill a short walk outside their camp. They were moving stealthily, not speaking as they picked their way through long brown grasses and scattered stones. Grace thought the stones might be the ruins of an ancient building, maybe a theater. She wondered if Gregori brought his men here to meet an ally. If so, she definitely wanted to know what was said. It was bad enough that Christian was down a man. Her one consolation was that neither Mace nor Oswald looked happy to be there.

Because it wasn't spring but autumn, the surrounding woodland formed a rolling carpet of red and gold. At the top of the hill, Gregori gave his men a signal, directing them to crouch behind a line of brush. First one man stiffened and then another as they peered through the scarlet screen. Needing to know what they saw, Grace drew nearer.

And then she heard it: the low but distinctive moans of people having sex. It was Philippe and Matthaus, stealing a moment to make up for their time apart.

"Do you see?" Gregori murmured, the light breeze carrying his voice to her. "These are the perversions my son condones. Switch allegiances to him and risk this taint sullying you. Men cannot fight side by side when such horrors are allowed."

Grace's heart sank as she looked around the watchers. Mace's and Oswald's expressions were just as shocked as the rest.

"We should kill them now," Lavaux said, hoarse and excited.

Silver-haired Timkin shook his head. "We should wait. Those sodomites can be taken care of in the battle."

The shiver that gripped Grace's shoulders was cold as ice. Timkin must mean the test of arms Gregori had promised would humble Christian.

"Timkin is right," Gregori said. "If we punish them before the pieces are in place, my son's twisted sense of justice will compel him to go after whoever was involved."

"We are stronger now," Lavaux said. "He would fail."

"Christian's rage would fortify him." Gregori laid his blockish hand on Lavaux's shoulder. "I am sorry. Perhaps I should not want to save him, but he is my son. When he is defeated, I pray God opens his eyes to his sins."

Christian's father appeared to mean every word. From where Grace stood, he actually looked devout.

You're the devil, she snarled to herself, not believing for a second that piety was behind the acts Gregori planned.

He was worse than her father, maybe worse than the vampire. Grace wanted to rip off his head like Oswald had the goat's. *I'd shower in your blood*, she swore. *And I'd enjoy it.*

Grace, said a gentle voice from inside her mind. *This is not what you're here for.*

She hung her head, contrite but still angry. She knew better than to look around for a speaker. *I know*, she thought to her angel, *but how could a normal person forgive this?*

She had to strain to hear the voice when it came again.

No one dies, Grace. This thing you call Death is not an end.

Maybe it wasn't, but her heart still tripped like a hammer as she raced off to warn Christian.

Twenty-five

❦

Christian's father was putting on a show, or that's how Grace looked at it when the second shoe finally dropped. Nim Wei and her escort had arrived in Florence the previous night, making camp in the bare fields outside the walls. In the morning, Gregori slipped away. On his return, he'd announced—as if they ought to slap him on the back for it—that the city fathers had agreed to let their group stage a spectacle, a test of arms that would display their martial prowess to prospective customers.

According to Christian, Florentines were great employers of *condottiere*. When it came to waging small-scale wars against rival families, mercenaries were the preferred means. Gregori's men would square off with Christian's on the Ponte Vecchio, the old bridge across the Arno. Whoever ended up controlling more territory would be declared the winner. Cosimo de' Medici was sponsoring the prize.

Grace would have been excited; the Medici family were

history's movie stars. Unfortunately, she was too busy choking down her terror.

She knew she was hovering too close to Christian as he and his men suited up in the shadowed corner of a *cortile*. On the other end of the bridge, Gregori's faction would be doing the same in the courtyard of another merchant prince's palazzo, probably with a similar marble fountain plashing in its center. Gangs of young boys were running back and forth across the river, reporting on each team's progress to the sharp-eyed, well-dressed men who were taking bets.

The cost of buying standing room in one of the butchers' shops that lined the bridge had increased by half since an hour ago.

"Peace," Christian finally said to Grace. His expression showed no fear, only determination. "We can defeat them. The advantages the vampire gave my father's men will only help him underestimate us more."

"Maybe you should go to her," Grace said, unable to prevent her ephemeral hands from clutching at his sleeve. "It's daytime, and she'll be weak, but maybe there's something she can do to even the odds."

"Grace," Christian said, an oddly sweet castigation. "You do not truly want me to do that."

"You could just go then. Run away with your men."

Ignoring how it would look to those who couldn't see her, Christian took her shoulders between his gauntleted hands. The articulated metal scales shielded the knuckle side of his fingers, and they were unexpectedly mobile. "You know I want to be the kind of man you are proud to love."

"I am proud. Always. But Christian—"

"No." He cut her off, calm but stern. "Trust me to know my business."

"All right," she said, swallowing back her protests. "I'll have faith in you."

He smiled with dazzling boyishness, his beautiful dark eyes gleaming with an emotion that clenched her heart.

"As I have faith in you," he said.

It was easier to talk of faith than to have it, but Christian did what he could. His men were armed with pikes, *zwei-hander* swords, and whatever their personal favored small weapon was. No missile weapons were permitted, for fear of injuring bystanders. In addition to this, they were expected to eschew killing blows.

None of Christian's men counted on his father's side honoring this—least of all Philippe and Matthaus.

"Do not worry about us," Philippe said as he wiggled two-handed into his visored helm. Matthaus adjusted its mail attachments to hang correctly around the neck and shoulders.

"We will look out for each other," Matthaus agreed. "We do not want you distracted."

Michael was beside the couple. He straightened up from buckling his second knee guard to clap a hand on Philippe's shoulder. He had yet to pull on his metal gauntlets, but he would soon. As with the visors—which they did not always wear—today the need for protection outweighed the need for less encumberment.

"You are ours," Michael said to Matthaus. "We will do whatever we can for you."

Christian had to turn away with his throat burning. Oh, he did not like this feeling. Someone was going to die today. He knew that in his gut.

Settle, he ordered himself. *You will get through what you have to—without dishonoring yourself in front of*

Grace. You need only take the step immediately in front of you.

"Ready?" he asked the others once he saw that they were.

As one, they nodded. Their strides rang in unison as they exited the courtyard for the broad *via*. A huzzah went up from the bands of boys, excited that the fight was going to begin. Christian ignored the noise. The fateful bridge stretched before them, its three graceful arches sinking into and reflecting off the Arno's small ripples. Caught by a sadness he could not repress, he turned to look back at the city. The sight he was seeking was the easiest to find: the beautiful egg-shaped Duomo soaring above the rest of the red-tiled roofs. For the better part of a century, the sanctuary had remained exposed to the elements, awaiting Brunelleschi's genius to figure out how to enclose it. Even after meeting Grace, Christian was not certain he believed in heaven. The dome reminded him it was possible to believe in man.

He had only paused for a moment, but it bolstered him. He did not turn again from his path until they reached their assigned staging area at the Ponte Vecchio's northern end. The crowd on either side of the bridge's length was thick, stuffed into the *boteghas* in their finest and most colorful raiment. This was a festival for the Florentines, an excuse to drink and bet and show off for their neighbors. Christian knew these Italians. They would not quibble if blood was spilled.

The stench of bloodshed was there already, thanks to the *ponte*'s predominant businesses. The river made a handy place for the butchers to dispose of their offal.

With an inward sigh, he continued forward without his men, to exchange formal greetings with his father. Gregori would not be fighting. Each side was restricted to six men, and with Hans gone, that meant he had to sit out. The crowd cheered as father and son bowed to each other. The official—a skinny, funereal man in a flat black cap with gold trim—announced that the contest would begin with alternating pike charges, the side who would go first to be determined by the toss of a coin. They were not to follow the assault with a "push of pike," as would be customary in battle, but only see what damage could be done in the initial collision.

"Agreed," Christian's father said silkily.

Christian did not know if Gregori rigged the toss, but it fell in Christian's favor. His men-at-arms would take the offensive first. He walked back to them, and they gathered round.

"No holding back," he said. "Any opportunity we have to exact a toll on them, we must exploit."

The success of a pike assault depended upon weight and momentum. Otherwise, the long blade-tipped poles would glance off their targets. To meet the charge, Gregori's fighters formed a small triangular schiltron. They settled on one knee with their pikes planted on the ground so the points rayed out in a hedge. For the first time, Christian noticed that their armor had been blackened, like dread knights spreading awe and fear at a tournament.

Christian barely refrained from rolling his eyes. He reminded himself the overly dramatic gesture would come in handy for telling the sides apart in any confusion.

He nodded, and his men tipped down their faceplates.

They took off together without a signal, without hesitation, even with a kind of joy at doing what they had trained for most of their lives. Halfway there, they leveled and aimed their weapons, their speed increasing in unison.

Christian sucked a breath and held it for impact.

When they hit, it was as if they had run full tilt into an immovable castle wall. Two of Christian's men fell over but none of Gregori's. Christian got a solid strike past Timkin's guard, though without doing injury. The best their attack accomplished was William splintering off Lavaux's pike tip. The hot-tempered man did not like that, but it hardly disabled him. He would simply replace the broken weapon.

"Excellent," praised the funereal Florentine as mostly Christian's men panted. "Now the younger Durand's team may form up."

"*Scheisse*," Michael cursed, exchanging a look with Christian. If this was how strong Nim Wei had made Gregori's men, they were well and truly in for it.

But there was nothing to be done about it.

"Defensive maneuvers only," Christian instructed as they set themselves. "Block all strikes. With the force they are able to put behind their blows, we cannot rely on armor protecting us."

Gregori's men did not charge with the same coordination as Christian's. Their strides were staggered, their acceleration uneven. All the same, the hollow clangor of them pounding forward was impressive. Christian's heart nearly burst with pride as his men braced each other shoulder to shoulder.

To his amazement, the collision did not level them. They skidded back on their knees until sparks flew from their poleyns, but none of them were knocked over.

Christian heard the cheers of their watchers through ringing ears. The surprised tenor of the sound said Christian's men were not the favorites, odds-wise. But he could not allow that to matter. According to the rules the Florentines had established, Gregori's fighters had to withdraw, to await the next stage of the contest. Christian could see most of Gregori's men would rather have pushed on now. The normally impassive Timkin looked as if he had swallowed a sour lemon.

And then the anvil fell, the signal that Christian's father

would not restrict himself to one underhanded trick. The official with the flat black cap was calling out scores for bettors when Lavaux pretended to catch his toe on a stone.

As he "accidentally" lost his balance, Lavaux was facing Christian's men—facing Philippe, in point of fact. Christian leaped to his feet, crying out, but he had no time to stop what was unfolding. There was a small opening between the plates that shielded Philippe's chest and right arm. Taken by surprise, Philippe had no chance to parry effectively. As Lavaux tripped, the sharp steel head of his pike found the chink in Philippe's armor, sliding through the chain mail underneath like it was butter. Pikes could be hard to handle; the poles were flexible and the ends would bounce. The angle of this supposedly happenstance thrust was flawless. Blood spurted up the shaft in a red fountain.

The whole affair took two heartbeats. Christian's cry was joined by Matthaus's, who had also jumped up. When Philippe toppled with the long wooden haft sticking out of him, it was William who caught him. Philippe was already dead. His head flopped bonelessly to the side while more blood—from his mouth, Christian presumed—trickled out from beneath his helm.

Matthaus looked at his fallen comrade, then at Lavaux, and then he attacked Lavaux like a snarling beast. Christian was more than ready to help him avenge his lover, but the Florentines intervened.

"Stop!" they ordered, swarming around Matthaus to pull him back. "*Fermate!* You cannot kill a man for an accident."

"Accident!" Matthaus cried, his voice echoing hoarsely behind his sallet. "This son of a whore killed Philippe on purpose!"

"It was God's will," Lavaux taunted from his protected sprawl. "God's *judgment* on a catamite."

Mace and Oswald had been looking on uneasily, but Lavaux's reminder of who he had killed shored up their wavering loyalty. The Florentines lost whatever sympathy they might have been feeling at the same time. So often accused of the crime of sodomy themselves, they could not be seen to approve of it.

"Obviously this is unfortunate," the main official said after an awkward pause. "Do you wish to continue?"

Christian looked to Matthaus, his visor now shoved up. Grief would come to him soon enough, but at the moment his eyes blazed with pure fury.

"Yes," Matthaus said, the words bitten out like gravel between his teeth. "We very much *wish to continue.*"

William returned from carrying Philippe's lifeless body to a watching barber-surgeon. The tunic that draped William's armor bore a long splotch of red.

"Yes," William seconded. "And, pray you, do not ask any of the *elder* Durand's men to retire. We would prefer to fight all of them."

The official stared at William's set expression, clearly gauging just how deadly it was. He must have known this fight had turned personal. A fresh spate of excited murmurs rolled through the crowd. Shouts for new bets rang out, and somewhere a woman let out a wail whose cause Christian could not discern.

"Very well," the grave-faced Florentine said at last. "We will observe a short interval. I recollect the melee is next."

Lavaux is mine," Matthaus snarled as they huddled together to strategize. "No one else may touch him."

"We will *try* to leave him to you," Christian corrected, "but we cannot afford to pass up an opening if one comes.

My father's men have proven they will kill today, and that means any of us might die."

His men exchanged glances at him putting into words what must have occurred to all of them.

"Heed me well," Christian said as Matthaus tried to speak again. "All of you. Lavaux always feints right when he charges. That will not change because he is stronger. Oswald has a blind spot because of his missing eye. Come at him from that side, and you may take him by surprise. Timkin is quick, but he is smaller than most of us, and he loves those daggers. If you keep him at a distance, the advantage of reach is yours. Mace is large and the best all-around fighter. If possible, he should be left to William or myself."

Michael opened his mouth.

"I know," Christian said. "You are as fell in battle as William or I am. I want you to fight with Charles as a team. Separate Jürgen and Graff from the pack. They have the worst technique of any of my father's men, though I realize that is relative. Together, your skill should trump their new strength, which is likely to have made them overconfident. If we can take those two out early in the melee, our task will be easier."

"If we have a chance, should we try to disable them?" William's tone conveyed a calm that Christian appreciated. William was not prejudging his answer. He simply wanted their mission clear.

"Every strike should aim for a kill," Christian said firmly. "Mind you, I am not certain we *can* kill them. Not easily. The vampire may have given them more resilience than normal men."

"Does your rule apply to Oswald and Mace?" This question came from Charles. Unlike William, his eyes held doubt. Though Charles had not managed to recruit them, he and the pair had grown friendly.

"They stood by," Matthaus interrupted in a low, dark voice. "They watched Lavaux slay Philippe in cold blood, and they strolled off with him afterward."

Charles's gaze cut to Matthaus before returning to Christian. His expression said he was willing to let Christian make the choice. Knowing that, in this type of situation, indecision was more often fatal than being wrong, Christian curled his gauntlet into a fist and lightly tapped Charles's chest with it.

"Your life is worth more to me than theirs. I expect you to defend it, no matter who that requires you to kill."

Apparently, Christian had chosen the words Charles needed to hear. He nodded, his freckled jaw firm again. He looked ten years older than he had a minute ago.

"I understand," he said.

Christian had done his best to prepare himself for his opponents' strength. The melee had not been under way for the time it took to say an ave before he realized their increased speed was more dangerous. For one thing, it meant the battle would move too quickly for the Italian officials to keep it within bounds, which—given that his father might have bribed them—they might only want to do for appearance sake. Worse, Christian could not follow the action peripherally, as he preferred to do. Though they were only eleven altogether, defending himself from moment to moment required all his faculties.

He knew Michael and Charles were not engaging Jürgen as he had requested, because Jürgen had closed with him. Christian found himself struggling against a man who, on an average day, was a far inferior swordsman. His arms were aching as he met each of the man's crashing strikes, as if a building were falling on him repeatedly. The only reason Jürgen had not killed him already was that he was swinging his two-handed sword with one, saving the other hand to bludgeon him with a club. His aim with both was thus compromised, though possibly not enough.

We are doomed, Christian thought, genuinely startled by the idea. *All of us are going to die today.*

And then the opening came. Jürgen dropped his arms a little to fill his lungs with air. Christian flipped his long sword around without so much as a pause to think, slapping his left hand around the *ricasso* where the base of the blade was blunt. The change in fulcrum turned a slashing weapon into a stabbing one. Jürgen had his knees bent in a slight crouch, putting him lower. Christian pushed off the ground as hard as he could, intending the weight of his body to compensate for the flagging strength of his arms. As he descended—falling from the sky, as it were—Jürgen's head jerked up. The tip of Christian's sword *thunked* straight through his visor slit.

It was an instantaneous killing blow. Christian crashed to the ground on top of his dead victim. He felt a rush of triumph, battle lust at its purest.

He used the moments it took to struggle upward to glance around. The crowd of watchers was spreading out, splitting up to follow the separate battles, which was adding to the confusion. In a distant corner of his mind, he hoped the Florentines had the sense to keep out of the soldiers' way. He did not see William, Oswald, or Mace. Mace was still alive, though, because Christian heard his new ball and flail whistling. This meant he was probably fighting William. As the beast that was the crowd shifted, he caught a glimpse of Charles and Michael circling Timkin together. Both his men had lost their swords, and Charles had blood running down one gauntlet, but they appeared to be holding their own against Timkin and his daggers. Not doing as well, Matthaus was rolling on the ground away from Lavaux, who was stabbing at him with an axe-headed pike.

Lavaux was toying with Matthaus. His speed seemed up to skewering him any time. Behind his breastplate, Matthaus's chest was heaving with exhaustion. Lavaux's prey was almost too winded to evade the jabs.

Christian's shoulders jerked at a flash of motion to his right. Some distance away, Gregori's last man, Graff, spotted Christian moving to help Matthaus at almost the moment he decided to. Graff began to run toward him to head him off.

A strange burning tingle suddenly engulfed Christian's back.

"Let me help." Grace's voice was a shock coming to him in the midst of a fight, the sound of it even odder because she was not visible to him. "Let me join my energy with yours and see if it strengthens you."

The tingle pushed at him urgently.

"Let me in," she insisted. "This is too much for you alone."

He no more knew how to stop her than he did to accept. Despite his befuddlement, she was inside him a moment later, the flood of her heat and vitality astounding. He did abruptly feel steadier, maybe even recovered from his fatigue—as if he had woken from a good night's sleep.

Happy to test the theory, he grabbed Jürgen's fallen cudgel, his sword still being stuck between Jürgen's eyes. Retrieving the simple weapon put him low to the ground. He twisted both his arm and torso back for momentum. When he unsprung the coil of his muscles, the club took Graff behind the knees. Swept neatly off his feet, Graff pinwheeled backward, the weight of his armor crashing him to the bridge. The impact stunned him long enough for Christian to clamber on him and swing the cudgel down on his head. His arms *had* recuperated. Graff's steel visor dented with the might of the blow.

Again, Grace said. *He's blinking!*

Again he swung, and again. Male voices cried out nearby, but Christian had to ignore them. Before he could help the others, he had to negate this threat. He could not know how long Grace's aid would last. Any other man would have been dead twice over, but each time Christian thought Graff was done for, the man renewed his struggles. Finally, blood began to leak from the breathing perforations in the snout of his helm. Graff's body twitched one last time.

Matthaus! Grace gasped.

It was like having two sets of eyes in one body. Christian sprang back onto his feet to find that Lavaux had finished playing cat and mouse with Matthaus. For one terrible heartbeat, Christian could only gape. He knew Lavaux was stronger than before, but he had spitted the other man with his pike, actually pinning Matthaus through both sides of his armor. Even more amazing, Matthaus was still squirming.

"I shall come after you from hell," he gurgled through his heart's blood to his killer.

Lavaux laughed at him.

"Lavaux!" Christian barked.

It was a challenge, and Lavaux knew it. Clearly, he did not care because his laughter rang out again, this time over Matthaus's death rattle. At first, Christian thought the burn expanding in his breast was his own rage. When

light began to shimmer through his armor, he knew it was
Grace's. Christian yanked his sword free of Jürgen's skull
and strode unhesitatingly toward Lavaux.

He saw Lavaux's gaze take in the two slain men, his
heart exulting in his breast as Lavaux's laugh faltered.
Gore dripped down Christian's upraised sword.

"No," Lavaux said, starting to edge away. "This is not
possible. You are supposed to be weaker."

Christian did not know if he was as strong as Lavaux,
but it scarcely paid to argue. Grace agreed, evidently,
because she was tossing coals on the fire she lit, so much
so that he had to squint through the spectral glare he was
throwing off. Seeing it, the whites of his enemy's eyes went
round.

"Tell me, Lavaux," Christian said pleasantly, "did you
really imagine only my father brought allies to this fight?"

The suggestion that the odds might be evening was too
much for Lavaux. Like most bullies, in his core he was
cowardly. He let out a sound very like a squeak and took
off running.

Every fiber in Christian's being wanted to give chase,
but he knew that was not strategic. Immediate threats were
what he needed to counter, not threats that ran away.

Grace shrieked between his ears an instant before a flying weight struck him. Christian's next heartbeat jolted his
whole body. The weight was a severed head. It bounced off
his stomach and then landed at his feet. Charles's wide green
eyes stared up at him through the decapitated helmet's slit,
their irises glazing over even as Christian gawked.

"Christ," he said, momentarily frozen by horror. "Mary
and the saints."

Sheer reflex snapped his sword up as a large armored
man ran toward him. The eyepatch behind the black visor
identified him as Oswald.

"Forgive me," he gasped. "I did not mean to kill Charles. I liked that idiot coxcomb. I am too strong now. I could not control the swing of my sword."

Christian's hands shook as they tightened on the hilt of his *zweihander*. Oswald was not the only one who feared he had lost control. Everything was moving too quickly. Christian had not known Charles was no longer fighting beside Michael. His voice pushed harshly from his dry throat. "You knew what sort of man you were fighting for. You chose to stay with my father."

"Please, Christian." Oswald dropped to his knees before him, his bloodied sword falling to the bridge with a loud clatter. "Philippe and Matthaus were sinners. Only they were supposed to die."

Christian wanted to scream at him. Did the cook not know Gregori was a liar? Could he not have shown Philippe and Matthaus the very mercy he now pled for?

"Christian," Oswald begged. "I am sworn to your father. I have my honor, too."

Christian drew back his sword for its longest swing.

Don't! Grace cried. *He's unarmed. Just tell him to stop fighting.*

Christian did not want to listen. He wanted to cut Oswald's head off just as the man had Charles's. Obviously at war with this inclination, Grace's energy felt like it was knotting inside of him. Had she not given him the strength it would take to enact revenge, he doubted he would have stopped. As it was, he was sorry his conscience would not allow him to make her his co-executioner.

"You surrender," he said to Oswald, the demand grating from him in frustration. "You leave the field this instant, and I shall let you live."

Oswald hesitated.

"*Now!*" Christian roared, his arm muscles readying.

Whatever reason he had for it, Oswald thought better of his reluctance, jerking back onto his feet and stumbling away.

Christ's blood, Christian thought, knowing he could not rest now.

"*Capitano*," piped a boy, nearly losing his hand in return for tugging at Christian's sleeve. Fortunately for both of them, he scampered back in time. "*Scusi*, I think one of your friends needs you."

Fearless now, even excited, the boy led him like an eel through the milling spectators. Hands patted Christian's back, congratulating him on his bravery. Each time they touched him, Christian's battle instincts urged him to lash out. Only Grace's murmurs that they were not threats kept him from doing it.

"There," said the boy, pointing.

William's fight with Mace had formed a clearing. Christian saw the epic struggle had battered both, William's battle-axe having done nearly as much damage as Mace's spiked ball and chain. Their armor was misshapen from the violent exchange of blows, but only William's bore spots of blood.

Bloodied or not, Christian could have wept at seeing William alive.

Stop, he wanted to say. *Pray you, everyone stop now.*

"I am all right," William called, seeming unaware that so many of their side had fallen. "Help Michael with Timkin."

Christian hesitated. He had his rule for battle: to deal with the threat right in front of him. On an ordinary day, Mace was formidable. Today he did not seem to be trying to kill William, but what if his control was as faulty as Oswald's?

"Go," William said, grunting as he blocked a swing. "Timkin has been cutting him."

I see them! Grace said.

Christian turned until he did, too. Decided, he shouldered through the crowd, sword up, mouth spitting curses to clear his way. The Florentines' attention was on the affray ahead, not on who shoved them from behind. Panic drove his legs faster. He saw the back of Timkin's black helmet, bobbing and shifting with the characteristic darting motions of a knife fighter. If he was meeting much resistance, Christian observed no evidence of it. To his dismay, he could not tell how Michael fared.

Help me, he thought to Grace. *I need to kill Timkin now.* This she had no objection to.

"Move!" he roared to the crowd as the heat that was her essence burst into full flame in him.

People screamed as they tried to obey his order, finally aware of the threat. Christian had reversed his sword, both hands poising it above his head for a downward plunge. The position left his front open to attack. Timkin spun toward him, crouched. Since the way between them was open, a dagger snapped from his hand, streaking toward Christian in a blur. Christian did not try to avoid it. He sensed it would glance off his armor. Instead, he focused all his strength and Grace's on driving every inch of his sword's forged steel into and through his objective.

Though the strike began high, it targeted Timkin's inner thigh, beneath his hip joint where plate armor ended and a layer of leather began. Naturally, leather was no match for steel. His leg speared through, Timkin fell with a cry. Going with him, Christian grunted, twisted, wrenching the sharp edge upward through flesh and bone. Timkin's left leg parted from his torso, showering everyone in the vicinity with blood. It did not matter then how strong Nim Wei had made Timkin. This wound was a death knell.

Knowing it, Timkin snarled and tried to swing his misericorde, a thin and especially nasty dagger, designed for sticking opponents through gaps in their armor.

His attempt never had a chance. Michael's boot slammed down on Timkin's wrist so hard that Christian heard bones snap.

"You . . . die," Michael said, his voice a moan between gasps for air. "You die, bastard."

Michael seemed to have used the last of his endurance foiling Timkin's attack. Lurching, he kicked the dagger away and then fell onto his hip.

Timkin began to laugh, a sound Christian had not heard him utter before. The noise was rusty and high-pitched, like a woman giving way to hysteria.

"*You* die," Timkin said through the eerie, hiccupping screeches. "You idiot pustule. Oh, wait." With his unbroken hand, he yanked his helm off his pale, sweaty face. "You have been dying for the last quarter hour, since the first little slice my special knife gave you."

Michael and Christian looked at each other, realizing what Timkin meant at the selfsame time. The blue of Michael's eyes, all Christian could see through his visor, burned like flames as the sun struck them.

"The idiots see it now," Timkin mocked, his laugh noticeably weaker. "My lovely misericorde was poisoned."

A shout swelled from the crowd surrounding the final fight, male and excited. Rocked by too many blows to handle, Christian's palm landed on the bridge beside Timkin's hacked-off leg. The leather glove to which his gauntlet was affixed splashed in the spreading blood. The sound of an armored body crashing to the ground suggested that his dread was well-founded.

Timkin wheezed in amusement.

"And so goes your precious William." Timkin's face was pasty as he strained for air, but—having spent so much of his life in silence—he would not relinquish his chance to gloat. "I poisoned Mace's flail as well, just as your father asked. Poor Mace will think he killed William."

Timkin died then, his curled lip going lax as one gush of blood too many ran out of him.

"Christian," Michael said. He was crying, but it was not sorrow for himself ringing in the word. "Christian, I am sorry."

Christian could not breathe well enough to speak. This was too much. His heart began to beat out of rhythm, sticking in his throat and then skipping crazily. The fight had not frightened him this badly. All his friends were dead or dying. Every one of them but him. He was going to disappear beneath the weight of this. Any moment, he would be no one.

"Help me up," Michael said more sharply, hardly able to lift his arm. "We will say good-bye to William together."

Grace could barely keep her ghostly self inside Christian. His emotions buffeted her like a choppy sea, trying to push her away from him. She didn't think Christian was aware of this. The strength she'd loaned him was ebbing. She could feel both men shaking as he helped Michael to his feet. Michael staggered, almost taking Christian down with him.

Grunting, Christian wrapped his arm more firmly on Michael's waist. Neither of the men was watching his back for threats.

Grace made that her job, but she didn't see any of Gregori's fighters—or not alive, at least. Timkin, Graff, and

Jürgen lay where they'd fallen. For whatever reason, the Italians didn't seem to want to take them away. Now that the fighting had ended, the locals' numbers were thinning rapidly. As they left the bridge in gesticulating fives and sixes, Grace thought a few of the watchers appeared ashamed.

Though they shot looks at Christian and Michael, none of them spoke to them. Of course, they also might have been leery because some had seen Christian glow. One monk in tonsure caught her eye when he crossed himself.

The boy who'd called Christian to William's aid was kneeling next to him. William lay on his back, big as a fallen tree, helmet off and eyes closed. A well-dressed woman who might have been the boy's mother cradled one of William's huge hands in hers.

"I am sorry, *capitano*," she said. "This brave soldier is dead."

For a second, Grace felt as if Christian were swallowing with her throat. He dragged off his headgear, holding it against his chest as if he were in church.

"*Signora*," he said, his voice almost too husky to come out. "Thank you for sitting with my friend."

And then Michael's knees buckled.

Christian caught Michael's body against him, hugging him to him as they both went down. Grace thought her heart would break right along with his.

"No," he pleaded. "Stay with me, Michael."

Michael's hands clutched him once and then fell away. Trapped inside Christian's feelings, an earthquake seemed to be battering Grace's soul. Michael was limp, a dead weight in Christian's hold. Christian flung his head back with rage.

"*No!*" he railed at the crisp blue sky.

The earthquake turned fiery, a thousand stingers pricking her as it rumbled. Though she had no lungs, she gasped. This was worse than what Nim Wei's aura had done to her. Christian was so sad, so angry, that his energy was at war with hers. Once she would have understood his despair. Once she would have felt no differently. She had changed since she'd come here, more than she'd realized. Now it was impossible for her and Christian to share space. Even as she clung to him, her consciousness flew from her.

The terrible fire of his grief had burned their bond to ash.

Twenty-six

Now and then, when *upyr* transformed humans against their wishes, the results were empty-eyed, shambling creatures without independent will. Christian looked a bit like one to Nim Wei as he lumbered toward the abandoned camp at twilight. Though he appeared uninjured, a puppet's limbs had more grace than his.

Only when he was close did she see the small, ice-cold flames burning in his eyes. Nim Wei's spine tensed, ready to defend herself, but he stopped an arm's length away.

"You know what has occurred?" he asked.

She nodded, unease coiling inside of her. She had seen the battle, hidden amongst the watchers with her immortal body bundled against the sun. Considering the slaughter Gregori Durand had arranged, staying alert had been less difficult than she thought. Certainly, the blood that had been flying everywhere kept her senses sharp. Looking back, she saw she had underestimated Durand's rivalry with his son—and the lengths to which it would drive him. The question was, would Gregori's son blame her for the loss of his companions?

"My father has disappeared," he said, his gaze unnervingly steady. "Along with three of his men."

"I could track them for you."

He stared at her, wetting dry lips before answering. "My friends are dead. My father and his men killed them. And she—" He shuddered, his hands curling into fists.

"She?"

He shook his head. "It does not matter. I am alone. All that is left to me is killing their murderers."

"I can help you with that."

Again, he gave her that cool, hard stare—as if he were looking at her through the length of a dark tunnel. The mystic inside her shivered: Fate was laying its hand on her. The tiniest prickle of excitement began to flower in her veins.

"It can be healing to have a purpose," she observed.

"You do not care if I heal."

This was more statement than accusation. Nim Wei denied the little dig of hurt it inspired. "I did not know your father would go this far. I would not have wished it so."

She was not sure he understood her implied apology. Christian looked at the tent behind her. It had been put up by the men last night, before this tragedy came to pass. A shadow fell across him, his eyes suddenly as black as the shelter's silk. "Are you still willing to change me to what you are? To give me the strength to kill all of them?"

In his grief, he was not thinking clearly. She had seen him fight, had seen him kill, for that matter. If he waited but a few days, when the advantage her bite had given the others faded, he would be strong enough to smite them down. She looked into his haggard face, the truth rising toward her throat. He was exquisite in his suffering, sorrow bringing out the perfect lines of his bones. Like the darkest of fallen angels, his shoulders seemed all the broader for being bowed. She knew what her maker would have advised, but could she truly bear to let such harsh and aching beauty pass forever beyond the veil?

He was hers, if she wished. For all eternity, whether he blessed or cursed her, he would know she had given this gift to him.

She held out her hand, fingers glowing in the swiftly descending night.

"I can give you what you need," she said.

Afterward, Christian fell to his hands and knees beside the cold remains of the previous night's cookfire. He had stumbled here from Nim Wei's tent, and she had not followed him. A stunted tree grew nearby, now shading him from the moon. To judge by that orb's position in the sky, mere hours had passed since his arrival.

It should have been longer. In the interval, not only he but the world had changed.

He breathed from his fallen posture, deeply, slowly, the action feeling as unfamiliar as the fragrances he drew into his nose. He identified the musty feathers of the ravens roosting in the branches of the olive tree, grapes fermenting in an oaken barrel miles away, the acrid smoke of a blacksmith's forge that had been lit early in the day. Most of all, he smelled humans. Their flesh. Their blood. If he closed his eyes, he could hear them. Each heartbeat was a separate person, drumming to its own rhythm. Where they gathered in the crowded city, all of them together sounded like the patter of distant rain.

Delicious rain, as it turned out.

He ran his tongue around his lips, around the two long teeth that had descended so sharply. His fangs throbbed as fearsomely as the cudgel between his legs. This new body of his wanted, hungered, with an urgency that spelled madness. Had he been in Florence, no woman would have been safe from his desire to rape and plunder.

Nim Wei certainly had not been.

He sat back on his heels, cold hands covering his face as he moaned. He should have guessed she would be beautiful naked, but the truth of her had come as a shock. Every curve had been an invitation to his newly starving mouth and fingers, every plane like polished marble sparkling with rainbows. He had seen her loveliness without a single candle, the smallest scrap of light sufficient for his transformed eyes. He remembered swiving her in half a dozen different positions, remembered coming so hard he bellowed for the relief of it. He had begged her to give him more of that delight. That much was crystal clear in his mind.

The rest, however, was a bit hazy.

His hands fell from his face as he realized he did not remember how she had changed him. She had bitten him. He was rubbing his throat—exactly as the others had—even as he thought of it. He remembered the stab of ecstasy her feeding had inspired, a violent seizure of an orgasm. There was something else, though, some secret act that caused the actual change. The lost knowledge nagged at him. He wanted to retrieve it more than he would have guessed, but she had stolen it from his mind.

"You think you deserve it?" he mocked aloud to the stars. "You think you deserve anything except eternal damnation?"

He was a betrayer just like his father. He had barely thought of Grace in all this. When he had, her memory had whipped such sadness into his heart that he had welcomed an excuse to push it away. The vampire had been happy to provide one, over and over again.

How could you leave me, Grace? he thought.

He grimaced, too aware of his veins burning, of his every cell clenching at the scent of humans that rode the air. In that moment, he was not certain he wanted Grace to return. She was too tenderhearted to approve of his decision. Maybe it was best that she not see how thoroughly he had damned himself.

With a groan that encompassed more than the stings of his altered body, he pushed, trembling, to his feet.

Nim Wei stood before him across the cold ashes of the fire. His heart gave a slower than human skip. That he had not heard her approach, even with his new ears, alarmed the soldier in him.

An instinct he could not control made him curl his upper lip back and growl at her. She did not flinch at the bestial sound. Indeed, she did not react at all. Though Christian might now be considered a threat to her, she did not appear afraid to be alone with him. He recalled her saying she was a queen.

"It was a ploy," he said, needing to speak his idiocy aloud, to punish himself for it. "Hiring my father's men. Pretending you needed an escort to protect you. You could have traveled anywhere you wanted without our help. From the beginning, you planned to seduce me."

She did not blink, but neither did she deny it.

Christian snorted at himself. "I hope the satisfaction of hearing me beg for your favors was worth it."

He could not read her expression, but some emotion tightened her face subtly. Perhaps she was considering reaching out. The muscles of her arms twitched, then relaxed again at her sides.

Had she expected him to like her better now?

"We should go," she said calmly. "You need to feed tonight."

Hunger exploded inside him, not only for blood but for more of the carnal pleasures she had shown him. Surely that was the worst betrayal of his beloved: that his body could long so deeply to sin again. Grace had literally been a part of him. Wanting anyone else, even for a moment, was a stain he would never be able to scrub off. His new fangs felt huge behind his lips, stonelike, curving, pulsing in his gums as his mouth watered copiously.

Aware that Nim Wei was watching, he swallowed and spoke carefully—*after* offering his maker a polite nod.

"I would be obliged for your instruction. It seems I have a powerful thirst for revenge . . ."

Gregori had not left Florence. Nim Wei tracked him to a room above a closed goldsmith's shop, following a trail Christian could not yet read with his new powers.

"In there," she said and left him alone at the door.

Christian's palm was damp, the sweat that coated it cold. He suspected this was a rare reaction for the kind of creature he had become, but he ignored it just as he would have before. The handle of the door was iron, which Nim Wei had warned him to avoid. He yanked a length of shirt from his hose and used it to wrap his hand. That done, he shoved inward hard and fast enough to snap the plank that barred the chamber from intruders.

The quick splitting of the wood did not wake his father. Gregori sprawled, snoring, in a carved and upholstered chair. The table beside it held the remnants of a meal some hireling must have brought him.

Apparently, killing all Christian's friends had not spoiled Gregori's appetite.

Christian glanced around him, not breathing or needing to. This was a room to hole up in for a while. It was richly furnished, though with tired objects. A single deep window, shuttered now, overlooked the street front. A second door might also serve as an escape route. Christian would have to ensure his father did not reach it.

His survey complete, he looked down at his sleeping sire, at the thickness of his muscles and bull-like chest, at the size of his sword-scarred hands, at the squashed appearance of his oft-broken nose. His lips were more sensual than Christian's—beautiful, really. Had Christian's mother ever touched that mouth with desire? Had there been a time when Gregori did not frighten her?

Would Christian have frightened her now?

Perhaps sensing a presence, Gregori's eyelids fluttered.

"Son," he croaked as they opened.

The inferno of rage Christian experienced at being called that, by this man, did not show in his face. He was relatively certain nothing showed there at all.

Receiving no answer, Gregori gripped the arms of the high-backed chair and pushed himself straighter.

"I know you are angry, son." Though his eyes were wary, Gregori was too proud to display fear. "Believe me, I am sorry matters had to come to this."

"You are sorry they *had* to," Christian repeated in disbelief.

"You forced my hand. How else was I to bring you back into the fold? You had to learn that I am still your master. You will never outmaneuver me on the battlefield."

Christian was breathing, his diaphragm surging slowly in and out. "*You* are the one who made this a battle. *I* was willing to take my men and go home."

"A coward's choice," Gregori dismissed. "Unworthy of our blood." Two stemmed silver goblets sat on the square table. To Christian's amazement, Gregori reached for the wine decanter and began to pour. "Come, Christian. We will drink to our rapprochement. To our long future at peace again."

Christian forced his throbbing heart to slow. "I would sooner drink with Lucifer himself."

His father looked up and truly saw him for the first time since he had come in. His gaze cut to the door where the broken wooden bar listed drunkenly. The neck of the wine decanter clinked on the second goblet's tarnished silver rim.

Christian had rattled him.

"The minstrel bit you," he said, his eyes widening.

"Oh, Father," Christian said, the words sliding from his throat with a strange richness. "Nim Wei did so much more than bite me."

His father moved like he was underwater, or so it seemed to Christian. His grip shifted on the glass decanter, wine splashing out in red ribbons as he reversed it. Gripping the throat securely, Gregori smashed the base on the table's edge, loudly shearing it off. Armed with the resulting circle of jagged edges, he jabbed his makeshift weapon at Christian.

Or he tried to. Quick as thought—and maybe quicker—Christian grabbed his father and flung him against the wall. The pompous chair he had been sitting in went with him, both it and his father's body striking the plaster hard enough to craze its full length with cracks.

His father slid to the floor in a daze. The broken decanter fell from his hand and rolled.

"S-son," he stammered.

"Do not call me that!" Christian screamed. He was not aware in that moment of feeling angry, but the scream said he was—as did the fingers he was constricting on Gregori's larynx.

He was not using his full strength. If he had, his father's head would have popped off. Instead, he watched, mesmerized, as Gregori's coarsely pored face turned ever darker shades of red. Christian crouched above his father with his heavy torso between his knees. The veins on Gregori's forehead were standing out in blue ropes, his big chest jerking with his fight for air. The thunder of his heart, of his growing terror, seemed to drown out every other sound in the city.

"You would do this to your own father?" Gregori choked. "Because I killed a few strangers?"

Christian growled, the struggle going on inside him one he did not perfectly understand. His body should have been calm and still, but it felt as if beasts were tearing him from within.

"*You* are the stranger," he accused his father. "*They* were people I loved."

An unexpected pain stabbed him in the stomach. Christian staggered up and back in surprise. He had not been wearing mail or armor; according to Nim Wei, the steel was not pure enough. Now the hilt of a small dagger was sticking out from his gut. Its pommel was wrapped in leather that was stamped with the Durand crest. Cool, thick blood welled out from its point of penetration. From this and the way the blade burned icily inside him, Christian concluded that the dagger's iron content was high.

Gregori must have concealed it in his clothing.

"My father's knife," Gregori rasped, crawling back from him like a crab. "My father, whom *I* knew how to respect."

Red washed across Christian's vision. His fangs punched from their sockets in an uncontrollable spasm. Seeing them, his father sucked in a breath.

"Devil," he said, his voice atremble. "You stay away from me."

Christian had fed before he came here. Nim Wei had made sure of that. *You want a cool head to face your father,* she had advised. *You are young and strong, but he is a wily dog.* So Christian had fed, and cooled his head, and had fully intended to do no more than snap his neck.

But when Gregori called *him* a devil, when he dared to cross himself and pray, those intentions fled.

Christian tugged the dagger from his belly, not caring how the wound hurt or bled. He tossed the weapon past Gregori's reach. Hands free, he yanked his father up to his mouth like a sawdust doll. Instincts deeper than a soldier's were guiding him. His teeth pierced flesh, found veins, and then he was swallowing.

It was a pleasure far beyond feeding from the sleeping thief whom Nim Wei had found for him. This was the life-giving feast of vengeance. This was a son's long-awaited declaration of freedom. This was joy itself running down his throat.

He worried at the punctures until the blood he could not drink spurted free. It was hot like summer, like the sun that was now his enemy.

He only felt sickened when his father's heart stopped beating.

Twenty-seven

Unlike the other times she'd been flung away, Grace retained no memory of where she'd been—not even a vague one. It seemed to her that she had simply ceased to be. She returned to existence on her feet in a narrow Italian street. It was night now and very quiet, so evidently medieval Florence was no New York. The buildings on either side of her rose four stories, and were plastered in a soft yellow. The one directly in front of her was set apart by a goldsmith's sign.

A black cat looked straight at her as it slunk across the cobbles. Grace wondered if this were a good or bad omen. Animals hadn't been able to see her before.

Well, now what? she thought.

A muffled sound drifted out from one of the floors above, a swallowed back cry of pain. Grace leaped for the window without thinking, her lack of corporeality allowing her to land on the sill *inside* the closed shutters.

She saw she had found Christian.

Her ghostly heart skipped a beat. She was looking at him in profile. He had one knee and both hands planted on the floor—like a runner poised to propel himself from a pair of blocks, except he seemed to be frozen there. His lower face and a good portion of his chest were splashed dark with blood. Strange gold lights flickered in his eyes, exceeded in shock value only by the pointy thrust of his fangs. Despite these jarring alterations, he looked strangely beautiful, even more than she remembered. The straight black hair that cloaked his shoulders could have been spun from the night itself.

He was a vampire. Somehow, in the unknowable amount of time she'd been gone, he had made this choice. At least, she didn't think it could have been thrust on him. Never mind the grief he'd been suffering. Christian wasn't a person who did much against his will.

Maybe a different woman would have run then, but Grace didn't know how to run from him. At a loss, she hopped down from the window. A noise broke in Christian's throat as he jerked his head around and saw her. He must have made the cry she'd heard earlier. It was hard to read his emotions through the partial mask of blood, but she didn't think he was grateful that she'd showed up.

"Grace." He stopped to laugh brokenly. "You *would* return to me like this."

It had been his choice then. She could tell from his rueful tone. With a shock she didn't need to pile on the rest, she realized a body was lying on the floor next to him. Its neck had been more than bitten. Two bloody gouges tore halfway down its length. Even in death, the barrel shape of the chest was unmistakable.

"Christian. Your father . . ."

Christian's broken laugh rose in pitch. "Well, his blood was already in me. What was a little more?"

He stopped laughing and began to weep—harsh, tearing sobs that sounded like they must have hurt coming out. He covered his bloodied face in both hands. The gesture was so graceful it reminded her of a statue.

"Grace," he cried. "Can you ever forgive me?"

Grace opened her mouth but couldn't speak. Christian didn't mean could she forgive him for killing his father. He didn't even mean for becoming a vampire. Her heart contracted as she finally understood what he was asking her pardon for. Nim Wei's mark was on him. Grace could see it with her spectral vision. The minstrel's dark energy twined through his like vines.

He had slept with the other woman. He had touched her and she had touched him. If Grace squinted, she could see the glowing prints of the minstrel's hands. They were all over him, too many to count. From their placement, she could not doubt how extremely intimate they'd been, nor did she have to be told that Christian had enjoyed it.

His look of shame made that obvious.

"Grace," he pleaded, his eyes too bright within their frame of spiky black lashes. "I feared you were gone for good."

Her hand was fisted against her breastbone, pressed tight to the hot, hard ache that was swelling there. Why would he think she wouldn't come back when she always had before? What he'd done was inexcusable. This, of all betrayals, couldn't be overlooked. Grace had trusted him. She'd loved him, as she hadn't any other living being. She'd relinquished heaven to be with him.

She waited for her angel's voice to come, to counsel mercy and compassion. She was fully prepared to curse it back to its cloud if it tried.

But her heart was the only voice beating in her ears, like the sea inside a seashell. Tears spilled over her lower

eyelids, hot and then cool against her skin. What was a
friend if a friend would not forgive a weakness? What was
love if it could be destroyed so quickly or turned to hate?
Grace knew those answers now. Maybe she always had.

Christian was not a person she could abandon.

The breath she pulled into her lungs was shaky but welcome.

"There's nothing to forgive," she said.

Grace's mercy pulled Christian to his feet. Could it be
true? Could she pardon him? Her face was tear-streaked
but not angry, as lovely as a Madonna's in the candlelight. An odd sensation crawled across his skin. When he
glanced down, an invisible wind seemed to be peeling the
blood off him. His old brown doublet was clean again, its
cloth as smooth as if the tailor had only then fitted it. Suddenly, he understood why Nim Wei had always appeared
so tidy. He turned his spotless hands back and forth.

This was part of his nature now.

"Christian," Grace breathed. "You're lit up as white as
snow."

Her voice drew his gaze to her, and he saw what he had
never been able to tell before. She was solid. He knew it in
a single blink. The shadows her body cast were different,
the feel of her vibration against the currents of the air.

Hope rose painfully inside him as he crossed the room
to her. She did not look away from him, did not retreat as
he came nearer. With motions that should have been jerky,
considering how frayed he felt, he took her warm face in
his cool hands.

He could have stared into her eyes all night, not just the
emotions they held but them. Their pale, clear green was
more beautiful than ever, living gems made magical by his

vampire sight. The delicate skin around her eyelids crinkled as she smiled at him.

"I'm here," she said.

Heat rose in him like a tide. He kissed her, deeply, slowly, loving the way she melted as his weight pressed her gently into the wall. He wanted to make kissing her a prayer, but in moments, his arousal pounded between them, so hard, so long, he did not know how he would wait to plunge it inside of her. As her arms slid around his waist, every nerve she brushed screamed with bliss. He felt so much when she touched him—too much, truly. It was impossible not to desire more. His hips surged closer, and he speared her lush red lips with his tongue. She was what he had been craving, the succor he could not live without. He moaned at how wonderful she tasted, and again when her palms smoothed soothingly up his back. Her hands slid apart when she reached his shoulders, as if she liked measuring their width.

"Grace," he groaned against her mouth. "Never leave me again."

"Never," she promised, and began gathering up her gown.

Quicker than she was, he helped her, pulling all that sheer linen to her waist. He trembled at the feel of her silken legs, then at the bump of her digging hand. She was freeing him from his underclothes, her fingers fire on his rock-hard prick.

The way *that* felt was enough to make every hair he had stand on end.

"*Grace*," he gasped.

She was stroking him, was pulling his aching hardness up from his groin. Fireworks spangled everywhere she rubbed, from his throbbing root to his drum-tight crest. He had not been this sensitive before, not even for Nim

Wei. His prick was leaking in little gushes, fluid spurting in pre-orgasmic spasms from its slit. His head fell back as the contractions rolled up him with her strokes. This was like coming, only he knew it would get better. He wanted it to, despite the near painful intensity of the sensations. Grace's thumb drew a maddening circle through his wetness, spreading it to his flare. That felt so good, he could barely stop himself from shoving her through the wall.

He had less luck holding back his growl.

"You're bigger now," Grace murmured.

She was looking down at him, female awe in every line of her face. He could not bear it an instant longer. He lifted her, so strong it took no effort whatsoever to grip and spread the back of her thighs. With her feet dangling off the floor, she was utterly reliant on him for support, but he did not wrap her legs around him. He had an image in his head of what he wanted: the length of her, the heat of her, impaled and held up by the massive potency of his cock.

If this was being a monster, maybe it would suit him.

Her fingers tightened on his shoulders, nails digging in as he worked the head of his prick slowly into her. Her throat released a sound, alarmed and longing at the same time. She was dripping down him, but he was almost too thick for her. Knowing what she wanted, he grunted and kept pushing. The walls of her queinte clung to him, molding, pressing those insanely sharpened nerves until he feared his knees would buckle. The feeling of her tightness, of her muscles flickering in reaction was overwhelmingly pleasurable.

She must not have known how close he was to losing all control—or must have been content with the dependence of her position. She slapped the soles of her feet onto the muscles at the back of his thighs, enabling her hips to move in a strong undulating roll. The extra bit of effort on her part drove him to his hilt inside her.

"Christian," she groaned. Her squirms around his very full penetration were a fresh torture. "Oh . . . my . . . *God*."

He could not speak. He felt like he had not come in a century, and that he would die if he did not do so in two heartbeats. God save him, but his balls were going to explode from the pressure building inside them. With a curse that was half prayer, he ground his teeth and held on.

He wanted to feel her coming around him more than he wanted to come himself.

"I am going to move," he gritted out. "I am stronger now, but I shall try not to thrust too hard."

She mewled and clutched him as he began. Bit by bit, stroke by stroke, he eased her tightness. Simple as the motion was, sliding in and out of her was heaven—made new by his new body. Her thighs tightened on his hips, and her hands tangled in his hair. He buried his face in the bend of her neck and shoulder, wanting to weep for how good she smelled. His fangs pulsed with his urge to bite her, but he would not give in.

He was determined to keep this sweet for her.

"Christian," she pleaded, clearly having her own ideas. "Please go faster."

His hands gripped her firm little bottom, curbing the way she was trying to thrash on him. The temptation to squeeze her was too strong to resist. She was so ripe, so hot, the petals of her vulva wet and soft around him. Those beastlike growls were coming from his chest again. Still, he did not—*would* not—lose all reason. He shifted her hips' angle, taking care to hit the swollen pearl of her clitoris with each calculated stroke. Though he was proud of himself for being able to do so, this was not wholly a blessing. She cried out at the change in target, her exclamation so purely carnal it drew an answering cry from him.

In one decisive tear, his lust ripped from his restraints.

He took her faster, farther, flesh beginning to smack flesh with the surrender. He did not know how to stop. This new body had become his master.

"Grace," he cried. "I am sorry. I cannot help doing this."

She did not seem to want him to stop. She seemed to relish his ferocity. Her inner muscles clenched like a fist as he hitched her weight up and drove deeper. Like a beacon that was shining only inside his head, he could sense the energy of her desire: where it focused, where she wanted to be pummeled, the extra moment she was wishing he would linger on that deep sweet spot.

He saw that this might save him. With a groan, he did as she longed, his sharpest pleasure tied up in pleasing her. As her cries came closer together, as they became her own breed of growls, his skin began to tingle, her essence lapping over his. He hardly needed the extra excitation. He was too close to spilling as it was. He could have screamed when she tensed her muscles and rocked harder, but all that wrenched from him was a grunt. His fangs were cutting his lower lip, the taste of blood fiery on his tongue. Utterly beyond his controlling, his hips threw themselves back at her.

His prick seemed to think that it could feed from her, too.

"Please," he urged, begging her to let go. If he hurt her, he believed he might die.

And then her queinte gushed heat and wetness all over him.

He came at the sign that she was coming, the release like lightning sizzling through his shaft. He thought the pleasure of it would blind him . . . until her energy burst hugely with her next climax. That was oil thrown onto an already raging fire. He peaked again, helplessly, swamped by her sensations bleeding over his. The chain that held the lightning of his climax snapped. As long as she came, he would, and she did not seem likely to stop soon. Scarcely wanting her to, he pounded into her ever more savagely.

It was madness, pure and simple. He felt himself swiving her, felt her climaxes soaring to dizzying heights. His jaw began to widen, his breath to pant. He could not throttle that one last instinct, could not hold back his need to feed from her as he came. Groaning as if Death itself had seized him, he plunged his teeth deep into her neck.

Grace threw back her scarlet hair and screamed.

The sound could not alarm him. She was too obviously in the throes of ecstasy. What came for him then was different, though in its way no less extraordinary. It was not hunger he satisfied by drinking from her, but a lifelong need for closeness. The fire of his orgasm quieted. Warmth spread through him as he sipped from her—like being wrapped in a soft blanket. Her love was in her blood, the comfort she had been wishing she could give him. *She* did not question if he deserved it; she only wanted to cherish him. He felt accepted, as he never had in his life. Tears stung his eyes as he pulled his fangs slowly out.

He knew she could not stand without his aid, so he kept her wrapped snugly in his arms. She settled as he held her, every muscle in her body relaxing.

"Christian," she murmured, her voice deliciously husky.

He *was* glowing. He could see the reflected radiance on her flushed face. He could also see the fissure his new strength had knocked from the wall behind her, straight down into the brick. He was fortunate he had not hurt her; his arms had shielded her from the worst of his aggression. He would have to be more careful in the future—a future they seemed to have, if he dared believe in this miracle.

He could bear almost anything, as long as he had her.

"Forever," he said, *his* voice more stern than soft. "You shall stay with me forever."

She stroked his eyebrows with gentle fingers, her beautiful lips curving. "Nothing could make me leave you. And now I want you to promise me something."

She laughed when he grew wary.

"Show mercy," she said. "At least to Oswald and Mace. I know it was—" She hesitated, shyness entering her expression. "I'm certain it was me forgiving you that let me be physical this time. It made me . . . a little more like my angel."

He smoothed a lock of her glorious hair from where it clung to her perspiring cheek. Grace was as close to an angel as he wanted to get. Nonetheless, her good opinion meant a great deal to him.

"We can have forever now," she coaxed.

"As long as I am a monster," he retorted with a dry snort.

"You are no more a monster than I am."

He knew this was not true, but it did not matter. He leaned her into the wall, her legs coming up to hug him around the hips. He was still inside her, still hard enough to stretch her pliable limits. He loved how comfortable she seemed with this. His shy little Grace, grown into a woman. Smiling softly, she rubbed their noses together.

"Doesn't it seem like heaven has taken pity on us? Couldn't you find it in your heart to let those two off the hook?"

"They helped kill my friends."

"I know." Grace stroked his hair and kissed his forehead. "I know they did."

She made no more argument, just gazed gravely into his eyes. While he made love to her, he had forgotten about his father's corpse cooling on the floor. Now it became a presence behind him, unseen but all too easy to picture. What Christian had done to Gregori horrified him, though he knew his father deserved it. Would killing Mace and Oswald horrify him, too?

"I shall not release Lavaux," he warned. "That son of a whore must die."

"That is your choice," Grace said.

"And if I *do* kill Mace and Oswald?"

Grace drew the pad of her thumb down the center of his lips, every whorl of its print now palpable to him. "You won't stop me from loving you. I'm yours, Christian. No matter what you do."

He stared at her until he was convinced she meant what she said. He had to embrace her then, if only to hide the tears that blurred his vision.

"I am yours also," he vowed thickly against her ear. "I shall love you forever."

Her arms were tightening around him, her throat echoing with a cry, when the darkest horror unfolded. Christian stumbled forward into the wall, abruptly holding nothing at all.

Grace had disappeared again, shocking his immortal heart into knocking frantically on his ribs. He told himself she would return, that this was no different from the other times she had gone. The faces of his friends rose within his mind, the empty chasm yawning in his life now that they were gone. Grace loved him, and she had promised him forever. She would not leave him when he needed her most of all.

He waited in the room above the goldsmith's shop until morning, then through the next night as well. Nim Wei arrived, but he cursed her so vociferously that she left. It was three nights later, when he had to bury his father, before he admitted Grace was not coming back.

The black rage that filled him could have swallowed the world. This was his reward for loving? For trying to be an honorable man? He had called Nim Wei a devil at midnight, but he was stealing the title back. Heaven and its angels—along with everyone else who had wronged him—had better look to themselves.

Christian Durand was at last becoming his father's son.

Twenty-eight

Grace became conscious of an assortment of throbbing pains. Her neck was so sore that even tensing her shoulders hurt. Her head felt like a sledgehammer was making a home in it. Her toes were icy, and her fingertips. Worse than any of these things, however, was the aching knot of loss in her chest, as if her best friend in the world had died. Even as she took note of the emotion, it dissipated. Oddly, she didn't think she wanted it to fade.

She realized she was lying on her back in a bed with a sheet and blanket pulled over her. Sounds came and went around her: footsteps, voices, rubber wheels squeaking on a linoleum floor. Bit by bit, she sorted the noises out.

When she smelled cleaning solution, she knew she was in a hospital.

I was almost a real ghost, she thought. *That's why the cat could see me.*

A second later, she thought: *What cat?*

Having succeeded in confusing herself, she opened her eyes—a feat that took two attempts, due to her lashes being stuck together. She turned her head gingerly.

Grace's mother slept in a vinyl chair pulled close to the side-railed bed. Helen Gladwell was wearing dark blue pumps, ladylike white gloves, and a pale blue polka-dotted dress with a belted waist. The long darts in the bodice faithfully conformed the rayon around the cone-shaped cups of her bra. For some reason, Grace thought she'd never seen an outfit so peculiar.

"Mom?" she said, the word scraping rough and strange from her throat.

Grace's mother jerked awake and cried out.

"Grace!" she exclaimed, tears immediately springing from her green eyes. "You're awake."

Grace tried not to wince but probably failed when her mother clutched her hand and forearm with her white cotton gloves. Fortunately, her mother wasn't paying attention.

"Grace, we thought we'd lost you! The medics tried to resuscitate you for six minutes. They told us you were as good as dead for a while."

Grace cleared her raspy throat. "*Us?*" she asked, trying to steer her mother to what mattered. Regardless of her confusion about the cat, she hadn't forgotten the incident that had sent her here. "Where's Dad?"

Her mother choked on a sob, dabbing at her nose with a handkerchief. "I've left him. I finally have. I'm taking you to my sister's. You never have to see him again, honey."

Grace remembered running to her aunt before. Her mother's older sister had a sour pursed mouth that liked nothing better than cutting at her sibling. According to her aunt, Helen never raised Grace right, *and* she'd gotten fat around the middle, *and* no wonder she couldn't keep a man. Naturally, Grace's father had found them there, and hadn't taken more than an hour to convince Grace's mother to reconcile with him.

"Don't look at me like that," her mother said.

Grace hadn't been aware that she was looking at her mother any way at all. Now that she thought about it, though, she was feeling . . . not calm exactly but steadier. Much steadier than she might have expected—as if her customary fear reactions had been short-circuited by her brush with death.

I'm not weak like she is, Grace thought. *I could pretend to go to Aunt Belinda's, then run away. I'm practically eighteen. I bet plenty of girls live on their own at that age.*

"Grace," her mother castigated, a pout in it. She smoothed her perfectly curled red hair away from her face. "I couldn't have known your father was going to throw you into that fireplace."

You didn't stop him, Grace thought. *And I can't count on you to try harder when he does it again.*

She felt no need to say this aloud. She knew her mother couldn't hear the truth. Instead, Grace patted the glove that still clutched her arm, marveling that she wasn't even a bit angry. But maybe that made sense. Grace's mother carried her punishments around inside her. Grace was going to be free.

"I'm fine now," she assured her mother. "You have nothing to be sorry about."

Grace meant every word she said. She might not be able to change the past, but she could change how her life unfolded from here on out.

SIX YEARS

Twenty-nine

1956

Two Forks, Texas, was a long way from Hollywood. Grace's boss, up-and-coming director Naomi Wei, had informed her the name of the town was "North Fork" back in the 1930s. Why they'd changed the *North* to *Two* was anybody's guess. Maybe so visitors would think they'd actually find someone they wanted to eat with in this deadsville burg.

Grace grinned to herself as she turned the flamingo pink Plymouth Fury off the minuscule main drag. The urge to floor the V8 past the Dairy Queen was close to irresistible. Although Miss Wei had disappointed Grace by not buying a convertible, Grace had once pushed the boatlike car to an eye-popping 120 miles per hour.

Miss Wei might be eccentric, but she knew her fast cars.

The road Grace had turned onto wasn't as well paved as the blacktop that cut through town. As sprays of gravel hit the custom whitewalls, Grace's employer stirred sleepily in the passenger seat. Because Miss Wei had been anxious to reach their goal, they'd gotten an earlier start than usual for them: at least an hour before dusk. Miss Wei had immediately sunk into a doze, bundled like Greta Garbo in her long powder blue silk scarf and her glamorous cat's-eye sunglasses.

"Thank God," she said now, tipping up the glasses to take in the lollipop red shards of sunset that were melting on the horizon.

Miss Wei was not, by any stretch of the imagination, a day person.

"We're close," Grace told her, as always enjoying the moment when her boss woke up. From their first encounter in the LA diner where Grace had been waitressing, she'd liked Miss Wei's company—in part because she was the sort of take-charge woman Grace wanted to be someday. "The cat at the Texaco said the Durand ranch is a mile west on the turnoff."

"The *cat*?" Miss Wei repeated, her perfectly painted mouth pursing with her smile.

Grace never got over how youthful her employer looked—her face unlined, her figure trim—and never mind she claimed to be old enough to be Grace's mother.

"*Cat* is what the kids say," Grace informed her.

Miss Wei laughed softly. "As if you weren't a kid yourself."

Grace's fingers tightened on the white steering wheel. At twenty-four and counting, she was hardly that. Sometimes she felt as if the sands in her hourglass were perpetually running out.

"Fine," Miss Wei teased with her uncanny ability to read expressions. "You're a woman of immense maturity and intelligence. Why else would I hire you?"

"Because I work for peanuts?"

"As I recall, I gave you a raise last week."

Because she had, Grace smiled to herself. The increase in pay had been generous.

"I'm worth it," she said blithely.

"You might be," Miss Wei conceded in the same airy tone.

She seemed happy tonight, her short hair ruffling in the wind from the open window, her dark eyes sparkling for the challenge in front of them. Filmmaking might be difficult for women, but the "old boys" at the studios never intimidated her.

"You're sure Mr. Durand is expecting us?" Grace asked.

"If he's not, he should be," Miss Wei answered, which wasn't exactly a *yes*.

But it was too late to worry, because the Durand ranch's wooden gate arched over the road ahead like a scene from a John Ford Western. The ground here was dusty. Flat as a pancake, too, with scruffy-looking grass a herd of dieting cattle could have starved on. An oil derrick poked up in the distance, black as night against the still faintly rosy sky, suggesting Mr. Durand could afford extra feed for his hungry cows.

"Longhorns," Miss Wei said. "Christian raises Longhorn cattle. He's one of the last holdouts."

"They're hardy," she added when Grace lifted her brows at her. "Shorthorns and Herefords need too much pampering out here."

"I didn't know you were interested in ranching."

"I'm not," her employer said. "But it pays to know your quarry."

Slowing as they got closer—because who knew if this Texas boy kept shotguns—Grace pointed the car toward a low-slung adobe house.

"Try the barns," Miss Wei corrected. "Unless I miss my guess, Christian is in that one over there."

The barns were a collection of worn-looking plank buildings. Grace parked in the rutted dirt beside the one Miss Wei had waved her arm at. Grace was wearing flats for driving, but her heels still sank into the dry earth as she got out. The wide double doors of the barn stood open. Caged bulbs were strung along the rafters to light the big space inside, though Grace wouldn't have said they lit it well. If someone was in there, she couldn't pick them out from the shadows yet.

Miss Wei came around the front end of the Fury and laid her cool hand on Grace's sleeve. "Just let me do the talking. Christian Durand . . . owes me his life, you could say."

For some reason, this request increased Grace's nervousness. She dried damp palms on her white pedal pushers, allowing her petite yet formidable employer to stride into the cavernous structure ahead of her. Grace followed more sedately and looked around.

Without question, this barn was a male domain. No cows resided between its walls, only a collection of automobiles of varying vintages and states of repair. Her mood improving, Grace spotted a 1950 Buick in the process of having its body "chopped" to reduce wind drag. The Harley-Davidson leaning on a hay bale also looked promising. Ever since Marlon Brando starred in *The Wild One*, motorcycles were big with kids.

Maybe her boss was onto something with this harebrained idea.

"Christian," Miss Wei called out. "It's Naomi Wei. I've come to talk in person."

Grace heard the clank of a wrench hitting the barn's dirt floor.

She saw the man then, or his bottom half anyway. He

was bent over the engine of a glossy black, two-seater, convertible Thunderbird. If the car hadn't made Grace's mouth water, the man's behind in those Levi's certainly would have. The metal-caged bulb above him shone a literal spotlight onto his butt. His legs were long and strong-looking. And the cowboy boots he was sporting didn't hurt, either.

He stretched farther into the engine, exposing two tantalizing dimples at the top of his hindquarters. Grace's mouth did its best to go desert dry. Maybe he sensed her attention, because he spoke. His voice was dark and smooth, with just a hint of a Texas twang.

"Told you on the phone I wasn't interested. All dozen times you called."

"You never heard me out," Miss Wei said.

Mr. Durand straightened, braced his arms on the side of the open hood, then slammed it down with a bang. Grace's heart began to beat faster as she took in how broad his shoulders were. A snug-fitting and oddly spotless white T-shirt clung to his tapered back, making very clear the fact that he didn't have an ounce of fat on him . . . exactly the way Grace liked her men, to be truthful. Despite Mr. Durand's leanness, the muscles under that clean white cotton rippled with contained power. His hair was long enough to need tying back, and just as black and shiny as the finish on his car. His hair would have to be cut, of course; leading men couldn't run around looking like Indian braves. For herself, however, Grace liked the ponytail.

As if to warn her how much she liked it, her panties dampened in a hot, quick rush—a tad embarrassing, she thought. If Mr. Durand looked this good from the front, she might be in trouble. Grace prided herself on always behaving professionally.

"I'm not an actor," he said, still not turning to her employer.

"And if I were, I wouldn't star in no damn flick called *I Was a Teen-Age Vampire*."

"It's bound to make heaps of money."

"I don't need money," he snapped.

"You owe me, Christian."

"I don't owe you shit, *Naomi*."

It wasn't so much his language as his unabashed hostility that had Grace sucking in her breath. The sound wasn't loud, but Mr. Durand spun around like lightning on hearing it.

He was facing her then, and his eyes went wide. Grace's heart slammed her ribs, but he seemed more shocked than she was. Knowing pretty well how she looked, she was used to men reacting to the sight of her. This man's response took the cake from them all. His head jerked back like someone had popped a knuckle sandwich into his chin.

He bit out a word she thought meant *shit* in German.

"Well," Miss Wei purred, her gaze shifting back and forth between them. "Isn't this interesting?"

Grace's brain recovered enough to realize that Mr. Durand's face was movie-star gorgeous, which probably accounted for why her pulse was pounding like a jackhammer. Oh, he didn't resemble James Dean or Marlon Brando, but he had that can't-take-your-eyes-off-him charisma. She judged he was about Dean's age, early twenties or thereabouts, a little lined from working outdoors but still young enough to pass for eighteen. His coffee dark eyes smoldered with hypnotizing hints of gold. His lips were thin, it was true, but a girl could slice her heart on those high cheekbones. Even his arms were sexy, the muscles graceful as they hung loosely at his sides. And, by golly, he was *tall*—six feet and then some, she was willing to bet. Neither the recently departed Dean nor the still-rising Brando could pretend that.

Best of all, from the toes of his cowboy boots to the dashing widow's peak of his hair, Christian Durand screamed *dangerous*.

"You're right, boss," Grace said, before she could worry how it would sound. "Every red-blooded female in America *is* guaranteed to sigh over him."

Christian couldn't wrench his attention from the woman who'd traipsed uninvited into his barn with Nim Wei. She was the spitting image of his Grace, lost to him for—*Christ*—nearly five centuries. This woman was a little older, but every year had given her a blessing. Her face had character to go with her prettiness: a shadow to make her glow shine brighter, a stubbornness to her peach soft jaw.

Her tidy outfit of pedal pushers and crisp white blouse was ridiculous, of course, a girl playing dress-up as someone far more serious and less sensual than she was. Her figure, on the other hand, was precisely the sweet temptation he remembered: a buxom, narrow-hipped torso set atop a pair of showgirl's legs. This woman's hair was shorter than Grace's, waving only to her shoulders, though it *was* the same deep, dark red.

Movie actress hair, he supposed.

Vampire that he was, with all the knee-jerk responses that went with that, he'd started hardening the instant he saw her. *Hardening* wasn't the word for what he was doing now. Running his eyes up and down her very warm-blooded beauty had his prick screaming for mercy inside his jeans.

It didn't care that she couldn't truly be his lost beloved. It was chomping at the bit to burn down this barn with her. On the bare floor right in front of him sounded fine, with his pike shoved up her pussy as far as it would go. He winced as his cock struggled harder against his zipper, but the erotic images wouldn't stop. It had been too long since he'd let loose with a woman. He had too little trouble imagining this gal's ankles around his ears.

"This is Grace," Nim Wei said in that insinuating voice of hers. As distracted as he was, he marveled that he made out the words at all. "She's my close personal assistant. If you agree to star in my movie, you'll be seeing her every day."

The girl seemed startled by her employer's promise, but she stuck out her hand gamely.

"Grace Michaels," she said. "I'm very pleased to meet you, Mr. Durand."

The name belatedly registered.

"*Grace?*" he repeated, abruptly hoarse. His normally cool palm turned fiery where she clasped it.

"Michaels. But please call me Grace if you like."

He couldn't release her hand. Her name was Grace, and her eyes were as clear and green as a peridot. All the times he'd stared into them rushed back like yesterday. He remembered these very fingers touching him with such kindness he'd feared he'd cry, remembered the way her ghostly energy could tingle straight up his cock. The nerves there were tingling now—jangling, really, like a telephone ringing off the hook. Grace wasn't a ghost anymore. She was as solid as the ground under him. Lord help him, if she brushed against him, his dick was going to erupt.

"Christian," he said, having to push his name past the constriction inside his throat. "My name is Christian. Please call me that."

"Christian," she agreed nervously.

When she attempted to tug her hand back, his fangs punched down from his gums, reacting precisely as if she were prey fleeing. Her accelerated pulse was lub-dubbing in his ears, a siren song he wasn't certain he could resist.

Alarmed by his out-of-control responses, he let her go and stepped back.

Grace massaged her palm as if he'd hurt it.

"So?" Nim Wei said to him.

He looked at her, and he had no idea what she was asking. He wasn't even certain what he felt. However it had happened, this *was* Grace, the same Grace who'd promised him forever and then abandoned him in his darkest hour. His face flashed hot and then icy. Did he hate her? Did he love her? Did he simply want to fuck her without stopping for the next ten years?

The painful surge of blood to his groin told him the answer to that was affirmative.

"Christian?" Nim Wei said, her lithe little arms folded. "Are you going to help me make this movie or not?"

She doesn't know, he thought. *Not who Grace was. Not what she means to me. All she knows is that her assistant has my cylinders running hot.*

Grace couldn't have remembered Nim Wei, either, or she wouldn't be trotting after her like a faithful girl Friday. Hell, the prissy sweater she'd tied around her shoulders was the same shade of powder blue as Nim Wei's scarf. The witch of Florence was Grace's goddamned mentor, as if Nim Wei weren't responsible for half the trouble that befell them both back then.

All of which boiled down to Grace not remembering him.

He stared into her wide green eyes, his immortal heart contracting in his chest with an emotion very much like terror. She wasn't putting on an act. He saw no recognition in her expression. She *was* flushed; attracted, unless he was mistaken, and embarrassed because of it, but only in the way—how had she put it?—any red-blooded American girl might be.

Without realizing it, he'd folded his arms in an echo of

Nim Wei's posture. He caught a flash from Grace's mind of how he looked with his muscles bulging in the white T-shirt. That definitely didn't help his blood pressure drop. When Grace extended her hand to touch his bare forearm, her fingers were trembling.

"We'd both consider it a favor if you'd agree," she said. "Miss Wei needs an ace in the hole to break out of making B movies."

"And you think I'd be your ace."

"Oh, *absolutely*," Grace breathed, her enthusiasm momentarily teenager-like. "I know you're inexperienced, but we could coach you. A person's presence is what matters for most movies. Acting is something plenty of folks can learn."

"And *you* could coach me," he said.

Grace shot an uncertain glance at her boss before turning back to him. "We both could. Or we could hire someone. Whatever you're comfortable with."

Despite feeling more discomposed than he had in five centuries, despite loving the peaceful life he'd built for himself out here, Christian sensed a rare canary-eating grin rising up in him. Love Grace or loathe her, he couldn't hate the idea of having her at his beck and call.

As the grin spread across his face, threatening to bare his fangs, Grace tensed warily back from him.

"*You* coach me," he said firmly, "and we might have a deal."

Yes, there is more to
Grace and Christian's story!
Stay tuned for

ANGEL AT DAWN

Coming January 2011 from Berkley Sensation!

Kissing Midnight

THE FIRST BOOK IN THE FITZ CLARE CHRONICLES
BY *USA TODAY* BESTSELLING AUTHOR

EMMA HOLLY

Edmund Fitz Clare has been keeping secrets he can't afford to expose. Not to the orphans he's adopted. Not to the lovely young woman he's been yearning after for years, Estelle Berenger. He's an *upyr*—a shape-shifting vampire—desperate to redeem past misdeeds.

But deep in the heart of London a vampire war is brewing, a conflict that threatens to throw Edmund and Estelle together—and to turn his beloved human family against him…

M413T0209